TELL ME MORE

D0873292

Also by Brad Kelln

Method of Madness
Lost Sanity
In the Tongues of the Dead

TELL ME MORE

A BLAKE WAITER MYSTERY

PAPL
DISCARDED

BRAD KELLN

INSOMNIAC PRESS

Copyright © 2018 by Brad Kelln

All rights reserved. No part of this publication may be reproduced, stored in a retrieval system or transmitted, in any form or by any means, without the prior written permission of the publisher or, in the case of photocopying or other reprographic copying, a licence from Access Copyright, 1 Yonge Street, Suite 1900, Toronto, ON M5E 1E5

Library and Archives Canada Cataloguing in Publication

Kelln, Brad, 1970-, author
Tell me more / Brad Kelln.

Issued in print and electronic formats.
ISBN 978-1-55483-216-3 (softcover).--ISBN 978-1-55483-220-0 (PDF)

I. Title.

PS8571.E5864T45 2018 C813'.6 C2018-905791-2
C2015-905792-0

The publisher gratefully acknowledges the support of the Canada Council for the Arts and the Ontario Arts Council.

Printed and bound in Canada
Insomniac Press
520 Princess Avenue, London, Ontario, Canada, N6B 2B8
www.insomniacpress.com

The Canada Council for the Arts since 1957 | Le Conseil des Arts du Canada depuis 1957

ONTARIO ARTS COUNCIL
CONSEIL DES ARTS DE L'ONTARIO

This book is dedicated to you. The reader. We all have stress in our lives. We struggle at times and need to escape from day-to-day problems. I wrote this book (hopefully the start of a long series) to be a fun, interesting form of literary therapy — to just escape and relax. Enjoy.

PROLOGUE

As a psychologist, I rarely get punched in the face.

I assume people have the urge to punch me in the face with some regularity, but it had never happened. I rely on other people's common sense, and self-restraint, to preserve my facial structure.

But not on that day.

The two gentlemen I found in my waiting room…

Nope. Stop. They were anything, but gentlemen.

The *assholes* I found in my waiting room were not respecting my personal space. They didn't respect the personal space around my facial region, nor even around my pelvic region (in case I'm being too subtle, they had punched me in the face and kicked me in the nuts). But the most significant damage was to my ego.

I'd like to consider myself a formidable opponent. I stand around six foot four, and I know I carry around some extra weight, but I'm still in pretty decent shape for a guy in his early forties. I keep my hair, most of which I still have, in a close-cut, nearly buzzed style that doesn't show any grey. Apart from a fair-sized belly, I'd always thought I looked like a big enough, fit enough guy whom no one would mess with intentionally.

Boy, was I wrong.

I now know that being tall and frequently watching mixed martial arts while on a treadmill does not prepare you for hand-to-hand combat. It looks like the proper preparation needs to include actual hands-on fighting experience. That's what sank me. My day job involves sitting and talking to people one at a time and, oddly, never had involved a fistfight. Even outside of my day job, I'd rarely found myself in a physical altercation, so overall I lacked hands-on fighting experience. That's a biggie.

But until that day, I'd always *assumed* I would be a pretty formidable opponent in a fight. It turned out that wasn't true and I was learning that the hard way. Because on that day, these two goons were beating the shit out of me.

My nose was pouring blood and I'd already dropped down to the floor in a heap. The advantage of being on the floor was that one of the morons could now kick me. So that was probably more of an advantage for him. I briefly lost consciousness on the ground, but one of the guys was kind enough to slap my face until I woke up.

"It's not sleepy time," the guy said. "Where is it? We know you have it."

The *it* was a magic silver ball.

A *singing* magic silver ball.

And I did know where it was, but I really didn't want to give it to him. Having the magic ball was probably the only reason I was still alive.

Lucky for me the room was about to explode into even more chaos and violence. The kind of violence where people lose body parts.

But that isn't the best place to start this story. The real story started a few days before.

CHAPTER 1

I'm a psychologist. Dr. Blake Waiter.

I've worked as a psychologist for over fifteen years — ever since I received my doctorate in clinical psychology. For the most part, I sort of enjoy the work. You meet a lot of people and hear a lot of interesting stories. Early on, I figured out that I couldn't be a typical psychologist. A typical psychologist might see a woman with depression, a man with anxiety, couples with marital troubles, or people struggling with substance abuse problems. Truth is, if I were in the office of a typical psychologist, then I'd probably be the one on the couch, not the one with the pen and paper.

So I actually specialize in a niche area of clinical psychology referred to as forensic. The field of forensic psychology can cover a lot of ground, but my specialty is working with adults in trouble with the law. This might not come as a surprise, but a lot of times adults get in trouble with the law because of sexual stuff, and so a big part of my work is with sex offenders. Over the years, I've also worked with the local police and more recently stumbled into a very lucrative, very secret contract with the military. More on that later!

On the day my story starts, I rolled into my private practice office for what I thought was going to be a normal Tuesday morning. It was actually going to be the last day that was even close to normal in quite a while. But you never appreciate those little things until they are gone. My private practice office is in a less affluent part of Dartmouth, Nova Scotia, the north end where there are pockets of family homes, but lots of cramped, low-income housing, and some pretty shady areas.

My little three-story building is on a busy street near a grocery store and a car dealership. I like the building even though most visitors describe it as ugly. I think that's unfair because it was likely a real stunning structure back in the 1960s when it was built. It still proudly displays the brown and orange brick and vinyl panel that was a popular construction method then. The fact that the owners clung to this original colour scheme probably reflects their opinion that style moves in circles and eventually brown and orange will come back.

There's parking in front of the building itself, but I never park there. People don't know how to park. I'm not sure why anyone bothers with lines in a parking lot unless they see them as a target to be parked over. People would park right on top of each other if that were possible. Jesus, watching some of the idiots wiggle their half-ton trucks into stalls drives me nuts. I can't handle it, so I never park there.

I park on the street near the building. That way people can't park next to me.

Not only can people not park next to me on the street, but there are also a few spaces along the road where there is just enough room to park two cars between consecutive driveways. If I center my Jeep

Wrangler just right, I can make it so only one car fits and boom! no one parks on either end of me.

It's a necessity for me to minimize things to worry about when I'm at private practice. I tend to catastrophize — meaning I assume the worst is around the corner — so if I were parked in front of my own building, I would be constantly checking to see if my Jeep was okay. And in recent years I've had more than enough things to worry about, so my vehicle's safety doesn't need to be one.

So, that day, I parked near my building and ambled down the sidewalk to the office. The entrance is a double set of glass doors that are wheelchair-accessible, which is hilarious because the three-story building only has a single staircase. I'm convinced that the installation of the automatic doors with a handicap button was a joke by the building owner. First of all, the doors represent the only wheelchair-accessible spot in the building, so what was the point? Once you get in those doors, you can only visit offices on the first floor. Second, if you make the mistake of using the big handicap door button, it takes almost three minutes for it to open. I guess it prevents the door from springing open violently and striking someone on the chin, but three minutes? Who's going to wait that long?

So most people just force the door open by hand against the resistance of the motor. Forcing the door tends to produce an unpleasant grinding noise for the effort, which probably accounts for the frequent service calls. So inside the entrance of the building is your standard greyish-white linoleum floor. I think it might have been just solid white at some point, but now it has interesting foot traffic patterns of the permanent grey variety. Across the patterned floor is a linoleum and metal-railed staircase, and at the top of the staircase is another lobby for the professional offices. That's where I am.

I share the third floor with a massage therapist, social workers, and an acupuncturist. It is a handful of offices arranged around the main waiting area. I don't want to brag, but my office is the biggest one on the entire floor. I feel a bit like the king of the misfit helpers.

Truthfully, if it all seems just a little too plain and boring, then it is doing its job. My office is supposed to look like nothing special because it is intentionally deceptive. I chose a nondescript building in a seedy part of town and wanted to be on a floor with a motley crew of health providers. I wanted it all to look common and uninteresting. So it's not until I arrive at my boring office, put the key into the deadbolt, and rest a hand against the doorframe that the first hint of something different is revealed.

My hand rests on a scanner, so perfectly blended with the doorframe that it is invisible. My palm is scanned, and this activates the deadbolt locking mechanism. My office key is also set to my biometrics, so it only works when it is in my hand. In other words, if you tried to use my key without my hand, it wouldn't work. Only it isn't just a deadbolt either. The door looks like a plain wooden door, but is actually steel and when locked has pins that covertly slide into place around the frame. Unlocking the deadbolt silently slides eight deadbolts away. So in essence, my office door is kick-in proof.

The local military base, 12 Wing Shearwater, installed the door (and the other neat stuff in the office). The modifications to my office were mandatory once I told them I refused to see my military patients on the base itself. It was all a part of the secret contract I mentioned earlier.

Inside the first door, I have a private waiting room, so my clients don't have to sit in the common area with patients of other clinicians on the floor. Actually, this was another non-negotiable from 12 Wing. My military clients aren't allowed to sit where they would be vulnerable. That's fine with me. It prevents me from having to do that annoying walk out to everyone and then asking, "Are you Mr. Smith? Is there a Mr. Smith here?" You know how that goes. No thanks. I'd done that before at an office years ago. It felt like some demented patient lottery where you scanned the faces of the people sitting there, just hoping that your patient was the least disturbed-looking. You kind of looked out the corner of your eye as you asked, "Is there a Mr. Smith here?" hoping that the weirdo with the droopy eye didn't bolt up.

But I don't have to do that anymore. I have my own private waiting room. It isn't much to look at. Six dark brown leather–armchairs — quite modest — with a dark brown coffee table in the middle of the room. A full-size armoire in the corner discreetly houses my microwave. An observant person might notice that the square footage of the room is slightly smaller than what you might anticipate from the outside dimensions. That's because 12 Wing insisted on installing sub walls, roof, and flooring that rendered both the waiting room and my office soundproof. I often wonder if the office is bombproof as well. Hopefully I never find out.

For now, I shut the outside door and headed to my actual office. On the opposite end of the waiting room is another door with a similar locking mechanism to the first. I rested a hand on the doorframe and used the RFID fob on my key ring. This door dispensed with the need for an actual key in the lock. It just looks like a normal doorknob, but when my hand is on the doorframe and I am holding the fob in proximity, it opens.

I went inside where I have a brown leather couch, leather ottoman storage bench, and leather bucket seat for myself. Against one wall I also have a computer desk and chair for my serious paperwork. The three large windows look like they have Venetian blinds, but are actually digital windowpanes that can be dimmed to blackout from an app on my phone. I can even cast my computer screen or phone to the windows to use as a secondary monitor. It's how I watch Netflix between patients. Very cool. When I casually mentioned watching Netflix on the windows to one of the 12 Wing techs, he scolded me and told me to never mention that again. He was probably just jealous.

So I opened my laptop and started an episode of the most recent sitcom I'd been watching and switched screens to play it across the office windows. I tend to watch the same few sitcoms over and over, as I prefer a bit of mindless TV in the background. Somehow it keeps my mind clear and relaxed. Maybe it just helps me stop my mind wandering to my own problems. Like I said before, I tend to catastrophize if left to my own thinking, so it's better to remain distracted. My first patient was due in fifteen minutes and I had to get ready.

I don't work with kids. I actually decided this very early on in my clinical training. It's just too hard. I always found it very difficult to get through to children in therapy sessions. Sometimes I provided the most succinct, brilliant observation on a child's behaviour and the kid simply said, "I know you are, but what am I?" What was I supposed to do with that?

And working with kids meant working with parents and teachers. I couldn't handle that either. There are too many bad parents and apathetic teachers around. It just made me want to pull my hair out. I remember when I was doing a practicum and a little shrimp of a dad was explaining why spanking his eight-year-old was the only way to "learn 'em." I asked him if he'd still be spanking little Johnnie when the kid grew up and was six feet tall in university. He looked at me like I was the stupid one and said, "No, he'd be too big. He'd probably hit me back." "Exactly," I said, and waited for the dad's light bulb to turn on. It didn't. I think that dad needed a new light bulb.

So on this particular day, my first appointment arrived on time, but it wasn't the patient sitting in the office with me. It was his parents. Hooray! Parents.

The patient was actually a nineteen-year-old named Geoff who still lived at home. Lucky guy. Therefore, I wasn't violating my rule against working with kids. Geoff was an adult. The parents were giving me their expert opinion on why their son needed a psychologist.

"We're just concerned," the mom was saying. "Ever since he got that computer in his room, he's been different."

"He spends all goddamn time on that Internet, locked up in his bedroom," the dad added eloquently.

"And we know he's surfing bad things," the mom whispered.

I looked up from my iPad, where I kept my notes. "Bad things?"

"Dirty pictures," the dad blurted. "The boy is looking at pornography." He pronounced it *porno graphy* like it was two entirely separate words. Honestly, the guy might actually believe that to be the case.

Before I could stop myself, I wrote *dirty pictures* down on the iPad and then circled it. It seemed funny to think people looked up *dirty pictures* on the Internet. If that was the extent of what adolescents surfed online, then we'd be fine. "How do you guys know what he surfs?"

"Because he's a moron," the dad answered. "The wife was cleaning up in that pigsty room, and he'd left the computer on with a screen full of porno-graphy."

I turned to the mom. "What did you see?"

Her face flushed a little and she leaned over to me slightly. "Boobies and downstairs areas." She nodded, just a little, towards her own downstairs to make sure I understood.

I kept a straight face. I don't know how, but I did. I deserved an award. I looked back at the dad to gauge his reaction to the screen content revelation. He was still just fuming, barely containing his anger. I wrote *boobies* down on my iPad.

"Are you guys worried he's surfing any illegal material?" I asked when I felt ready to speak again.

"Illegal?" the dad barked.

"You know," I continued. "Like maybe underage images."

"Oh dear," the mom gasped. "I hope not."

"He better not be," the dad bellowed. "Or he'd get a swift boot in the ass out to the street."

I nodded. I wrote *swift boot* and *ass* down. "So Geoff is spending all his time in his room, and you're worried he's looking at dirty pictures too much."

"That's right," the dad confirmed. "He'll come home from work or university, and next thing he's up in his room and we don't see him."

"Wait," I said. "He's working and going to university?"

"Yes," the mom answered. "He's still got his job at the Tim's, and he started attending engineering at Dal." Tim's was Tim Hortons, a popular chain of coffee shops and Dal was Dalhousie University, one of Halifax's largest post-secondary schools.

"So the biggest concern is that you saw *dirty pictures* on his screen one time?"

"That's a pretty damn big concern," the dad snapped. "And every time the wife or I tried to ask what he was up to, he ignored us. He told us it wasn't our business, but it certainly is."

A thought occurred to me that might shed some light on the gravity of the situation. "Are you guys religious?"

"What's that got to do with it?" the dad asked.

"Just curious."

"We're Catholic," the mom answered. "We normally attend Mass during the week and then again on Sunday."

Chronically surfing Internet porn can be a big problem, especially for a younger brain. Unfortunately, religious types tend to have a bit of a skewed perspective about what is normal or problematic when it comes to sexuality. I was starting to get a clearer picture of Mom and Dad.

And poor Geoff.

"Do you believe in Jesus Christ?" the dad snapped at me. It was almost an attack.

"There's nothing more important than faith," I shot back with equal intensity.

He nodded his agreement as I breathed a sigh of relief on my dodge.

"Maybe I should have a chat with Geoff now," I said, and stood. I walked the parents back to my private waiting room and motioned for the son to come in. He was a normal-looking nineteen-year-old. Jeans, basketball shoes, and a T-shirt. He wore black-rimmed glasses and kept his hair a little longer, but otherwise you wouldn't pick him out of a crowd.

As we stepped back into my office, the dad called to Geoff with a final warning. "You be honest in there. I don't wanna waste my money on this shrink."

I shut the inside door and turned to my young patient. Geoff had an embarrassed smile on his face and shrugged. I just smiled back and motioned for him to sit on the couch. When we were both settled, I said, "So what's going on?"

"My parents are both idiots," he said.

I wrote *Geoff displays excellent insight* on my iPad.

I spent the rest of my session with Geoff, just making sure he was okay. He was doing fine and agreed to spend less time in his room and make sure his parents never found anything on his computer again. I couldn't justify booking another session and having the dad *waste* any more money on a *shrink*, so I left things open for the family to call if needed.

I was happy the session ended right on time because I had to take a little trip. I tend to be overly generous with my therapy times and frequently let them run over, so it was nice to be out exactly at the fifty-minute mark today. I needed to drive down to 12 Wing to meet with a case coordinator. It didn't hurt that the case coordinator was cute, so I enjoyed spending a bit of time down there. I met with her fairly regularly as part of my secret contract with a military division that didn't officially exist.

That's right. Here comes the top-secret business.

CHAPTER 2

So if you were from Atlantic Canada, then you would already know 12 Wing Shearwater is a naval aviation base and part of CFB (Canadian Forces Base) Halifax on the southern point of the Dartmouth peninsula in an area called Eastern Passage. It runs national and international operations and is a natural point of departure for many Atlantic missions regardless of where that mission originated.

That's the part that most people know — the stuff you can Google.

Here's the part only a handful of people know. The base is also home to a division called Special Services Coordination for High-Value Assets, or SSCHVA (pronounced Shiva). Shiva is obviously a god in the Hindu religion and the one most frequently associated with the practice of yoga. So that kind of health angle makes sense and is pretty clever. But Shiva is also associated with being a creator and destroyer, which maybe doesn't make as much sense. Either way, the secret program has a cool name.

SSCHVA is a military respite program for U.S., Canadian, and other allied military personnel who work with high-level clearance, generally on projects that are above top secret. So this includes black ops soldiers and military scientists and any other members who, for security clearance reasons, could never openly discuss their stress and occupation with a typical health care provider.

CFB Halifax base is the ideal spot to house SSCHVA for a number of reasons. It is more or less out of the way, being located in Nova Scotia, Canada, but still an area that is highly trafficked and, more important, easily accessible. The base is already home to national and international military personnel, so any additional military traffic wouldn't be suspicious. It is within a three-hour flight to thousands of military personnel up and down the Atlantic coast and only a six-hour flight over the Atlantic to our British allies. Shearwater also has its own landing strip, so personnel can fly in and out without having to use commercial airlines. Plus Halifax is a big enough city to offer more than enough services, accommodations, entertainment, shopping, and, so on for members staying here during their treatment.

But the SSCHVA program itself is a secret even to other military personnel at 12 Wing. The program is staffed by a very small group of soldiers, all of whom keep other duties on base to maintain a cover story. I am the only one who works off-site, so every so often I end up visiting in person.

From my private office in North End Dartmouth it is a straight drive down to Eastern Passage, maybe twenty minutes. Once I was in Eastern Passage I pulled off Main Road onto Bonaventure Street and slowed as I approached the military checkpoint.

A uniformed soldier started towards me, but then recognized my shiny white smile and nodded back towards his partner in the booth. The gate swung up and I kept driving. It was an expected part of my routine to come down to the base and check in with the SSCHVA program, so I was a regular at this gate. The soldiers on the base also knew I was a psychologist, but no one ever asked any questions about why I was there. There's something about working in mental health that makes people assume they shouldn't ask questions. It worked to my advantage in this case. I didn't even need a cover story.

The base itself has a family health clinic somewhere, so if I ever need a story, that would be it. So far I haven't, but I keep thinking I should at least figure out where the family health clinic is located. Just in case.

I parked near one of the main buildings and headed inside. The outside signage indicated this building was engineering and operations, and for the most part it was, but not the whole building.

There was more security inside. First there was an officer behind bulletproof glass in a small lobby. He looked up, saw it was me, and buzzed me through the next door. Unlike the traffic checkpoint, this officer knew about SSCHVA and knew why I was here.

I went down the hall past engineering and other aviation offices and turned the corner to find an old elevator. The building was only two stories tall, so the elevator was a bit of overkill, but necessary. I got in and used a security fob (the same one for my private office door, actually) and swiped the elevator panel before hitting *B* for basement. You need a RFID fob to be able to select the basement level otherwise you can only go up to the second floor. Chances are no one who didn't know about SSCHVA would bother to try the basement anyway. For years it was just a junk room full of old office furniture, discarded files, and other crap soaking up dust. SSCHVA turned it into a heavily secured base of operations with offices, common rooms, and even a little living suite.

As I stepped off the elevator, I almost bumped into Anne Petrost. I don't mean that as a bad thing. In fact, a little bump into Anne would've made it onto my daily list of highlights. She was quite the stunner. Mid-thirties, dark brown hair, olive skin. Blue eyes. Petite. And flirty with me.

"Oops," I said as I pulled up to keep from colliding into her. "Sorry."

She smiled. "Dr. Waiter," she said in an intentionally over-formal way. "To what do I owe the pleasure of your company?"

I smiled back. "I came to see you." We started to walk down the corridor towards her office. "It's the only reason I come here."

"Is that right?" she asked in mock surprise. "So I can have payments to your account stopped?"

"Oh." I recoiled. "Although seeing your smile is rather priceless, the world has not yet reached the point where such beauty is recognized as currency."

"So you choose money over beauty?" She frowned. "I'm devastated."

I nodded. "But you are a close second."

Anne was actually a pretty high-ranking officer in the Canadian military. She was a colonel who'd worked across Canada and briefly overseas. Her current official posting was something to do with the military police even though she spent most of her time in the SSCHVA office.

We reached her office and the door was already open. We went in, and she took a seat behind her desk while I dropped down into one of her uncomfortable guest chairs.

She held her hand out across the desk to me. I feigned a look of surprise and reached out to take the proffered hand. Anne pulled back before we connected.

"You're such a jackass," she managed through a smile. "The USB?"

I knew what she was reaching for. I dug in my front pocket and pulled out a rather largish USB drive in a steel rectangular case. It was about as long and thick as a giant French fry, which was big considering it held only sixteen gigabytes. But it wasn't an ordinary flash drive. It was encrypted with a combination lock built right onto the hardware. The encryption was military grade with multiple redundancies. When you slid the metal cover off, you found the actual numerical buttons and had two minutes to enter the proper code before the device was wiped. In addition, you had only five chances to enter the correct code before — you guessed it — the device erased. The code was a minimum of six digits and a maximum of twelve, meaning that there were over a trillion possible combinations. Don't bother to Google that, it was a lot of combinations.

Surprisingly, Anne opened the USB drive up and entered the combination correctly on the first try.

Actually, that wasn't surprising. The SSCHVA program set the code on this USB. It's technically their property. SSCHVA didn't use paper files — everything needed to go on a secure USB like this one. So that day, Anne was giving me three new *folders* by transferring them onto my stick.

She tapped a few things with her mouse after putting the unlocked USB into her computer and then turned back to me while the files transferred. I could see the little dialog window with the status bar on her screen. "So how's the wife?" She grinned.

"Good," I said. "How about your husband? Is he still a cop?"

She nodded. "I think so. At least he still has a pretty big gun."

It was too easy, so I ignored it. "Any new stories of muscleheads hitting on you at the gym?"

Her expression relaxed some. "Actually, I gave up on that gym out by Larry Uteck. I'm sticking to the base gym. The guys around here know better than to mess with a superior officer."

"Sounds like a conundrum," I offered, and smiled.

She shook her head and changed the subject yet again. "The General continues complaining that you don't use an office here on the base. We still have space for you."

"Nope. That's not going to happen."

"He's all about that option being more secure and better for SSCHVA. He might eventually insist on it."

"Then I'm going to have to explain why he's wrong all over again. The people I help don't want to stay on base. Normally it was a military base that helped create their stress and dysfunction. Having that physical separation helps them clear their heads — creates a more therapeutic milieu."

"Therapeutic milieu," she mocked. "*Ohh la la*, Dr. Waiter. Such fancy words."

"Oh, I can be fancy. You'd like it."

She turned back to her monitor and then used the mouse to safely remove the USB before tucking it back into the metal sleeve. She reached across the desk and dropped it into my waiting hand.

"So tell me about the new transplants," I said.

"First new transplant is a civilian computer genius." We called the SSCHVA patients *transplants*. I'm not sure why. "He's off work from some super top-secret research thing in Nevada. Sort of a nervous breakdown. Lots of anxiety and panic. It looked like his family was going to meet him here."

"Sounds like fun."

"I hope he is. I took the liberty of sticking him in your schedule for tomorrow morning."

I kept a few spots in my schedule that SSCHVA could book directly. They tended to let me book my own patients, but sometimes a case was a bit more urgent or the patient was anxious to get the date and time, so Anne put the person in. We did it on a shared cloud calendar, but only used code words to represent transplants, so there weren't any issues of confidentiality.

"Well, aren't you just ever so considerate?" I said, and gave her a giant fake smile. "What other transplants are coming?"

She glanced at her screen, but I knew she didn't have to. She took her job seriously and knew the details on these cases well. "There's an off-book shooter on his way. He's coming back from some dark runs in the Middle East and apparently not doing great."

Those guys were often bad news. Frequently boozers. An off-book, or dark run, referred to a mission that didn't run through normal channels and probably involved a lot more risk and violence than typical engagements. The soldiers could end up in a pretty psychologically damaged state.

"Great," I said.

"He isn't here for a few more weeks," she continued. "I guess there are some logistics on his travel slowing things down."

"Okay," I said. "Anyone else?"

"It's your lucky day. Another civilian scientist. Female. British. I know how much you like a British accent."

She was right, of course. I did enjoy a British accent, some of them. "What's she here for?"

"We actually didn't get a lot of detail on her. There's not much in the file on your USB there."

I frowned. "Really?" I didn't recall having a case with almost no details before. That wasn't how SSCHVA worked.

"Yep. This is sort of a handshake across the Atlantic. I'm really not sure what's going on. I guess you'll find out when you meet her. The request came in very specifically for you to see her ASAP. I put her in your schedule a couple of days from now. Hope that's okay, too."

"That's why I leave the spots there. You can either book a transplant in or even add your own name."

She looked up at me. "And what reason would I have for putting my own name in your schedule?"

"We'd figure something out," I said, and smiled, but I'm pretty sure it ended up looking dorky.

"Thanks." She smiled. It was more genuine. "Just give me a quick update after you see this British one, so I can put something in the files on this end."

"Will do," I said, and then started to stand. "We done?"

She nodded.

"Are you going to walk me out?" I tried to smile again.

"I think you'll be fine," she countered, but she matched my smile.

I turned and left, tucking the USB into my pocket.

As I walked back down the hall towards the elevator, my mind lingered on Anne. Attractive. A bit of an edge to her. Smart and playful. Such a nice combination of features. And her butt… yummy. It would be the perfect dessert to enjoy after.... But I stopped myself as soon as my mind went there. I shouldn't be having those thoughts. I reached up to my forehead with my fingertips and grabbed all the inappropriate thoughts and jerked them away, flinging them into the air around me. This was a bit of a strange habit for me, pulling unwanted thoughts out and tossing them. I had learned to do this to cope with any errant, unnecessary, or foolish thoughts. I physically pulled them out of my brain and discarded them. It was silly, but it worked.

CHAPTER 3

Thirty minutes after I left SSCHVA I arrived home in my suburb community on the outskirts of Halifax. Capilano Estates is a small community bordering Ashburn golf course. Technically, it's located in Windsor Junction, but most people consider it more like Fall River since that is a fancier area to associate with. They're all just a collection of large homes on big lots where you can't see your neighbour. But you can hear your neighbour. On a beautiful summer night you can hear them cursing each other out over finances.

Or sex.

Or the rotten kids.

Or all of the above.

There's something about big houses that seems to breed boredom and bad tempers. The bigger the house, the unhappier the occupants. But I might have the causation backwards. Maybe unhappy, bored people buy big homes to try to get happy and find something to do.

It doesn't work.

Arriving home was not my favourite thing in the world. Don't get me wrong. I love my wife and my house is nice, but sometimes I just sat around feeling guilty that I didn't love my beautiful wife *more* and didn't appreciate my big house *more*. And because I don't like feeling guilty, I then either got bored or mad. And then to burn off that excess energy, I would mow the lawn (summer) or shovel the driveway (winter). And then I was tired and went to bed, so I could start it all over the next day.

Don't listen to me. I'm just being negative. It's not that bad. Sometimes I'm just an asshole. Ask my wife. She'll vouch for that.

I used an app on my phone to open the garage door and pulled my Jeep inside, shutting the door right behind. My wife's Audi Q5 hybrid was already parked in the next space, plugged into the outlet we had to have installed. It's kind of funny that she spent all kinds of money on an Audi hybrid to protect the environment. Wouldn't it have been better to give that money to an environmental group and carpool with the neighbours? Maybe then our power bill wouldn't be so high. I reached up and pulled those thoughts out of my brain and flicked them away.

I headed into the house and dropped my keys on a table before stepping out of my shoes. Around the corner from this entranceway was the living room and kitchen. Lisa was sitting in the living room.

"Hey," I said.

"Hey."

She didn't look up from her iPad. She was probably on Pinterest or Facebook. I doubted she was surfing porn even though that was why the iPad was invented.

She put her iPad down and turned, putting her bare feet down on the rug. "How was your day?"

"Good enough," I said. "A nonstop stream of mentally deranged people. Who could ask for anything more?" I smiled sarcastically. My wife knew that part of my work involves the military, but nothing more. She wasn't allowed to know any more, actually.

"And were any of these *deranged people* able to help you work through your many issues?"

Banter. I do love this woman. "Actually," I replied in a most serious voice, "I'm a psychologist, so technically I'm supposed to help them." I paused. "But, yes, one of the pervert peeping toms did help me with a few questions I had about what teenagers look like when they shower."

"Oh God!" she said, standing. "Shut up. I'm sorry I asked." She came over and briefly touched my arm before continuing into the kitchen.

We still have sex, but we aren't generally affectionate. The touch on the arm was about as close as it got. But we have a good excuse for that. What we've been through normally ends a relationship, so we're beating those odds.

So far.

"How was your day?" I asked. My wife is a physiotherapist at a sports medicine clinic.

"Fine," she said, and continued into the kitchen where she turned on the Keurig and reached for a Starbucks coffee pod. Without looking back at me she asked, "You want one?"

I told her, "I'm good," but watched her from behind for an extra minute. She was wearing yoga pants and a tank top. Her dirty blonde hair trickled down to touch the swooping back of her top. She'd either just come home from, or was soon heading out to yoga. I was tempted to go over and embrace her from behind, but that would be awkward and probably result in a fight. She'd flinch. I'd feel hurt and blame her. She'd blame me for surprising her. I'd tell her that a husband is allowed to hug his fucking wife from behind, and she'd tell me to calm down.

Fingers. Forehead. Flick.

Bye-bye stinking thinking.

"I'm going to change," I announced, and started towards the staircase.

"I'm leaving for yoga shortly," she called after me. "Are you okay for supper?"

Thankfully she couldn't see my frown of annoyance at her patronizing question. I'm a grown man with a doctorate and I won't be able to figure out how to eat if she leaves? "I think I'll survive," I called back. She didn't respond.

And now I was thinking I had no idea what I might eat. Please let there be something leftover in the fridge or I might starve!

At the top of the stairs I rounded a corner past our son's room. The door was closed. I didn't even think about opening it and hurried past to our bedroom. We had a set of walk-in closets that faced each other. Lisa's was the bigger one. I flicked on a light as I entered mine and quickly changed into basketball shorts and a T-shirt. As I slipped the shorts on I vaguely noticed the scars. The longer basketball shorts nicely covered some nasty purple scars on my thighs. I have an odd collection of them on different parts of my body from a car accident a few years ago. It's weird because I can't remember the accident very well, but I sure have the scars to prove it.

I left my closet and briefly lingered at the door to Lisa's. My eyes drifted across the clothes and shoes lined up on shelves. I could feel memories drag along with my gaze. I was tempted to go touch the clothes, hold a shoe in my hand — look for the fine imprint of her toes.

Nope.

I stepped back and headed downstairs. I felt a bit like a dog getting easily distracted by the sight of a squirrel. Back on the main level, I heard, and felt, the rumble of Lisa's garage door closing. She'd gone to yoga.

I ducked into the kitchen and opened the fridge, leaning on the door as I peered inside. Fridges are one of those appliances that aren't perfectly designed for the tall guy. Inevitably, the thing I'm looking for is either on the back of the top shelf out of my line of sight or down so low that I can't get to it easily. We even have the fridge with the freezer drawer on the bottom. That doesn't help. There were no obvious leftovers to be seen. At least none in my direct line of sight. I might starve after all. I shouldn't have been so quick to tell Lisa I'd be okay.

I shut the top and opened the freezer drawer. Salvation. Frozen pepperoni pizza. I yanked it clear as I used a knee to shut the drawer. I turned the oven on to 375 degrees and put the pizza on a baking sheet before setting the timer to twenty-two minutes, more time than it needed, but the oven wasn't up to heat. That's the creative side to my cooking. There was nothing left to do in the kitchen, so I headed out to the garage.

On the way I slipped into a pair of older Nikes and grabbed a basketball off a shelf before using the garage side door. We had a basketball net on the side of the driveway and I still came out here to shoot baskets to kill time or just clear my head. It had taken me a while to feel right about using this hoop again, but it felt okay now. Someone should use this hoop.

I'd only taken a few shots when something in my peripheral caught my eye. My neighbour Roland, was ambling down towards me. He's a rotund, cheery guy from across the street, where he lives with his equally rotund wife and three butterball kids. He was all smiles as he lumbered over. I briefly had a flash of inviting him to a game of one-on-one and crushing my crotch in his face as I jumped over him to dunk. I think I saw that in a movie. I laughed, but immediately pulled that thought out and chucked it away.

"Hey, Roland," I called tucking the ball under my arm.

"Yo, Doc." He was breathing a little heavy from the trek down the long driveway. "I've got a business question for you."

I nodded, inviting him to continue.

"You're a psychologist. You work with people with sexual problems, right?"

Oh God, don't ask me about your love life. "Yes," I answered hesitantly.

"There's a guy at my office..." Roland was an accountant or something. I actually had no idea what he did. "...that got suspended for surfing dirty pictures on the company computer. We aren't going to consider him for a return to work until he gets a psych assessment about his problem. I wondered if that was something you did?"

"Yep. I do that kind of stuff. But why are you asking about it?"

"He's on my caseload. I need to make a recommendation for him."

Oh right. I remembered now. He was some kind of human resources guy. For an accounting firm? No idea. "Sure," I said. "I've got a pizza in the oven, so I have to go back in. Come with me and I'll get you my card."

He thanked me and hustled behind. He probably thought he could scam a piece of my frozen pizza after he got my card.

No way.

CHAPTER 4

There are three kinds of appointments I generally have when working. The first is an assessment appointment. In those, I meet someone and try to figure them out, sometimes using psych tests to help with the process and ultimately writing up a report that explains why the person is so messed up. Those are the best kinds of appointments. They last only as long as they need to — even if it is stretched over days or weeks — and they have a very specific, and achievable, goal. Plus, people are pretty interesting to meet, and the luxury of being a psychologist is that I can ask literally any question I want.

"When was the last time you and your wife had sex?"

"What was it like?"

"How much do you drink?"

"When was the last time you did something you regret?"

"How many fingers am I holding up?"

That last question is a joke. I have cards with fingers on them that they have to count — I never hold up my own fingers.

The second kind of appointment is also pretty cool — meeting someone for the first session of therapy. It is a bit like an assessment appointment in that I'm just trying to get to know, and understand, the person before we get down to the serious healing. So the first few sessions with a new therapy patient are all about the question and answer. So all and all, still a very interesting appointment because ....(See above note on people being messed up.)

The worst sessions, the ones that are the most difficult, are the ongoing therapy sessions. I'm talking about sessions that have gone on for weeks or months. Sessions that often start the same way, "How are we doing today?" and then each session involves rehashing the same key points of recovery over and over and over:

"Well, Mr. X, you know that being alone in the house is a trigger for surfing porn, so why didn't you go to the mall with your family?"

"Now, Mr. Y, we've talked about hanging out with Jimmy and how you can't resist drinking."

Within those categories of activities, about fifty percent are transplant referrals from SSCHVA. Less than ten percent are general mental health referrals, and the rest of my patients come from the forensic world and mainly consist of people charged for sex stuff and going through court.

That day, I was meeting a new SSCHVA transplant for the first time. He was a civilian quantum computer pioneer (whatever that means), and Anne had booked the appointment, so I'd never even spoken to this guy on the phone. I'd only glanced at his USB file. His name was Nathan Zwicker, or, more appropriately, Dr. Zwicker since he had a couple of PhDs in computer science, quantum physics, things like that. He'd been working at some secret project in Nevada until three weeks before when he took a leave of absence for stress, anxiety, and panic attacks too. No wonder he was transplanted here to SSCHVA.

I tend to review my files on new people just before they arrive, especially the SSCHVA transplants. For one, the information is on the secure USB drive, and it almost never goes home with me. So the flash drive is either here in this secure private office or being transported back to 12 Wing to be updated or swapped out. It isn't a smart idea to carry confidential data, even encrypted, around town. So that means most of my SSCHVA contract work has to happen in this office. But I also prefer to have file details fresh in my mind when a new transplant is in front of me. That lets me focus on what they are saying and focus less on trying to figure out who they are.

This Zwicker guy was a family man who seemed pretty preoccupied with his academic career. His C.V. listed lots of awards and invited presentations at high-level academic events. The term *quantum computing* came up over and over too. I needed to make sure I asked about that. I was still flipping through the pages on my laptop when my phone buzzed, indicating someone had opened the waiting room door: Nathan Zwicker had arrived.

I grabbed a clipboard and hopped over to my door, opening it to find a thin guy in one of the chairs. He wore tiny wire-rimmed glasses, and although he was balding, he looked to be a bit younger than me. As I recalled from the file he was late thirties. He looked up and then stood.

"Dr. Zwicker," I said, and extended a hand.

He nodded and we shook hands. His grip was a bit wet and not very firm. He looked kind of pale and stressed. Actually, he didn't look stressed exactly; he looked more afraid.

"Are you okay?" I asked as I took my hand back. I subtly let my arm drop to my side where I could wipe my palm against my leg.

"I'm okay," he said, but it wasn't convincing.

"Well, listen," I started. "I have these forms here for you to review and sign off. I'll just leave you here to take care of that and then we'll go back into my office and chat. Sound good?"

I handed him the clipboard and pen. He just took it and sat back down without a word. I hesitated a moment and then shut the waiting room door and returned to my office. The paperwork was just some basic personal info and a contract outlining the nature and limitations of the therapy arrangement. I generally had all my patients fill them out in the waiting room so they could read the documents without me staring at them. I didn't want to rush them.

Once in my office, I sat back at my laptop and flipped through a few more pages on Zwicker. I wasn't sure why the guy was so spooked. I thought he was just an anxiety case and assumed it was a typical perfectionist getting overloaded. Now I wondered what else was going on. I had only a few minutes before I heard him call for me.

I poked my head back into the waiting room. "All done?" I asked.

He nodded and stood as I motioned for him to come into the inner office.

Once seated back in my office, I brought my phone out and used an app to seal the outside door and then the inside door. Most people assume I'm just setting the phone to silent or something, but I can control some of the safety features from here. I set the phone down on the little side table next to my bucket seat and addressed him on the couch. "Any questions about the forms you just filled out?"

He shook his head.

"And you are aware that these sessions are covered under the North American Classified Information Schedule?" The North American Classified Information Schedule (or NACSIS, as it is pronounced) is a complicated agreement that essentially says that people covered under it cannot discuss any of their work with anyone other than another person covered under NACSIS. Unless they want to disappear from the face of the earth — and, no, that isn't an exaggeration. Even the NACSIS policy doesn't exist to anyone not covered by it.

He nodded.

"So what's going on?" I asked as informally as I could manage.

He sucked in a big breath, but remained quiet with no eye contact. This guy had a lot on his mind.

I switched gears to get his lips moving. "Your family's here in Halifax with you?"

He nodded.

"You guys ever been to Nova Scotia before?"

"No," he said.

SUCCESS! He spoke.

"Where are you guys from originally?"

"I'm from Ohio, but I did my grad school at MIT, which is where I met my wife. She's got a doctorate in mathematics."

"Kids?"

"One daughter. Cassie. She's twelve."

His face didn't exactly light up when he talked about his family. Maybe they weren't pleased about the current situation.

"What are they feeling about coming to Nova Scotia?"

He shrugged. "It's fine. We lived outside of Boston for a few years. It feels a bit like that."

"When did you move to Nevada?"

His expression noticeably darkened. My segue was not as subtle as I'd hoped. "I took a contract with the government and was transferred there about six months ago. There was research underway and they needed me."

I let that just sit in the room. Sometimes the most effective question a psychologist can ask is no question.

Eventually he felt the weight of the silence and continued. "There were some computer interface issues that they were pretty motivated to chuck money at, and I got swallowed up in it."

"It sounds like the job might have contributed to the difficulties you're having now."

He snorted a sarcastic laugh. "The job *is* the difficulties I'm having now. If I didn't think my family and I would be killed, I would have gone to the police or the media or someone. Hell, I don't even know. Who do you go to when you have a science fiction story about government conspiracy with big business?"

"Who is that fat documentary guy?" I offered with a smirk. "Michael Moore?"

He laughed. A real one this time. "Exactly. That might have been a good choice."

I let the silence fill the room again until he continued, "The way the world works is pretty fucked up, you know? The general public doesn't know even one percent of what's actually going on and how fucking corrupt everything is."

I nodded, not entirely sure whether to agree with that or gently challenge it. Whenever a psychologist isn't exactly sure of what to say he has two choices: nod knowingly, or say, with a fantastically curious expression, "Tell me more about that." This time I chose the nod. And I don't want to brag, but I'm fucking excellent at doing the nod.

He was staring out my high-tech windows. I had them set to clear, so they just looked like windows. "Do you know what antigravity is?"

I liked this guy already. I did not see that one coming. "It's what makes spaceships fly. It's stuff that goes up instead of dropping towards the Earth."

He snapped towards me. I think he was trying to gauge if my answer was a joke or not. "No. That's a common misconception." He slid to the edge of his seat and became more animated, holding his hands up, demonstrating the principles at play. "Gravity is the attraction of one body of a particular mass to another. For us, gravity is the result of the mass of the Earth beneath us. The force of gravity is exerted on our mass because of the mass of the Earth." He moved his fist towards his palm, simulating the attractive force. "People often mistake antigravity as opposite force, where instead of mass attracting mass, it repels." He again used his hands to illustrate his fist flying away from his palm.

"Antigravity is the idea that a form of matter can exist that is unaffected by the force of gravity. It isn't repelled, but simply unresponsive. It ignores the mass of the Earth or whatever mass it is near." To illustrate this he let his fist hover over his palm.

"So if I set the antigravity object here, two inches above the ground, it simply sits there in space until another force acts on it. Like wind or another object striking or moving it. Antigravity, as a concept, is not propulsion, but absence of adherence to gravitational waves."

His voice was pressured, agitated. I nodded. I was tempted to say, "Tell me more about that," but my head hurt.

He dropped his hands and sat back on the couch. "I know it sounds like crazy science fiction stuff and you're wondering why I'm telling you this." He paused to confirm this in my expression.

Confirmation received.

He took a long, deep breath again. "I'm telling you because the military has antigravity material. That was part of the project I was working on. Well, that's what they originally told me, anyway."

So at this point you've got to wonder if we're dealing with a psychotic person or whether shit just got real interesting. Two things point to the latter. One, this guy was referred to me out of a top-secret military program, and, two, you're reading about this in a book, so it's a good bet it wasn't just delusions.

I decided on my fail-safe question. "Tell me more about the antigravity."

He straightened his glasses. His pointy nose was having trouble holding them up. "What do you want to know? I'm pretty sure it was a fluke. They weren't trying to find it. They had no idea what the hell they were doing!"

He had just crept up the freak-out scale a little more. I needed to calm him.

"Right," I started. "Let's just figure this out together. You help me understand what was going on."

That approach didn't work. He started yelling again. "I don't even understand. It's all bullshit. The project leader tells me one thing, but the general in charge tells me another. I never knew who to believe. It was always just *fix the computers! Fix the computers!*"

This time I just left the words in the air around us. I wanted the silence to help calm the situation. I needed this guy calm. I'm a psychologist, but I hate heavy, dramatic emotional scenes.

"Let's switch gears," I tried. "Let's talk about you and how you're feeling."

"I'm feeling like I'm a dead man walking," he shouted. "They don't let people out of that base once they're involved in this project. I shouldn't be here. I need to hide. I need out."

"Who's going to kill you?" Jesus, I was wishing I'd read this guy's file closer. This wasn't going the way I had expected.

"That Slim guy. The military. Anyone. You, maybe? Are these walls soundproof?" His eyes darted around the room.

The walls were soundproof, but I opted to avoid that line of questions. "Okay. Let's breathe for a second."

He slumped back in his chair and covered his face with his hands, twisting his glasses awkwardly as he did so.

I spoke very quietly, setting a peaceful tempo. "You're safe here. You're safe in Halifax, in general. This isn't the kind of place where people get killed. You're here specifically to be kept safe and to take some time out. You're obviously very stressed."

He sighed as he dropped his hands. "I'm sorry. I've just been expecting to die ever since I asked for a leave of absence off that goddamn base. When I met with the doc down there... I expected to get shot when I left her office. When the car picked me up to take me to the airport...I thought they'd bury me in the desert. When I got on the plane, I thought it would never arrive here." Tears fell unrestrained down his cheeks. "I've been waiting to die for close to two weeks."

I hate crying. Why did he have to start crying? Was I supposed to hug him? No. That'd be weird. I'll try soothing words, I thought. "Well, it seems like they've had lots of chances to kill you and haven't so far, so I'd say you're safe right now."

In an almost hysterical voice, he yelled, "Slim refuses to allow loose ends on his little kitten project. He's the real monster here. He's the one people need to be afraid of. All he does is lie and lie and lie!"

Well, that created far more questions than it answered.

"Slim?" I asked tentatively, hoping not to set him off.

"I don't know. Whatever his name is." He sniffed, but the waterworks started to dry up. "He was the project lead. He wasn't even military, so I don't know why he had so much control at that base."

"We've got only about fifteen minutes left. Why don't you tell me why you wanted this leave of absence?"

"It doesn't matter," he said after a brief hesitation.

I just waited.

"Look, I think that's all I can do right now. Can we start again tomorrow or something?"

I flipped my iPad screen over to Calendar view. Anne had booked another transplant in for me tomorrow.

"I can't do tomorrow, but what about Friday?"

"Sure," he said weakly as he stood.

I stood too and picked up my phone, so I could open the app to unlock the doors. We walked through the inner office door and paused together at the next.

"Just try to relax. You're safe here, and we'll work on this stuff together. I'm in your corner, okay?" I extended my hand.

He smiled and took my hand and looked at me with an odd expression. "I can trust you, can't I?"

I suppressed a frown of surprise. "Yes."

He took a big breath, obviously contemplating something. "I think I'm going to introduce you to someone." He partially stumbled over the words.

"Who's that?"

He nodded, confidence growing in his decision. "Yep. I'm going to set you up. I need to know someone else is with me on this." He paused and then added, "In case something happens."

I had no idea what he was talking about. "Let's pick this up again Friday." I realized we were still shaking hands. I pulled my hand back. "You go get some rest."

"Thanks. I'll try." He stepped out into the corridor and turned back. "See you Friday."

"Absolutely. I'm counting on it."

He turned down the hall, and I saw him pulling his phone out as he left. Strange guy. Probably a typical genius type. I figured we'd cover a lot more ground next time. I turned back into my office.

Little did I know that Nathan Zwicker was going to

walk down the stairs to the lobby, leave the building, and immediately be run over and killed.

CHAPTER 5

I watched the accident aftermath from my office window three stories above. The ambulance, the police, the countless gawking bystanders. It was a scene.

But I couldn't go down. I wondered if I should, but I knew that I couldn't answer questions about how I knew Nathan Zwicker or why he was at this address.

Even if I just said I was his psychologist and didn't go near all the military stuff, it would just leave a trail of questions that eventually led to areas that I couldn't talk about.

No. It was better for me to stay out of it, so I watched from up here.

Goddamn it.

Was that a coincidence? The guy was paranoid about being killed and then this. I knew life could be random and ridiculous, but this stretched random to extremes.

Just in case I had any doubt this was a set-up, a black sedan rolled up and parked along the intersecting side street. It was one of those painfully obvious government cars with tinted windows. They had no intention of being subtle. Two agent-looking guys got out and headed over to the nearest police car. They flashed credentials at the cop and had the briefest of conversations. The cop pointed them to another officer near the ambulance, so the agents made their way over and flashed credentials again. Now they spoke to the cop and the ambulance driver. One of the agents pointed south and the ambulance guy nodded.

And then the weird part happened. The ambulance pulled away. No siren. No lights. And headed the opposite direction from the nearest hospital. Then the police conferred quickly and retreated to their patrol cars — there were two units on scene. And they left. They didn't stay and canvass the neighbourhood to try to get an eyewitness to the hit and run. They didn't protect the crime scene for forensics to come to do measurements. They just left.

And then the crowds left.

And it was just the two agents standing on the sidewalk outside my office. I keep referring to them as agents, but I had no fucking clue who those guys were that they could just sweep in and shoo everyone away. What the hell?

As I watched, one of the agents turned his head slowly and dragged his view up my building until he was looking right in my window. I ducked, reflexively, and then I felt like a tool. My high-tech windows are set to view out, but you can't see in. I was just being paranoid. I stood again, but buddy was still staring up at me. Creepy.

Then the agents meandered back to their secret-agent-mobile and left, and I stood at my window, watching the peaceful street below. Not even so much as a bloodstain to mark the spot where Nathan Zwicker was just murdered.

I dropped back into my bucket seat and let my arms hang over the sides. Now I needed a psychologist. I wished a good one worked in Halifax, but I know them all and none are as good as me.

Could I be my own psychologist?

"So tell me," I began out loud, like a lunatic. "How are you feeling right now?"

"I'm pretty stressed," I replied. "Someone I was just talking to died in front of my building. Someone who I basically guaranteed safety to."

"Tell me more about how you're feeling."

"I'm thinking that I have two choices. One, take the USB file on this guy back to SSCHVA as soon as possible and get myself off this pilotless plane, or, two, reread that USB file a little more closely."

I folded my arms contemplatively. "You're going to opt for the risky choice, aren't you?"

I shrugged noncommittally.

"Is your recklessness because of what happened to your son?" I asked, knowing the answer already.

I leapt to my feet. This guy was good. "Fuck off," I yelled because I was not quite ready to go there yet. I'd rather live in my recklessness a while longer. "This session is over and I'm not paying you a nickel for this bullshit."

It was kind of what I expected from this patient. He seemed a bit unstable.

I reached up and pulled these thoughts out of my

brain and chucked them away. I had to focus. I went over and flipped open my laptop as I retrieved the USB out of a locked drawer. After tapping in the numerical code, I inserted it and waited for the dialog window to pop up, so I could open the folder on Zwicker.

His electronic file was sparse. It didn't take long to read that he had been stationed in Nevada at an unnamed project for only about six months. He was a civilian recruit to the science project, but the exact nature of the work was labelled as *Classified.* That seemed odd since I was supposed to have pretty high-level clearance, as were the rest of the people at SSCHVA, but I guess some things even we weren't allowed to know.

It seemed that Dr. Zwicker had anxiety issues shortly after arrival at the project and was being seen by the base GP. They tried him on a low-dose anxiolytic, but the base discouraged very aggressive pharmacological treatment because of the nature of the work. In other words, they didn't want people doped out on drugs operating dangerous machines. Made sense. The file was thin on the exact details, but Dr. Zwicker became increasingly anxious over his six months and eventually was approved for a respite. That's where SSCHVA entered the picture.

The file didn't mention antigravity, but that didn't mean that wasn't the research of interest.

The rest of the electronic folder held personal details with things like his C.V., original application to join the Nevada project, background files on him and his family, etc. I'd already looked at much of this stuff, so I went through it again quickly. There were only a few files left when my cell rang. The called ID showed *Private Number.*

"Dr. Waiter," I answered after briefly considering letting it pass over to voice mail.

"Blake? It's Anne."

"Hey."

"Did you know Dr. Zwicker died? You were supposed to see him." Her voice was slightly pressured.

"Yeah. He died outside my office here. Hit and run."

"Jesus! Did you see it happen?"

"Nope."

"So had you seen him first? Did you talk to him?"

"Yeah. We'd just finished our first session."

Silence. Then, "How soon can you get that USB back to me?"

"Why? What's going on?"

Silence again. She was weighing each answer. "There's something of a shit storm going on."

I waited, assuming she'd continue. I was wrong. "A shit storm about what?"

"Listen," she started up, sounding pressured. "Dr. Zwicker shouldn't have been here. He shouldn't have seen you. I think it is better if you never saw him and you just get that USB back here ASAP."

"But I did see him and he was worried that someone was going to kill him."

"*Nope!*" she basically yelled into the phone. "Don't talk about it. Don't talk to me. You didn't see him. He didn't make it upstairs to your office. That's going to be best for everyone here. Trust me. Just get that USB back to me and let's just delete this one."

Obviously I had a thousand more questions, but now wasn't the time. "Sure. Fine."

"When?" she demanded.

"Right away."

"Good," she said, and hung up.

As I pulled the phone off my ear, I noticed an open dialog window on my screen. It was a text box that just said, *Hello, Dr. Waiter.*

That didn't make any sense. I put a finger on the box and swiped it away. My phone was supposed to be military grade secure, so I shouldn't have a virus. Whatever. I tucked my cell away and ejected the USB from the laptop after I closed out all the files. My current priority was eliminating Nathan Zwicker from my caseload. The sooner I passed the USB back to Anne, the better. I didn't need it.

I locked up my inner office and headed to the other door, opening it with my phone as I walked. When I opened the next door, all light from the corridor was blocked by an enormous mountain of a man who had been standing there.

And he did not look amused.

CHAPTER 6

The man mountain standing in front of me was Chuck Peligro, and I'd forgotten about our appointment.

"You going somewhere, Doc?"

He stood close to six foot six, and his shoulders literally touched both sides of the doorframe as he stood there. Shaved head and stubble on a face permanently fixed in a scowl. He wore those Oakley Blade sunglasses that make anyone instantly look like a tool. Chuck liked to wear the sunglasses inside too and frequently wore them through most of our appointments.

And we had lots of appointments. Three per week to be exact: Monday, Wednesday, and Fridays at eleven a.m., sharp. Never late. Rarely early. He arrived exactly for eleven o'clock and I needed to be ready. If I was even the slightest bit late, it could set him off. When we first started meeting, I was on a long-distance call that ran over eleven a.m. while Chuck was in the waiting room. He broke my coffee table in half on his way out the door at three minutes past.

So, no, I wasn't going to tell Chuckles that I forgot about our appointment. "I was just making sure the door was open for you, Chuck."

He pushed into the room intentionally bumping into me. I'm not small, but when that much muscle bumps into you, you get tossed. I stumbled back and hit my calf on the corner of the coffee table.

"Shit," I said quickly.

He paused and turned to look down at me with his ridiculous sunglasses. "Problem?"

"Nope."

I grimaced ever so slightly and swallowed my urge to rub the pain out of my leg. When you show any emotion or reaction like pain, sadness, fear, or anxiety, Chuck mocks you. Even now he looked down at me a second too long and then a grin creased the corner of his mouth before he headed into the inside office. The guy hated emotion — other than anger.

Out of his line of sight, I flipped him off quickly and then followed. My cell phone was still in my hand with the door app opened, so I locked the outer door and tucked the phone away as I sat.

"How're things?" I started.

He sighed. The couch creaked under his weight as he shifted. He didn't always answer my questions. I had to figure out the right question, or sometimes just the right way to ask a question, before he would answer. He stretched his arms out to lay them on the back of the couch and deliberately looked away from me.

My patience was pretty slim that day. I wanted to get out of there and drop that USB off. My head wasn't on Chuck's numerous problems and annoying quirks. For one, the guy was brain damaged. He was volatile, memory impaired, impulsive, and generally an asshole. I guess getting a metal plate put in your head can do that, but from the reports I'd seen, he was an asshole long before the brain injury.

He didn't look at me as he finally spoke. "You know what they used to call me before I ended up in this faggot town?"

Here we go. He's going to tell me the story he tells at least once a week. "What's that?"

"Chuck the Fuck." He grinned widely. He couldn't help himself. He loved this story. "You know why?"

Because you've always been a fucking jerk? "No, why?"

"I used to fuck people up. That was my job and I was good at it." His smile increased and then just as quickly slid away.

He wasn't kidding. It was his job to fuck people up. He was a black ops, off-book operative for U.S. and other allied interests. He did some shit that no one can ever know about. Killing people. Torturing terrorists or even the family of terrorists to get info. I've only seen parts of his classified folder and that was more than enough. His brain injury eight months ago left him as just a shell of his former self. No longer able to do the kind of stuff he was trained for.

"Now I'm sitting here," he announced, holding his hands up to indicate the office. "All because of this." He knocked roughly on the side of his head to indicate the steel plate. "What's that about?"

At some level he knows his old life is gone. You can see it in his face. But he doesn't acknowledge it. He can't, really. He has a condition that affects a significant number of brain-injured patients — anosognosia. He literally doesn't have the capacity to acknowledge the deficits he now experiences as a result of his brain injury. He knows he was in an accident, but in his world there weren't any lasting effects from the injury and the military is just punishing him by putting him off active duty.

"What's on the schedule for this week?"

He pulled his phone out and flipped through screens. "Gym, physio, meeting with HR guy. Just wasting time."

Chuck lived by his calendar. He thought he did it because his commander ordered it, but really it was one of those things he needed to do to keep track of his life.

I didn't care about his schedule. I knew what was on it. His electronic schedule showed up on my computer and at SSCHVA. We all knew what Chuck was doing and when. But he was also required to take note of angry episodes on his calendar.

"Any blow ups on there?"

"Nah, man. I'm not like that."

I knew he freaked out just yesterday at the manager at his apartment building. "Oh yeah? Can you just give your calendar a look over?"

My job with Chuckles was to monitor his outbursts and help him with anger and impulse management while continuing to build any skills around his cognitive rehab. The guy was a real wreck, but had been an enormous asset to the military when he was functioning. It was a bit sad that he was left like this, and I think that's why someone was paying for me to see him three times a week even though there'd been virtually no progress in close to a year. Sometimes I felt bad for him.

"Why don't you look over your own calendar, you fancy gay-boy?"

And sometimes I didn't feel bad for this giant asshole. This was one of those days when my job sort of sucked.

I took a slow breath before answering him. "If I looked at my own calendar, I'd find that I did have a blow-up at the apartment manager just a few days ago. That guy's an idiot."

Chuck turned on me. Something struck a little chord in his broken brain. Still holding his phone, he glanced down at it. "The super at my building is an idiot." It almost sounded like a question. He was working it through in his cloudy mind.

But now we were moving. I could angle a bit of a conversation about anger management out of the next thirty minutes.

And then I could drive like a maniac to meet up with Anne and be done with Nathan Zwicker.

CHAPTER 7

I made record time arriving at Anne's office and tossed the USB down on her desk.

"What the hell's going on? Was that military people who came and tidied up the murder scene?" I asked.

She took the USB and handed me another in its place. "Don't say murder. Don't talk about Nathan Zwicker. Did you chart him on this?" She held up the USB. All charting and patient notes were supposed to end up on the encrypted USB.

"I hadn't gotten that far before he was murdered."

"Jesus. What did I just say? Don't say murder. It was a hit and run."

We just stared at each other for a bit. Finally, I broke the silence. "So he doesn't exist and I never saw him."

She nodded. You could tell she wasn't entirely comfortable with this either.

"How can something be above our clearance level? I thought that was the point of SSCHVA. Total clearance."

"I don't have the whole story, but reading between the lines, I don't think he was supposed to leave the Nevada project. I think there was a screw-up that got him in our program."

"What do you mean he wasn't supposed to leave the Nevada project?"

"It looks to me like the Nevada project was so top-secret that no one was supposed to go off base. They should have dealt with Dr. Zwicker's issue down there and not let him get all the way to Halifax. I think that was the screw-up."

"A screw-up they needed to fix by killing him?"

She rolled her eyes. Hard. Then she continued. "The other two cases we talked about are on that new USB. Just carry on. Business as usual."

"His wife and kid are here. He has a twelve-year-old daughter."

She didn't say anything.

"What happens to them? Another accident?"

Still nothing from her.

"I guess we're done talking about it."

She either couldn't, or wouldn't, say any more about it. I stood and left her office. She wasn't walking me to the elevators today. Part of me wanted to keep pushing, almost felt like it was my duty to dig a bit more. I basically promised the guy he was safe here in Halifax and now he was dead. I know it wasn't my fault, but still…I felt like shit about it.

I punched the *up* button and waited. The elevator in this building was deliberately ancient in appearance and operation to reduce suspicion. That meant I often waited here.

Even if I wanted to pursue this Nathan Zwicker mess, I didn't have any clues left. The USB file was gone now. I had no clue where his wife and daughter lived, and they were likely already scooped up by whatever clandestine branch of the military was taking this over.

Case closed. My hands were completely washed of the matter.

The elevator arrived, and I stepped on just as my phone beeped. A tone I didn't immediately recognize. I pulled it out as the doors of the elevator slid shut.

A text box. *Hello, Dr. Waiter.* And a blinking prompt for me to enter a response.

What the hell? I reached to hit the basement button again. I might have to get SSCHVA to check my phone. I should have mentioned this virus to Anne when I was with her. There was no way I should be getting some mystery text box on my phone. No way. I used a finger to swipe the box away, but it bounced back and re-centered on my screen.

Hello, Dr. Waiter and the blinking prompt.

Fuck! I pulled up a menu from the bottom of my screen to revel recently opened apps. The phone dialler and email were the only apps that showed. I quickly swiped them away, closing out everything, then I hit the home screen button.

Blank — just my screen background of a beach scene (actually, Clam Harbour Beach — I'd taken the picture a few summers ago). The elevator stopped and the doors opened onto the basement again. I stepped out, determined to tell Anne that something weird was going on with my phone, and then I hesitated. I'm not sure why, but suddenly I had a wave rush over me about who I could trust at the moment. I knew Anne wasn't telling me everything.

Then *bing!* and the text box was back. But a different message this time.

Dr. Zwicker thought I could help you. He asked that I make contact. And the blinking prompt.

Now that was weird. I backed into the elevator and hit the button for the first floor. The doors eased closed, and the car rose up before the doors opened again. I stepped out and glanced back in, taking note of the cameras. Then I glanced up and down the corridor. I suddenly felt like I was being watched and felt very self-conscious. Was I being set up with this reference to Zwicker?

I clicked the box, bringing up my virtual keyboard, and typed, *Who is this?*

I am Talus, came the immediate reply

I kept walking and tucked the phone into my pocket as I passed the security station at the entrance to the building. I decided not to use my phone again until I was safely in my Jeep. I did a little Olympic speed walk and slid back into my car before I typed again. *How r u sending these messages?*

Through your cellular network.

Nice. This guy's a comedian.

Funny, I typed. *I meant that my phone is secure and u shouldn't have access.*

Nothing is secure. Do you require my assistance?

With what??? I typed.

Dr. Zwicker instructed me to work with you.

On what?

No parameters were set. At the moment you have unlimited

access.

What's this guy talking about? *How do u know Dr. Zwicker?*

Mentor.

What do u know about his death?

Officially listed as hit and run, but no active police file open. Case appears closed.

You hacked the Halifax Police? That didn't sound good.

Police server lacks significant security. Was not much of a hack.

So did u hack my phone? R *u a hacker who works with Dr. Z?*

Yes and yes.

Fuck. *Get out of my phone. This could get u in serious trouble.*

The dialog box was idle for a moment and then an address popped up. A house on Henry Street in South End Halifax, near Dalhousie University. I knew SSCHVA owned some houses around there for transplants coming in with families. They kept the furnished residences (along with a few furnished condos) as safe houses because often the transplants were here for months, not just a few days. Psychologically, it was better to recover in something like a home. I was pretty sure I knew whose address this hacker just put on my phone, but I typed the question anyway. *Whose address?*

A winky face emoticon was my answer. Pretty cheeky bastard, this hacker. I tossed the phone onto the passenger seat. I didn't have any more time for these games. Now I wished I had left my phone with Anne to be debugged or whatever. I only had a few patients booked in after lunch, and thankfully none of them were transplants, so no more drama. I really couldn't handle more patients getting murdered outside my office. I have a strict one murdered patient per day rule, and I wasn't about to break that.

Jesus, what's wrong with me? Sometimes my head just drifts to weirdness. I pulled those thoughts out and tossed them away before I started driving. I wanted to grab something to eat before I got back to my office.

CHAPTER 8

Comfortably back in my office in the afternoon, I was sitting with my next patient, Gary Ryan. He was a recent addition to my weekly sessions. Somewhere in his mid-fifties and slim with thinning grey hair, he was seeing me because of an addiction to visiting escorts. A less sophisticated person might call them prostitutes.

To me, being addicted to seeing escorts was a grey area of concern. On the one hand it was a questionable pursuit, legally, since the police could charge you even though it was a debatable law and many police forces didn't pursue it too hard. I suppose that's why so many escorts can simply advertise on mainstream buy and sell sites like craigslist. You can surf some pretty explicit ads for local escorts and then meet up with the lady you pick within a few hours — if even that long.

On the other hand, being addicted to escorts was a difficult thing to pull off when you'd been married for twenty-eight years. That's how long Gary had been married when his wife stumbled onto his Internet history of surfing escorts. That led her to investigating his email and cell phone to find the messages where he'd set up the dates. It also seemed odd to me how men rarely cover up their tracks. It was so easy to find out what Gary had been up to that it begged the classic psychology question — did he want to get caught?

And maybe he did. We'd had three sessions so far, and much of that had been exploring his family and relationship history. Before I can help someone, I need to know who they are. Gary's father had passed away when he was young, and his mom and a much older sister raised him. He hadn't dated as a teen, claiming he was always shy, and then married the first woman he dated in his twenties. They had a couple of kids early on, but both were gone off to university now.

Gary was fighting to stay in the house and to stay in the marriage. When his wife found out that Gary had slept with about twenty escorts over the last three years, she didn't take it well. After dodging a few kitchen plates and a coffee pot, he'd moved out to a motel for three weeks. He was back at home now, but slept in the basement.

"Things are still pretty tense at home, then?" I said because stating the obvious was one of my specialties.

Gary nodded. He was a bit of a sad sack, often tearful throughout our sessions. Thankfully the waterworks never fully turned on, not yet anyway and not if I could prevent it!

"What's your earliest memory of sex?" I asked.

He considered the question for a moment. "That's tough because I think I was curious as a pre-teen or early teenager, but I can remember my sister and my mom talking about it."

"And what were they saying?"

"After my dad died, my mom didn't want anything to do with men. She didn't date or anything, and my sister had a bad experience with a boyfriend in high school and didn't like men either. I guess the message I got was that men are bad and sex is just one of the bad things men push on women."

"How'd that make you feel?"

"It made me feel...." He paused to find the right word. "Guilty. I always felt like apologizing for being a guy. I felt like men had been to blame for them feeling bad and I was guilty by association."

"And how old were you when your dad passed away?"

"I was twelve."

"That's a tough age to lose the only male in your life. An important age for a boy just about to turn into a man."

He nodded. "It was terrible. I'm not sure...."

He kept talking, but I kind of zoned out. As I was talking to him, I realized that Nathan Zwicker's death left a twelve-year-old without a dad. And Zwicker's daughter might not ever know the truth about why her dad died. I was quite sure the Nevada project was well on its way to covering up this whole Halifax trip. But even I didn't know the truth about why he died. All I knew was little snippets that might not come close to the truth. Zwicker told me it had something to do with antigravity, but that can't be a real thing, can it?

"...why I never really felt like I could go on dates like a normal person," Gary said.

"Tell me more about that," I said, and Gary started talking again.

I was holding my iPad on my lap, taking notes, and I clicked the home button with my thumb to return to the main screen so I could open my Internet browser. I glanced up to make sure Gary couldn't see what I was doing and then I typed in "antigravity." You find a bunch of wiki type websites with info and an impressive number of drawings of antigravity devices. There was no shortage of websites devoted to the topic, and many seemed legit. It wasn't just UFOs and aliens. People were actively trying to find ways to thwart gravity.

"...and she was kind of abusive early on. She always told me how lucky I was to be dating her, and I suppose I believed it. I mean, she was really good-looking, at least she was back then."

I glanced up. "And somewhere along the way you stopped feeling so lucky to be married to your wife."

"I'm not sure I ever fully bought into that. Can a person be bullied into marrying someone?"

"It's probably more common than anyone acknowledges," I said, and then shifted gears. "Talk to me about the sex in your relationship. How did that change over the years?"

"It was always on her schedule. I learned pretty early on to let her initiate things or it would cause an argument. I remember one huge fight...."

I tried to listen. I even leaned forward and nodded, which is sure sign your psychologist cares about what you're saying, but my eyes drifted back to the iPad. The browser was still open with pictures of antigravity devices. I couldn't focus. Goddamn Zwicker! I leaned back in my bucket chair and added Nevada, to my antigravity search term. That brought up a bunch of attractions in Las Vegas. There were plane rides you could take that simulated zero gravity and other things like wind tunnels but nothing about a research project. That made sense, though. I shouldn't be able to find a top-secret military research project just by Googling it. I clicked the browser closed and turned my attention to Gary. I was done with Nathan Zwicker and the foolish claims of antigravity.

⧈

My second, and last, patient of the afternoon was Lionel Outhouse. Believe it or not, Outhouse is a reasonably common surname in Nova Scotia. I didn't grow up around here, so I thought it was kind of weird until I met the fourth or fifth person with that name.

Lionel was seeing me for psychotherapy as a condition of his probation. He was a twenty-three-year-old computer science student at Dalhousie University who was caught at a local grocery store trying to take up-skirt pictures on his cell phone.

I imagine, for some of you, that requires an explanation.

Internet pornography knows no bounds, and the limitless material has expanded to every possible niche, and for every niche there exists exclusive sites devoted to it. Up-skirts is a porn category phenomenon made possible by the fact that everyone carries a camera in the form of their cell phone these days. Up-skirts are photos taken discreetly and without the knowledge of the victim. The intention is to get a picture under the dress of the female in the hopes that she is without underwear or wearing something revealing. The perverts taking these photos frequently don't have constraints on who they target, so underage girls in dresses are at the same risk as any other female. The photographers frequently upload their images to a porn website or a like-minded Internet discussion group.

These up-skirt offenders are normally porn addicts of some variety and may even justify their photographs as a victimless crime.

Enter Lionel Outhouse. Porn addict at the age of twenty-three, but unfortunately he wasn't the exception to the rule. In this day and age, most people have Internet access continually. Internet used to just be something associated with computers, but now phones, tablets, gaming systems, watches, fridges, and almost anything connects us. And connects our kids. More than fifty percent of males these days admit to surfing hard-core porn before the age of fourteen years. Is it any wonder that they're addicts by their early twenties? Addicts whose porn diseased brains think up-skirt photos are sexually exciting and worth the risk of taking. Addicts like Lionel Outhouse.

In this session, we were beginning to review his disturbing porn history.

"It's not like you can avoid the Internet," Lionel said. "Almost everything we do requires a connection. Most of the video games I played growing up were online."

"That doesn't mean you couldn't avoid porn online," I suggested.

"It kind of did," he argued. "I mean, from early on we hear about sex, and there's sex on TV shows and in movies, and then kids are talking about it. Then people are talking about porn, and your parents are saying it's bad don't watch it, and your friends are laughing about it, and eventually you need to see what all the fuss is about."

"Okay," I said, but didn't sound convinced.

"Let me give you an example of what I mean. Ever heard of drugs?" he asked.

I raised an eyebrow, but nodded.

"Now let's imagine there's a secret room in your house full of drugs. Even if you weren't an addict, don't you think you'd check out a room that was full of every drug imaginable, especially since it was all free?"

"What do you mean *check out*?"

"I mean just pop your head in. Have a look."

I shrugged. "Sure. I'd have a look."

"So you pop your head in a few times. Then maybe you go in the room and have a look, maybe pick up a joint and smell it. Don't you think at some point you might get up the courage to try something? I mean, it's in your house and it's totally free and totally anonymous."

"I see your point," I said. "Pretty hard to resist taking the first peek at porn, but then it's a slippery slope from there."

"Especially to a twelve-year-old," Lionel said. "A twelve-year-old that doesn't know any better and doesn't have any other outlet for his horniness."

"You were twelve when you started up with porn?" I asked.

"Yeah, I was an early bloomer, I guess."

There's that age again. Twelve. Same age as Zwicker's daughter. Damn. It's like there's a conspiracy to not let me forget about Nathan Zwicker.

"When did the interest in porn turn into an interest in up-skirt?" I asked.

"I kind of got lost in computer stuff around the same time I got lost in the porn stuff. I was never really a jock or anything, so when I finally started figuring out what computers could do, that was it for me. I was hooked. I spent all my time on them. They were my hobby, my work, my socialization, my sex. Just everything."

"How was it your work?"

"I was just messing around and figuring things out like HTML and other web-based languages, and I put a few sites together for friends and stuff, and then by the time I was fourteen, I was doing web set-ups and maintenance fairly regular. It wasn't a lot of money, but it was fun."

I was tempted to ask a personal question, but that wasn't fair to Lionel. Oh, screw it. "Hey," I said. "With all your computer know-how, have you heard of any famous hackers?"

He frowned, confused. "I guess, why?"

"Ever heard of a hacker named Talus? He might be newer."

He thought for a moment. "Nope. Doesn't ring a bell."

"Okay, never mind. Tell me more about what computers meant for you growing up."

Lionel started talking again, but I couldn't hear him. I was distracted and discreetly brought my web browser up. There was one more thing I was going to check and that was it. I would be done with all of these distractions.

Lionel hadn't heard of this Talus guy, but that didn't mean he wasn't a famous hacker. The guy hacked my super-secure cell phone, so he had to be pretty good. I Googled his name on my iPad.

Nothing.

Not for hackers anyway.

Talus is a rock climbing term for a type of terrain. It's also a lodge in the Rocky Mountains of British Columbia. It also has something to do with a device that emits light and can be clipped to a monitor. I could find no reference to a hacker named Talus. Shit.

"...and started to care more about my online life than my real one," Lionel said.

I looked up from my iPad. "Have you dated?"

He looked embarrassed as he answered, "No."

"It can be tough, eh? Tough to get started on stuff like that." Before he could answer, there was a strange tone on my iPad. I glanced down and nearly yelped. There was a little dialog box and a message. *Are you looking for me, Dr. Waiter?*

"Everything okay?" Lionel asked.

"Yeah, sure," I said, and looked back up. "How close have you gotten to actually asking a girl out?"

He started telling me about a dating site he was on and some of the text relationships he'd had. I looked back down at the iPad and the message with the blinking cursor awaiting my response. I typed, *How'd u get on here??*

I have monitored your electronic devices and was aware you typed my name into a search engine.

Jesus. I double-tapped the home button and then swiped the dialog box off my iPad to close it. I reopened my note-taking app and looked back at Lionel, who was still talking.

"...we had a lot in common, but I never really knew who she...."

My iPad made another tone, and I looked down to see the dialog box back with the same address on Henry Street. The message below said, *You need to visit.*

I closed that dialog box again, but made a decision. Once I was done with Lionel, I would take a drive down Henry Street. What could be the harm in that?

Fifty minutes later I was driving down Henry Street. This was considered the affluent end of Halifax. Close to Dalhousie and Saint Mary's University. Also close to downtown shopping and restaurants.

Henry Street was a narrow, tree-lined road with unique, well-kept homes on either side. Some of the houses along here were probably over a hundred years old. The mature trees stretched across the street so that their branches touched, creating the impression you were travelling through a tunnel. In 2003, Hurricane Juan tried to rip these trees out, but didn't do a very good job.

I neared the address and slowed. I didn't see any black sedans, secret agents in suits, or any other obvious signs of concern. The street was quiet.

I drove past the Zwicker house with just a quick swivel of my head to check things out. A woman stood on the front porch, obviously watching me. She waved at me. I snapped my head away and kept driving.

What the hell? I'd never seen that woman in my life. Why would she be waving at me?

My phone beeped, so I passed the next intersection and pulled over to the curb before picking it up off the seat. Guess who?

The text box read, *I notified Dr. Marie Zwicker of your arrival. Did you miss the address?*

I let the phone fall against my chest and just sat. I turned the car off, but made a quick promise not to get out and walk back to the Zwicker house.

Then I promptly got out of the car and headed back towards the Zwicker house.

She was still standing on the porch and watched me approach with an overly casual nonchalance that I didn't share. Now that I was out of the car, I could hear music growing increasingly louder as I approached. She had a bluetooth speaker playing music on a small patio table.

Dr. Marie Zwicker was a pleasant-looking woman in her early forties. Longish, brown, greying hair, pulled back in a ponytail. Slightly overweight, with glasses and the general look and dress of a university professor. Overall, she looked more smart than fun with a fixed serious expression (although her husband did just die that morning).

As I walked up the path, I raised a hand. "Hi. I'm Dr. Waiter."

Her expression didn't change. "Okay."

"Are you Nathan Zwicker's wife? Marie?"

She nodded.

"I thought maybe we should talk."

"About what?" she asked.

Now that I was at the foot of the porch steps, the music was quite loud and distracting. "Could we turn that down?" I nodded at the speaker.

"Only if you want other people listening to this conversation."

I frowned.

She motioned for me to come closer. I did.

She continued. "I used to think my husband was paranoid until I found a device in a light bulb that my daughter accidentally broke. That was back when Nathan and I were still at MIT, but I assume that this house is also bugged. I'm not even sure having this speaker going does anything. They can probably still hear."

Before I could ask anything else, a girl appeared at the screen door behind Marie. The spitting image of her mom, she spoke through the mesh. "Mom, I'm done homework. Can I watch Netflix?"

Marie turned. "Sure, honey. Watch in the basement though."

And the girl disappeared again.

"That's my daughter," Marie said with the hint of a proud smile.

I nodded and felt compelled to say something about how she'd seemed like a lovely girl, but I generally don't like kids. "Is she doing okay?" I asked instead.

Marie looked genuinely surprised.

"I mean because of what happened to her dad?"

"Oh. She doesn't know about that."

She said it so casually, and with the music playing, I wondered if I'd misheard. "You didn't tell her about what happened?"

She ignored the question. "Did you actually see my husband this morning? Did he make it that far?"

I hesitated. The official story was supposed to be that I didn't see him. "Briefly," I said. I guess I'm not good at official stories.

"He's not a normal guy," she continued. "He's a genius, but he's paranoid and unreliable in every other way. Cassie barely knows him. I barely know him, especially in the last eight years. He frequently took on special projects and was gone from our lives for months on end. It was hard to really consider him as a husband or father."

This is a new take on the grieving widow. "So Cassie doesn't know about what happened?"

"As far as she's concerned, her dad is just gone off

on another project. I knew we shouldn't have agreed to meet him here. Now I just want to get the hell out of Nova Scotia."

"What do you mean *meet him here*?"

"We got dragged up from Boston as support during his *recovery*." She put air quotes around the last word. "We were never in Nevada."

Curiouser and curiouser. "So do you believe it was a legitimate accident this morning?"

Her expression dropped to one of exasperation. "That's not why you're here, is it?"

I didn't have a fucking clue why I was here. "No. I mean, I guess I was just checking in on you."

She made a loud buzzer noise. "Nope. Wrong answer."

I felt like I could book this woman into my office for a year of daily therapy and never even scratch the surface. She was a tough nut. "Listen, I have no idea what's going on. I was hoping you'd shed some light on it. This all seems a bit out of my league."

She nodded. I guess that response was closer to what she expected. "My husband wasn't a great husband or father, but he wasn't a bad man either. I don't know exactly what the military and government were up to, but if he didn't trust them, it was probably for a good reason. And whatever reason that was — it got him killed."

"This is about the project he was working on in Nevada?"

She nodded. "I assume it is about the antigravity."

"You know about what he was working on?"

"A little bit," she said flatly. "Does that mean you have to kill me now?"

"I'm not authorized to carry a gun," I said back, equally deadpan. Although if I did carry one, I might have been tempted to shoot this woman. "But why would that project get him killed?"

She looked at me with what could only be considered disdain and ignored the question. "Do you have a PhD?"

I stumbled over an answer. "Uh, ye…yes."

"Was it university based or like an online thing?"

"University."

"But it's just psychology, not a science-based program."

"Yes," I said, impatience creeping into my voice. "It's a doctorate in a social science — not a *real* science like math or physics."

"It's just that the significance of finding antigravity should be pretty obvious, just as keeping it secret while they're researching how to use it to make money or weapons would be worth killing for. I don't have trouble wrapping my head around that. We're talking about something that will fundamentally change the entire world."

God, she was arrogant. No wonder Nathan took projects and stayed away from home all the time. "Okay, right," I said to placate her enormous need to be superior.

"My daughter and I aren't dead because they don't think we know anything, and with my husband gone and our having never even been in Nevada, we aren't much of a security threat. They likely think I'm just some dumb woman who *lucked* into getting a doctorate in mathematics from MIT, a typical male assumption."

This felt a lot like a therapy session, and I bet I wasn't going to get paid for it. I hate pro bono.

She continued her rant. "They arrived here shortly after they killed Nathan. The morons in their suits and secret agent car. They pretended it was about notifying me of the accident, but then used the access to the house to search it with all kinds of gadgets and tools. They were looking for something."

"What were they looking for?"

"They took some papers and a laptop, but there wasn't anything here. Nothing they really wanted. I think they had to conclude that everything was just with Nathan."

"Everything, like what?"

She just stared at me for a moment. Her condescending appraisal seemed to indicate she was trying to decide if I was smart enough to be let in on the plot.

I just waited.

She did a quick scan around the street before addressing me again. "My daughter was at school when all of this happened. I suppose it didn't make any sense to search her. What could she possibly have, right?"

I shrugged.

"Exactly," she said, pleased with my ability to follow the conversation. "So I checked her backpack when she got home."

I waited. Expectant. Like a pregnant stripper.

"Nothing there. Just Cassie's school stuff."

Fuck. I wished I was allowed to carry a gun.

"But then I talked to Cassie, and she said she'd found something when she was packing up to come home after school. It was sort of jammed into the lining of the bag. She was playing with it on the way home today." She leaned back and reached into the front pocket of her dress and pulled something out.

"You can have this," she said, but didn't open her hand. "We don't need it, and once we leave Nova Scotia, we're done with all of this intrigue and Nathan's bull-shit."

I leaned forward.

She glanced around again and then opened her hand to reveal a perfectly round metallic ball. It was about two or three times the size of a golf ball and basically filled her palm. The metal was smooth and polished to a mir-ror-like finish. It was actually somewhat difficult to look at due to its reflective qualities. Something about it seemed almost to suggest it didn't have a finite border. As she revealed it, her eyes had stayed firmly fixed on my face.

I wasn't sure what I was supposed to be looking at. I continued to stare at it as I spoke. "Yep. That's a nice shiny marble. Pretty cool."

She opened her hand a little more so that her palm didn't cradle the ball, and she spread her fingers. The ball rested precariously for a moment and then she slowly lowered her outstretched arm.

But the ball stayed where it was. Hovering, if you can call it that, a few inches over her hand.

Now my expression changed. "Holy shit. Is that…?"

She nodded and took the ball back in her hand, looking around the neighbourhood again. I think we both expected the military to swoop in and take us to the ground to retrieve their antigravity ball.

She reached over and put it in my hand. I gripped it tightly, irrationally worried that if I let go it would shoot off into space and be gone.

"Now you can leave," she said.

I looked down into my hand and gingerly opened my fingers and let the ball float for a second before I took hold again. Holy shit.

"Goodbye," she said, a little more snot in her tone. "Try not to get killed, and you better not tell anyone that you have that. No one."

CHAPTER 9

I went home. I almost ran to my car and I broke a few speed limits on the way. I was nervous as hell. Every dark sedan behind me was an assassin. I should never have gone to see Marie Zwicker.

Plus she wasn't very pleasant. You could call her rude, but maybe that was harsh considering her husband had been killed that day. Either way, I was now holding a magic ball. I glanced away from the road at my hand where I gripped that ball like my life depended on it.

Oh shit. That was a bad way to frame it. My life might actually depend on having this ball.

Or maybe it was the other way around — maybe my life was in danger now because of this goddamn magic ball.

But how cool was this thing? I was cruising along the Bi-Hi, or Highway 102, the road that connects Halifax proper to some of the suburbs and outlying districts, and it seemed like I was in the clear. At least there weren't any obvious government sedans trailing me. I carefully held my right hand up and opened my fingers. There it was. The magic ball. I lowered my hand a bit and the ball just sat there — floating in the air.

So goddamn cool.

I put my right hand on the steering wheel and left the ball floating, but I could barely focus on the road. I didn't want to take my eyes off the thing. I felt protective, like it could disappear if I wasn't watching it, but I was also baffled by it and just wanted to stare.

It was only a few seconds, but I had to snatch it back into my death grip. I held it there until I pulled into my garage in Capilano and watched the door close in my rear-view mirror. I have a little workbench in the garage, and I headed over there and pulled shut the banged-up blinds that hung over the window. I flipped on the work light and sat the ball on the bench — well, actually, in the air over the bench — to have a good look at it under the light.

By applying my keen powers of observation, I quickly learned the metal ball was…

…round…

…very shiny, almost like a mirror…

…and it was not affected by gravity.

In other words, I learned nothing new, so I decided to just play with it. I let it float and waved my hands around it. That made it sort of wiggle and move a bit. I could push it gently, and it would glide across the room and slowly come to a stop, but only if it hit a wall. It seemed that even though gravity didn't draw it down, the object still had mass that was marginally affected by air. You could push it down and it would move at the speed of whatever force you used, strike the floor, and bounce up. I guess bounce isn't exactly right — it kind of ricocheted up a few inches and then hovered again.

I did a few magic tricks in my reflection against my wife's car window. I held the ball out in front of me and then waved it around before quickly tucking my hand behind my back. Once out of sight I could let go of the ball and it would float behind me until I retrieved it. Voila! I could make the ball disappear and reappear.

It was during the rehearsal of this trick that my wife spoke from the door to the house. "What are you doing?"

I had no idea how long she'd been watching. The trick looked so cool in the car window, I was oblivious to everything else. I snatched the ball out of the air and spun to her. "Oh, hey. Nothing."

"Why are you out here? I heard you get home like twenty minutes ago."

"I...I was just trying something."

She kept on watching me. I think she was trying to gauge my expression. "What's that thing?" She vaguely pointed at my hands wrapped around the ball.

Oh shit. "Uh, nothing," I said because I'm an idiot.

She raised an eyebrow sceptically and waited for a real answer.

"It's just a thing I picked up. I was trying it out."

"Oh," she said sarcastically. "It's just a *thing* you picked up. Why didn't I figure that out?" She tapped a palm against her forehead.

"It's...it's like a magic ball," I finally said. My shoulders slumped.

"Is that what you were practicing in the car window?" A little smirk in the corner of her mouth.

She thought it was an actual magic trick prop. Excellent. I dropped my eyes to try to look a little sheepish as I answered, "Yes. I just wanted to see how the trick looked."

"Why'd you buy a magic trick?" She was genuinely confused and with good reason. I don't hate magic, but I'd never shown an interest in being a magician.

"This thing…" — I held up the ball in one hand — "is pretty cool, so I don't know. I just wanted to try it."

She still looked sceptical. She needed more convincing.

"Watch what it can do," I said as I began dramatically moving my outstretched hands around the ball until I threw my hands back and the ball stayed there in the air. I gestured all around it to show there were no strings and then looked back at her.

She clapped. "Very nice. Where'd you get it?"

"Um, a magic shop down on Spring Garden." This is the long main drag in downtown Halifax full of shops and restaurants. I didn't even know if there was a magic store there, but neither would she since we hardly ever go to Spring Garden.

She turned to go back into the house. "I hope it didn't cost a thousand bucks." And then she was gone.

For half a minute I just stood there watching the doorway. The ball still hung in the air. I couldn't believe it. That was easy, but it showed how careless I was being that she was just standing there and watching me with it. I grabbed a clean rag off the bench and an empty brown coffee tin (I keep them around for storage) and tucked the ball away. I set it on the floor behind my driver's seat and threw an old blanket over it.

I was definitely going to take this thing into the

private office tomorrow. Until I decided what to do with it, I didn't want it around the house.

I came down from changing to find Lisa in the kitchen. She was standing at the sink, her dirty blonde hair trailing over her tan shoulders, exposed by her yoga top. I paused at the entrance and admired the view from behind. She sure looked great.

She glanced back over her shoulder. "What are you doing?" she asked with a hint of irritation. "Why are you just standing there?"

"I was staring at you."

"Don't be weird," she said with some humour creeping back.

"That's funny," I said. "Because I was thinking about something weird I could do to you."

She took a towel off the counter and pressed it between her hands as she turned to me. "Like what?"

I moved over near her and leaned against the center island, folding my arms over my chest. I knew she liked me being close to her because it emphasized our size difference. She said it made her feel tiny and she liked that. "Well, I need to check if we have all the proper ingredients for my idea."

She nodded for me to continue.

"I'll need some chocolate. Maybe a little massage oil and some candles. We'll need to put on some music."

"I'm not hating this idea," she purred.

"And I'll need to get a big jar of mayonnaise — it

can't be Miracle Whip. I'll need about two meters of heavy-duty rope and a towel that we don't care about, preferably a towel we were just about to throw in the garbage anyway."

She turned away back to the counter. "Nope!" she said. "You lost me."

"Wait," I cried. "I'll also need a Tupperware container with a lid that fits really well. Like really well. And do we still have that webcam that tracks movement?"

She started to walk out of the kitchen, and I was hot on her heels.

"Are you saying *maybe*? Is it because of the mayonnaise? We could use butter."

She stopped fast, and I ended up bumping into her. It wasn't much of a bump, but the size difference meant she would have gone flying except that I put my hands on her shoulders. I pulled her back against me and leaned down to kiss the top of her head. God, she smelled good.

I turned her around and kept her body pressed against mine. She didn't resist. Her head tilted up and I bent to kiss her. It wasn't totally comfortable for me, but the reward outweighed the neck cramp.

I pulled back enough to speak. "I missed you."

"I missed you, too."

"Want to go upstairs to the bedroom?" I asked.

Her sleepy smile faded ever so slightly.

"What?" I asked, trying to hold onto this moment.

"Nothing," she said.

Holding her shoulders, I moved her back to arm's

length. "What?"

"It's the anniversary next week."

I let go of her. "Oh Jesus."

"I'm sorry," she pleaded. "It was just standing here with you. Having you hold me like that.... It's just where my head went."

"Well, put your head someplace else then." I went to the fridge and opened it.

She swivelled in place to watch me. "That's not how the mind works. You're the psychologist."

"You don't have to remind me which one of us is the psychologist."

"What the hell is that supposed to mean?"

"Nothing. Forget it. I'm just going to grab something to eat."

She was silent. Working up something mean to say to me. Finally she got it. "Not everyone can just turn off emotions and make a big joke out of the world, like you. Not everyone can pretend to be a sarcastic hard-ass just so people think you're cool."

I had to stand and frown at her for that one. "Are you psychoanalyzing me?"

She didn't respond.

"I'm not pretending to be a hard-ass with no emotions. I'm not pretending to be anything."

"Oh," she said in mock surprise. "So then you *really* don't care that Gabe disappeared three years ago. You're totally fine not knowing if he's alive or dead."

I swivelled to stare at her.

"And if he's alive, is he still getting treatment? Do

you wonder about that? Because I do."

Our son had a rare genetic disease that caused muscle weakness. Before he disappeared, it was starting to get worse.

"I'm not having this conversation with you," I announced, and turned back to the fridge. I could feel her eyes burning into me from behind and then she stormed out of the kitchen.

This wasn't the first time we'd had had this exact argument and I wasn't about to do it again. I grabbed a club soda and a container of leftover Chinese food and got out of the kitchen. Thankfully she wasn't there to see my eyes full of tears. I retreated to the basement to watch Netflix and let my brain go numb.

CHAPTER 10

The next day, I was at my private office with my magic ball and the coffee can. I had a new transplant coming in for her first appointment shortly, but I just couldn't bring myself to put the antigravity ball away.

IT WAS TOO COOL!

I was presently letting it sit in the middle of the room. Hover, really. And I was noticing that it never stayed perfectly still. It was quite difficult to let go of it and not inadvertently push it with a finger as you detached. This always sent it sliding along in the air. But even if you did manage to let go of it just right, it rarely hovered in precisely the same spot for long. It eventually drifted in one direction or the other. Sometimes it drifted up and sometimes down. I guess it was slight air currents. Sometimes it didn't move, but that was rare. The ball was completely unaffected by gravity, but it was still susceptible to the movement of air, however slight. I could partially circumvent that effect by spinning the ball. If I could get just the right amount of spin and let go of it cleanly (which was very difficult) the ball would sit in one spot, endlessly — or with my lack of patience, about ten minutes.

My phone announced, "Excuse me, sir, it's time for your appointment," in a pleasant female voice. It was the tone I had set to my calendar, and it meant it was fifteen minutes until my first patient of the day was expected to arrive. I swept the ball out of the air, wrapped it in the cloth, and tucked it back in the coffee can before placing it into the storage ottoman. Then I checked my phone to make sure the outer door was set to unlock so the patient could get into my waiting room. It was.

I popped over to my laptop and opened the secure USB to recheck my new transplant, the civilian British scientist with the sparse file. All I knew was she'd been off work for two weeks and had requested respite out of country for her treatment. Nova Scotia certainly fit the bill for her.

She was forty-seven and had no family. No other details. Not even a name.

I was expecting some variation of a prematurely old Margaret Thatcher type with bad teeth. She would probably smell of fish and chips and have one of the gross British accents so thick I'd have to keep asking her to repeat herself. I chuckled and reached up to pull those thoughts out of my head just as a beep on my phone indicated someone had entered my waiting room. She was early. I had a camera in the waiting room that I could view from my laptop (or phone), but I rarely bothered.

I grabbed the clipboard with the registration forms, opened my door, and stepped out. A tall, physically fit woman sat in one of the leather chairs. A magazine partially obstructed her face. She let it drop on hearing my entrance. She was beautiful. Straight dark hair over pale skin. Blue eyes and high cheekbones.

"Good morning," I said.

"Hello," she answered in a lilting northern accent. One of the British accents I found attractive as hell. Shit.

"I'm Dr. Waiter," I said. "And you are?"

She stood and reached for my hand. It was a firm handshake, warm and soft. Yummy.

"Constance Blanc. An absolute pleasure to meet you."

"Likewise." I reluctantly let go of her hand. "I've got some forms for you to fill out." I held out the clipboard and waved it like a moron, but didn't move to hand it to her.

"Shall I fill the paperwork out right now?" she asked, the accent giving me goose bumps.

She'd left the outer door open a crack, so I went over and pushed it shut. "Um," I said. "No. Why don't you head into my office and we'll take care of these together."

I motioned towards the doorway, and she stood and moved off. That gave me the opportunity to reach up and pull the impure thoughts out of my head as I followed her shapely figure into the back.

I didn't get all the thoughts on the first try.

After we were seated with my door closed and both doors secured from my phone, I handed the clipboard to her. "Just have a look at these and let me know if you have any questions as you go."

I watched her read the forms. They're just standard psychotherapy contracts and confidentiality disclaimers with modifications specific to SSCHVA. I enjoyed watching her read them over and sign. She eventually finished and looked up at me. "No questions?" I asked.

She shook her head and handed over the clipboard. She was staring at me pretty intently.

I took it and had a quick peek to make sure her signature was in the right spots.

She started up again before I could. "How are you getting along, Dr. Waiter?" She pronounced my last name *Wahter*. I liked it.

"Um," I answered. "Generally, I get paid for *asking* the questions."

She laughed. Not a giggle, but a laugh. She didn't give off a girlish vibe. She was more woman. Confident woman. She just nodded her acquiescence and raised a hand, beckoning me to carry on.

"So," I said with a smile. "How are you getting along, Ms. Blanc?"

"It's Dr. Blanc, actually. I'm a surgeon."

"Oh, I'm sorry. My file on your background is pretty slim."

"Not a problem." She was still looking at me pretty closely.

I met her gaze for a moment and she looked away. I decided to start with some non-threatening rapport building. You laypeople call it small talk. "How are you enjoying Halifax?"

"It's lovely."

"First time here?"

"No," she said, and suppressed a smile. "I was here

before. Working."

I nodded. "I feel like maybe you just want to get down to business." It was a guess on my part, but she didn't seem like a beat-around-the-bush lady. "So you work with the British military?"

"Do I work for the military?" she reflected aloud. "I guess." She paused, still considering the question. "They certainly don't work for me."

I pretended to write on my iPad and spoke out loud: "Patient appears to address questions with cryptic answers."

She laughed again. "I apologize, Dr. Waiter. I don't mean to be so vague. I don't know how to answer most questions these days. I was involved in a research program out of the Cambridge University Hospital that got scooped up by a division within a division of the Elite U.K. Forces. It's the SFSG — the Special Forces Support Group, but most of the work wasn't on the books — I think that's what people say: not on the books."

"Top secret stuff?" I smiled.

"I suppose I wouldn't be here otherwise."

"So what kind of work did you do?"

She made eye contact with me again, and a smile stretched over her face before she corrected it. "The program was researching spinal cord injury and paralysis using some very new implants. I suppose I did some quality control around that program. Checked on things."

I smiled back and waited for her to continue.

"The original research was ethics approved. They went through all the appropriate channels, but that kind of concern with ethics ended when SFSG got involved. They sped up the research timelines. It went straight from computer models and animal trials to human subjects — semi-volunteers from the British Forces and elsewhere. With the SFSG, they always wanted faster and faster, more and more."

"And that made you uncomfortable?"

"I tend to avoid feeling uncomfortable. It's not something I do."

"Okay," I said with some hesitation.

She smiled. Or maybe she smirked. Her expressions were hard to read. "I suppose I'm really here to meet you."

"Me?" I said with surprise. "Why?"

"Just to check on you."

A knot appeared in my stomach. "I'm not sure I understand."

She shrugged.

My phone made a noise like a doorbell. It was the proximity alarm that someone was standing at my outer door. I need the sensor because someone could hit that door with a hammer and I likely wouldn't hear it back in this office because of all the soundproofing. "I'm sorry," I said. "Just give me a second."

I opened the camera app. The picture was terrible — full of static, but I could just make out a middle-aged woman standing at the door. She had greying hair pulled into a loose ponytail.

I stood. "Would you excuse me for a quick minute?"

Dr. Blanc nodded.

I unlocked my door and the outer door as I headed out. By the time I was in the waiting room, the mystery lady was opening the door and entering. Her eyes found me and she said, "My apologies, Dr. Waiter. I may be slightly tardy." Her English accent unmistakeable. (And not one of the sexy ones, more a cockney accent than the pleasant Yorkshire.)

"Oh," I started. "I'm sorry. You are?"

"I'm Dr. Carol Smith. We had an appointment."

"But I...." I turned back to my office to find Constance moving towards me, at speed. I almost ducked, but she simply swept past.

"I'm on my way," she announced cheerily. "Talk soon." And she was past the new guest and gone.

"Hold on," I said without effect.

Carol watched the other woman disappear out into the hall and turned back to me with a puzzled expression. "Did I interrupt something?"

"Um, I'm not sure." Which was actually a far more confident answer than I felt at the moment. "Can you have a seat for a second?" I motioned to the chairs in the waiting room. "I'll be right with you."

And then I popped back into my office. I grabbed my clipboard off the ottoman. It was empty. She'd taken the forms she'd signed. I sat down at my desk and woke my laptop to bring up the camera feed. My office recorded the video on a loop, so I always had access to at least the last forty-eight hours. I started the video from the waiting room and ran the time slider back. It quickly turned into static when Constance was in the room. She must have had an electronic jammer on her.

Of course.

I went back to the waiting room and invited the new lady back in. She smelled a bit of fish and chips. Once we were seated in my office, I asked, "Do you have any ID?"

She presented me with a British Special Forces ID: Dr. Carol Smith, civilian consultant.

It turned out that this transplant, the real transplant, was actually a surgeon seconded from the Cambridge University Hospital for her groundbreaking work on nano implants.

"I'm sorry, Dr. Smith. It's a bit of a weird day," I said as I handed her ID back.

"Was the woman who just left a part of the weirdness?"

I nodded. "Let's not worry about it. I have some paperwork we need to fill out and then we'll get started." I put some fresh consent and contract forms in the now empty clipboard, and she signed off after we briefly went over the SSCHVA agreements.

Then we started talking again. I asked, "Why don't you tell me a bit about what's going on? What brought you in here today?"

Dr. Smith explained that her medical research on the use of nano implants was taken over by the British forces, and initially that seemed to help with advancements in research, but it quickly grew into an ethical quandary for her.

"How so?" I asked while experiencing an acute case

of deja vu.

"Well, the military never much cared about going through ethical boards. They were more about doing first and asking for forgiveness later. That never sat right with me." She paused and then continued. "Especially when the "so-call" *volunteers* were young army recruits who didn't seem overly enthusiastic. The military didn't have any trouble trying things out on their own personnel, including civilian members contracted to them. I heard stories about people using my research even outside of the U.K. and on people who weren't even aware they were guinea pigs."

"Like random people on the street?"

"No, people who had a connection to the military."

"And what was the British Forces hoping to accomplish?"

"Super soldiers, I guess. The nano augmentation should make people faster and stronger, but it was never a hundred percent successful." Tears welled up then.

I'm probably repeating myself to say I hate crying. A tissue box sat on the end table between my seat and the end of the couch where she sat. I plucked it up and dropped it on the seat next to her. She eagerly grabbed one out and held it to her face until her sobs slowed.

She finally continued. "And then a few weeks ago there was an accident." She held off tears for a moment. "One of those *volunteers*, a young army recruit, was paralyzed from the waist down. It was a surgical procedure from a sister team of mine. I wasn't doing the operation, but technically all the procedures were supposed to be overseen by me." The crying started again, and she pulled out another tissue to join to the wet mess the first had become. The newly created tissue ball was immediately pushed back on her face again.

This woman was an emotional wreck. She should probably see a psychologist.

Oh wait, never mind.

I waited another moment and then said in a quiet, calming voice, "Take your time." I'm pretty sure that's what you say to people who are crying. I know because I saw it in a movie.

And because I'm a psychologist.

But mostly because of movies.

"I'm fine," she said. "I've always been a bit of a crier. It runs in my family."

That's perfect. We should schedule tons of appointments, then.

"Anyway," she said, "I never got to examine this poor recruit or even review the charts. I don't know whether it was a sloppy surgery to install the nanos in the wrong spot or maybe someone just nicked a nerve. I have no idea. I only found out because a nurse from the surgical team mentioned it to me and then she got the sack."

"They fired the nurse for mentioning the botched surgery?"

"Yes. Security and secrecy were huge with these people. I had to sign so many NDAs it was ridiculous. Even my mum and dad don't know what I'm really doing."

An NDA was a non-disclosure agreement, but in military circles, a breach of an NDA was often treated like treason, so it was pretty serious. I suppose firing the nurse was letting her off easy.

"Now that poor kid can't walk."

The tears welled up again, and this time she didn't even try to stop it. The soiled tissue sat balled up on my couch. If that disgusting tissue hadn't been so distracting I would have probably felt really bad. I involuntarily glanced at my desk where I kept a pump bottle of hand disinfectant. I might have to wash down the couch.

God, I'm an ass. I reached up and discreetly pulled all these misguided thoughts out of my head and flicked them away. "You're in a really tough spot. A research project you care about, but can't talk about. And now it seems like control of things is slipping too." That's called an empathic summary statement. A psychologist uses it to show he's heard and understood you, and the result was that it bumped you along to tell more of your story. Boo yah!

She answered through tears. "The Forces has taken my career from me. I don't know if I can go back to the military hospital there. I can't keep taking chances with people's lives, but they're going to keep doing this no matter what."

I leaned forward and put my hands on my knees. "I don't know any magic answers for this, but I do know you're here now, and we're going to work together to figure something out. This is your time, here in Halifax, to do some thinking and planning for a next step."

She made eye contact with me and gave a partial smile.

Twenty minutes later I was back out on the road. I wrapped up the session with Dr. Smith and booked her for next week and left. I was heading back to 12 Wing. This must have been some kind of record going there three days in a row.

It's a good thing Anne was so cute.

But this visit wasn't going to be about Anne. The real mystery now was this Constance Blanc person. A woman who seemed to know about my appointment with Dr. Smith and also knew about the supposedly top-secret nano research. That kind of breach wasn't supposed to be possible, but I knew SSCHVA needed to be on high alert in case the leak had originated there.

In the excitement, I forgot about the anti-gravity ball in a coffee can in my office. That should give you an idea of how much excitement we're talking about.

CHAPTER 11

The moment I mentioned an information leak, Anne immediately took me down to the General's office. I was sitting next to Anne and across a massive oak desk from General Walter Belaire. He was a distinguished man in his mid- to late sixties who kept in shape, but couldn't hide the age in his wizened face or balding grey hair and moustache. I always teased Anne that he looked like a 1970s porn star who specialized in grandpa fetish. She always frowned at me and told me to "grow up."

"So this British woman knew about the research the real patient was involved with?" General Belaire asked.

"That's the shit she was talking about when she was pretending to be a patient. Almost word for word the same story the actual British doctor talked about."

"But what would be the point in that?" he barked. "Why would she go to the trouble of getting in your office and pretending to be this Carol Smith doctor only to run off when the real doctor arrived?"

I shrugged.

"She was obviously sending a message," Anne said. "She wanted you to know that she wasn't accidentally in your office. She knew exactly who you were, who Dr. Smith was, and what was going on in that office. She wanted you to know she knew about SSCHVA."

"Goddamn," General Belaire spat. "This is exactly

why your office should be here on-site. This woman would never have gotten away with that little trick on this base."

I was not getting into that one right then. "So we have her message then," I said. "Now what?"

"What did you say she looked like?" the General asked.

I cleared my throat. "Long dark hair. Fair skin. Blue eyes. Looked pretty fit." I dared a sideways look at Anne. She was grinning like a maniac.

"Was she good-looking, Dr. Waiter?" she asked in the most non-innocent voice I've heard.

I shot her a death stare. "She was a handsome woman, yes."

"So you thought she was attractive?" she pushed.

"Well, she wasn't ugly," I said.

"Excuse me," the General barked. "What is the point of this ridiculous banter? Does it matter if she was fucking Brigitte Bardot?"

I almost asked *Brigitte who?* and then remembered that I liked my balls just where they sat right then.

"My apologies," Anne said snapping back to her boss. "I was just wondering if maybe Dr. Waiter found this person attractive and maybe let his guard down. Maybe that's why he didn't realize she was an impostor."

I frowned. "Um, no, I don't think so."

"Oh." She spun on me. "So she wasn't attractive?"

"Jesus H. Bartholomew Christ on a stick!" General Belaire shouted. "You two sound like an old married couple. Can we get back to this British mystery person?"

We both turned to the General sheepishly, but stayed quiet.

"So," he continued with a quieter tone, "why didn't you know she wasn't the real client?"

"The file Anne gave me on this particular transplant was thin. Very thin. I didn't have a description or a picture or even a name for the woman. I knew the woman was supposed to be British, but not much else. Her initial appointment with me was also booked direct through the SSCHVA office straight into my schedule."

"So she strolled into your office, told you she was Dr. Carol Smith, and—"

"No," I cut the General off. "She didn't call herself Carol Smith. She actually gave a different name, which is kind of weird if she was really trying to send a message about her intel."

"Well, what name did she give you?" he asked.

"Constance Blanc. Sounds kind of French if you ask me."

The colour instantly drained from General Belaire's face. I thought he was having a stroke or a heart attack. "General?" I asked out of concern.

Anne noticed it too and had jumped to her feet to lean across the desk.

He held up a hand to us. "Don't. I'm fine." But his breathing was rapid and shallow, and his face was still pale.

"What's wrong?" I asked again.

"What name did she give you?" he asked in a hushed voice.

Anne looked totally confused.

"Constance Blanc," I repeated. "Why? Does that mean something?"

He drew in a big breath before answering. "It just sounds like something. It's probably nothing."

I pursed my lips for a second. The scepticism dripping out of every pore. "I'm just going to go ahead and call bullshit on that, General. Excuse my French."

Anne wasn't as blunt. "What are you thinking, sir?"

He sighed and looked away. He seemed reluctant to make eye contact. "There's a rumour that's gone around for a few years in international circles," he started. "A rumour about a high-level fixer who runs off-off-books black ops. She's supposed to be good at her job. Very good."

"High-level fixer?" I repeated. "Off-off-books black ops? What are we talking here? She's a soldier of some kind?"

Anne turned to me. Her face creased with concern. "He's talking about an assassin. Not a solider. A fixer is someone the military, or government, will use to keep things completely away from any official channel."

The General nodded at this. "But not just any assassin. If this is the woman I've heard about, she's brutal in every way. No mercy. Completes any and every job she takes, and from the crime scene she leaves — relishes every moment of her work. Someone with all the skill and patience of a trained killer, but with the passion of a murderous psychopath."

I stared at him a moment longer and then looked at

Anne before returning my gaze to him. "What makes you think that's this woman?"

He shrugged half-heartedly. "The assassin I've heard whispers about has a code name. No one knows her real name."

"A code name?" I asked.

"She calls herself Constant White."

I sat back in my chair. "Well, then it could just be a coincidence. The name, I mean."

"Constant White," he spat back. "Constance Blanc? I don't think it's a coincidence. That woman was either the fixer or knows enough to pretend to be her."

"By why would she be in my office?" I asked. "And if she's this amazing *fixer*" — I put air quotes around the word — "what was she fixing? I'm not dead. She didn't hang around and kill Dr. Smith."

The General frowned. "That's true. It is strange that you aren't dead."

"Great," I said. "Thanks for the moral support."

Anne finally jumped back in. "You know, it might not have been this Constant White person. Maybe it was just someone screwing around with SSCHVA."

The General shook his head. "Pretty far lengths to go just for screwing around."

"But still," I urged, a little too desperate, "it might not be Constant White. You said no one knows anything about her."

"Why is she called Constant White?" Anne asked.

"I think it's partially a reference to her leaving almost no evidence behind. She never leaves fingerprints or any physical evidence. She evens carries an electronic jammer so that she doesn't show up on any video monitors. Just static if she's in the room."

Oh shit. That sounded familiar. "The video in my office was all just static after she left. I didn't capture any images of her."

Everyone was silent now. Processing that.

Finally the General spoke. "Do you want to move yourself and wife onto the base?"

"Do you think I need to?"

He stared at me for a moment and then answered. "Constant White knows who you are. She obviously has some interest in you, and normally the people she is interested in end up dead."

"If I move onto base, will that mean she can't get to me if I'm really her mission?"

General Belaire looked away and slowly scratched his head as though contemplating the question. After a moment he shook his head. "From what I've heard, son, being on base wouldn't make a goddamn bit of difference."

I glanced over at Anne and saw moisture in her eyes before she turned to avoid eye contact.

There was only thing I could say, under the circumstances, and I think it summed up how we were all feeling. "Fuck me."

Unfortunately, neither the General nor Anne felt able to offer any words of encouragement. Not even a weak attempt at telling me everything would be okay. Instead, Anne shifted topics. "That might tell us *who* the person was, but it doesn't get us any closer to *how* she knew about anything. Is there a leak at SSCHVA?"

The General reflected on that and then said, "I think it does, actually. If it really is Constant White, she only operates under orders from the highest authorities. People with clearance to anything going on here. If she was sent here to...." He stopped, aware that his line of thinking was about to get grim — grim for me.

"If she was sent here to kill me," I finished for him, "then she'd be provided with whatever she needed to make that happen."

The General offered an uninspired shrug of agreement.

Anne's eyes darted from me back to the General. "But she didn't kill Blake," she blurted. "Is she just teasing us before she does. What the hell?"

I have to say her concern for me was kind of nice. I was tempted to give her one of those *Oh, you love me!* lines, but luckily I still retained my common sense.

"Why else might she be in Halifax?" the General asked. "Why else might she be in Dr. Waiter's office?"

A light went on for Anne. "What about Dr. Nathan Zwicker? Can it really be a coincidence that you saw him and he died only moments later?"

Wow. That was sitting right there the whole time. The three of us were temporarily frozen by our own oversight.

"Zwicker," General Belaire said. "Of course."

"She was sent to clean up that case," I said. "Maybe she even killed him. Arranged the hit and run."

"Or drove the car," Anne added.

"But why is she back in your office?" the General asked. "If she came to get rid of Dr. Zwicker, what does she want with Waiter?"

"Blake was the last one to see him alive."

Oh, I was getting a bad feeling right about now.

"She's tying up loose ends," the General announced.

"I'm a loose end?"

Anne stared at me. "Did she ask you about Zwicker? Anything?"

"Nothing. Not a word about him."

The General looked puzzled. "It's the only thing that makes sense. I don't believe in coincidences."

"But she didn't mention Zwicker," Anne argued. "What's her game?"

"We're missing something," the General said. He fixed his gaze on me. "Was there anything else that stood out about your meeting with Zwicker?"

Shit. I knew exactly what he was talking about. I got the mysterious message from a hacker, I went to see the widow, and I got the magic floating ball. "Nope," I said as a bead of sweat on my forehead betrayed me.

"Did Zwicker give you anything or leave something in your office? Is it possible Constant White is looking for something and that's why she didn't just kill you?" Anne asked. She was still wrought with concern.

Oh God. Should I tell them? It's my only ace in the hole right now, and Marie Zwicker told me not to tell anyone. But these two are on my side. If I could trust anyone, shouldn't it be them? "No, Nathan Zwicker definitely didn't leave anything with me." And that was the truth. Nathan didn't give me the floating ball; his wife did.

We were all silent. The General and Anne working hard to figure out what was going on, and me sweating hard hoping they didn't.

I glanced at my watch. "I need to go. I have other appointments."

"You're going back to the office?" Anne asked in surprise.

I shrugged. "I have people to see." She started to protest, but I stopped her. "We've all agreed that if Constant White was going to kill me, I would be dead already, so I'm going to assume there's something else going on. Something bigger than little old me."

Anne shook her head in frustration.

"He's right," the General said, and turned to me. "But be extra careful. Watch your back and keep your eyes open. I'm going to dig a bit on my end to see what I can come up with."

"I appreciate that," I said, and got up to leave. "Besides," I said to Anne, "I'm so cute that no one could ever hurt me once they've met me."

I turned and got out of there, but I thought I heard a whispered *Dick!* as I left the general's office.

CHAPTER 12

I couldn't get out of SSCHVA fast enough. Jesus, why didn't I just tell them about that magic ball? Better yet, I should have brought the damn thing with me and handed it over to them.

Washed my hands of this whole nightmare.

But I'm stupid, and who doesn't love a good adventure? Especially one that almost certainly ends with your being killed by a super hot British assassin. I'm hoping she chooses some kinky sex torture to kill me because.... I reached up and touched my fingers to my forehead and chucked those thoughts away. What's wrong with me?

I slid back into my Jeep and sighed. It was going to be tough to focus on my patients this afternoon. Fortunately, I only had two appointments left, and one was a sex offender, so I needed only half a brain in the room. I'd worked with so many guys just like him that it was autopilot.

My phone vibrated and chirped, a tone both familiar and unfamiliar. I pulled it out to find the expected dialog box. It said, *Can I be of service?*

Who is this? I typed even though I knew the answer.

Talus.

But who r u and y r u doing this?

I work for Dr. Zwicker.

He's dead.

No answer. I typed again. *So who do u work for now?*

My last instruction was to work with you. I work for you now.

And y would I want 2 work with u?

I have access to a significant amount of data. I have extremely high levels of computational power.

The way this guy texted he sounded like a robot. Jesus. *I don't think I want 2 work with a hacker. Tks.*

Talus is not a hacker.

Now I'd offended him. Hackers have pretty thin skin. I swiped the text box of the screen and tucked my phone away. I really didn't have time for Talus.

I should have just cancelled my afternoon. Now that I was sitting in my private office, I realized that my concentration was shot. I had a Netflix show playing across my windows, but it wasn't helping to distract me. Ordinarily, a mindless show in the background was just enough to rebalance me regardless of what stressors nipped at my heels. Oddly, a TV show didn't provide much distraction when the threat of a British assassin lingered.

It didn't help that my first case of the afternoon was a sex offender in denial. He was a successful executive with a big company and had a lot to lose. No doubt about that. He had charges of possessing, distributing, and accessing child porn. This trifecta of charges was pretty much standard these days because of how people found their dirty pictures and videos: torrents. A torrent is a fragment of a video, or picture, file, and when multiple people seed that file, it makes for fast and easy downloads. All you need is a torrent engine / program and then you can search for anything and have the file in a matter of seconds or minutes. The problem with this is that as soon as you have a fragment of the file downloaded, you immediately became a seeder and started sharing it with other users. So the moment Mr. Business Executive found his dirty little underage video, he was *accessing* it, and as soon as he had even a sliver of it downloaded, he was now *distributing* it himself, and then once he had the whole thing and looked at it, he now *possessed* it. So that means he was charged with accessing, distributing, and possession of child porn.

Anyway, Mr. Grant Nelson was one of those guys who went online looking for an underage torrent and found it. But he found one that was planted by a police agency. Probably not even a local police force. The Internet doesn't know borders, so when the police track a file, it can be from anywhere. Once they figure out the IP address and the jurisdiction, they generally pass the details to the appropriate agency to follow up. So goes the global war on child porn.

But Mr. Grant Nelson had money and spent lots of it on a lawyer. Money well spent, I suppose, because the Crown was now agreeing to drop some, or all, of the charges if Mr. Nelson got help. The help part was me. I was supposed to see him for some specialized psychotherapy and help him develop insight. I'd only seen him twice so far and he was a piece of work. He took very little responsibility for his actions and pulled out excuses like chewing gum.

My phone chirped with a doorbell chime, and I knew Mr. Nelson was here. I checked it on my video feed anyway. The picture was nice and clear now. No static from Constant White. I went and brought him back into my office and secured the doors with my phone before setting it aside.

The fiftysomething slickster sat in his expensive grey suit and offered the warmest, most genuine smile. He was very well rehearsed in such things. His grey hair was perfectly touched up to retain a mostly blond colour that likely represented the original shade.

"How we doing today?" he asked, and clapped his hands together to signal his readiness to kick things off.

"Pretty good," I lied, all the while trying to hide my involuntary cringe at the way he spoke. "Did you give much thought to our last discussion? Anything come up for you over the week?"

He leaned forward and got all serious. "Yes, about that. You seemed pretty aggressive last week. You pushed pretty hard. I have to say I was a bit rattled when I left." He was talking about the fact that I wouldn't roll over and accept excuses from him like:

I think all bodies are beautiful.
I just prefer slimmer bodies with less hair.
Sometimes I have a couple of glasses of wine in the evening.

I nodded just so he'd feel like he was being heard because this guy needed lots of ego stroking or he was too defensive to work with. "I was pretty tough on you. I guess I'm just concerned and really want you to figure this stuff out and put this bad experience behind you as quickly as possible."

He leaned back, satisfied that he'd properly scolded me. "Thank you," he announced a little too loudly. "I do want to put this bizarre situation behind me."

He often referred to his charges as *bizarre* or a *one-off*, or otherwise minimized and distanced himself from them. It was another way to avoid taking responsibility.

I decided to try my dumb-guy routine to get him to talk. I shook my head like it was the biggest mystery in the world and said, "We just need to try to figure out why you would have been looking for sex videos of underage girls."

That took the wind out of his pompous sails. He dropped his gaze and went silent for a moment. Now his voice was barely a whisper. "I didn't know that stuff was underage. I told you that."

I made a big show of flipping through something on my iPad. I was bringing up his electronic file to find the Crown file. The Crown file was the police account of the charges and evidence they found, including any witness statements that might be relevant. In a case like this, the document also included what was found on the computer. I used a finger to theatrically trace down the screen, looking for something. "Right," I finally said. "But it says you used search terms like *teen*, *preteen*, and *young and innocent*." And those were the least offensive terms this guy used.

He mumbled something, but now his voice was so low I couldn't understand him.

"What's that now?" I asked.

He still didn't look at me. "I was drinking. I didn't know what I was doing. It was just a mistake."

I nodded again. I was so sympathetic. "I know it was. You were drinking, so you could have searched for almost anything. It wouldn't have meant you were into it. Not sexually, anyway."

He liked that. He looked up. "Exactly."

"How much gay stuff did you look at?" I asked quickly.

Now he was surprised. "What?"

"How much granny porn or bestiality?"

"What the hell are you talking about? None." He was offended. That's good. That's what he needed to be.

I returned to being dumb and confused. "I don't understand. You didn't search for hard-core gay porn?"

"No!" he barked back. "I'm not gay."

"So then you wouldn't search for something that was totally out of character? Even if you were drinking?" Boom! Suck on that, Mr. Nelson.

His voice was a whisper again. "I..I..."

But there was no way out of this.

I supposed I could go easy on him, but I might get killed by a sexy British assassin in the next day or two, so I figured I didn't have time to play games.

And it was kind of fun.

The rest of the session with Mr. Nelson was typical. Lots of denial and rationalizing met head-on by my skillful reframing and challenging. He'd come back next week and not be any further ahead, probably. He was pretty committed to his own little story of how he was falsely charged and doesn't have a problem. We'll see.

My next appointment was my last one for the day. A referral from the Department of Fisheries. It wasn't a huge source of referrals for me, so I'm not sure how it ended up here, but oh well. It was this early twenties guy, basically a kid, who worked on a seasonal fishing boat. It was one of those jobs where the crew goes out for two-week tours, catches whatever, and brings it back for a huge cash score. This happens on a heavy-duty schedule when the season is on and everyone makes a lot of money and then they all go on Employment Insurance during the off-season. A simpler way to explain it is: work, work, work, party, party, party — repeat.

This kid was seeing me because he got stoned on the ship a few tours ago and was immediately suspended. Substance use on the big boats is not tolerated because of how dangerous it can be. The Department of Fisheries takes it pretty seriously, and since they control the insurance and the licenses, the fishing crew needs to keep them happy. And what the Department wants now is for this kid to be seen every time the boat is in dock to ensure his head's on straight. So I see him, write a little report on his mental state, and he goes back to sea.

And now it was five minutes past three, and the little shit was late. I hated late, especially today.

I strolled out into my waiting room and it was empty. I continued through there and poked my head into the hall and it was pretty dead out there too.

I'd already called him and left a message on his voice mail, so now I just had to wait. I'm terrible at waiting around despite what my last name suggests.

There aren't any hard and fast rules about how long you need to wait, but it was creeping up on ten minutes past the hour and I still hadn't seen or heard from this kid. It was a bit odd since his job depended on meeting with me, but ultimately what could I do? I wasn't going to run around the city looking for him.

Plus, I felt a growing urge to just get home. With all of the uncertainty about what was actually going on, I was feeling more and more like I should be home with Lisa. I hadn't even bothered to check on her. I knew she was working that morning, but I thought she had most of the afternoon off. That settled it for me. Ordinarily I would walk down to Tim Hortons, get a coffee, and come back to check on my no-show, but not today. It was time to go home.

I went over and logged out of my laptop and opened the secure filing cabinet under my desk where I locked the military USB drive away, and then I made sure all the lights were off. I used my phone to lock the doors as I left and took the stairs two at a time to get out to the street.

Within seconds I was in my Jeep and on the road.

Another fifteen minutes and I was driving down my Capilano street. On the way, I was justifying my failure to try to call Lisa on the basis that I couldn't tell her anything anyway. Military confidentiality and all that. It was a weak excuse, I know.

As I neared my house, I was telling myself that there wasn't anything to worry about. I was just making a mountain out of a molehill, and why would any of it come back to haunt Lisa, anyway? I do have a tendency to assume the worst, so maybe there wasn't anything to worry about.

I was wrong.

There was lots to be worried about.

And I'm a shit who should have called home to check in before this.

There was a black sedan parked sideways across my driveway so as to block both sides of my double car garage. It was obviously parked that way so no one could shoot out of the garage and escape. I pulled in and parked my Jeep behind the sedan, but didn't turn it off. My head was going a mile a minute. I thought about backing up and taking off. I was trying to think of where I could get a weapon or if maybe I should go back to the private office and get the coffee can so I had a bargaining chip. Maybe the coffee can was all these guys wanted (or at least the antigravity ball in the can).

Screw that. I turned the Jeep off. I needed to get inside and check on Lisa. I walked up to the front door. I hardly ever entered my own house through the front door. I tried the door — locked — so I opened it with my key and cautiously stepped inside.

All clear in the entranceway. The house was quiet.

"Honey," a male voice called from the living room. "Is that you? We're in the living room."

I frowned, but slowly made my way down the hall to the intersection where the kitchen and living room met. My wife was seated on a couch opposite a man in a dark suit. A big guy, almost my size from the looks of him. Movement caught my eye, and I turned to see a second suited guy in my kitchen, bent over to look in the fridge.

"You got a pop or something in here?" that guy asked.

I ignored him and turned back to Lisa. "What's going on?"

She looked shaken, but not panicked. "These guys say they know you."

The couch guy stood. He wasn't as big as me. "You remember us, right, Doc? We're friends of Dr. Zwicker. I think he asked you to hold onto something for us?" He winked at me to encourage me to go along with this story.

I hadn't looked away from Lisa. "Are you okay?"

She nodded.

Now I turned to Couch Guy. "I'd like it if you two guys left now. I don't have anything for you. There's been a misunderstanding."

"I don't see it that way," said Fridge Guy. He'd come up behind me and was close enough to reach out and touch me. Or hit me.

I was hoping he wouldn't hit me, but I took a step

away just to be sure and also so I could see both of them. "Whatever you think is here, isn't."

"Where is it then?"

"Where is what?" I said.

"Whatever you were talking about?" Couch Guy said.

"I don't have anything," I said.

"What's the thing you don't have?" Fridge Guy asked.

"*Jesus Christ!*" Lisa shouted. "What the hell is the matter with you guys?" Tears blew out from her eyes and she stood. "I'm going upstairs."

"Sit down!" Couch Guy shouted at her.

"Go fuck yourself!" she shouted back, and left the room.

Couch Guy and Fridge Guy just looked at each other and shrugged. They probably weren't used to that level of resistance from a petite five foot six woman in yoga pants. It was pretty cool. It made me want to follow her upstairs and pull those yoga pants off. Fingers. Forehead. Flick.

"Hey," Couch Guy yelled at me, and snapped his fingers. I was staring at Lisa's ass storming down the hall. Fridge Guy was too. "Dr. Zwicker left you something. Perhaps something shiny with some very unusual properties?"

"Unusual properties?" I asked. Do you see how good I am at playing dumb? Most people can't believe I have a doctorate.

Fridge Guy pulled a gun out from inside his jacket

and pointed it at me. "Where is it? We know he left it with you."

Couch Guy strolled over and put an arm around me. "You don't need this kind of stress. I know it. You know it. Just give us the ball and we'll be gone. We don't need anything else from you."

I was silent.

"Did Zwicker tell you that that thing is dangerous?" Couch Guy asked. He was close enough now that I could detect a faint smell of garlic (or salami) wafting out with each word. "The thing will eventually explode. It doesn't belong here. We need to get it back to protect you. To protect that lovely wife of yours." He looked down the hall in the direction Lisa had just gone.

I still didn't say anything. I didn't say anything, partially because I didn't want to and partially because I didn't want to get his salami breath in my mouth. Gross.

"If you hand it over," Salami Breath said (he used to be Couch Guy), "it will just save time. If you don't, then we'll tear your house apart and get it anyway. The first way is just way more pleasant for you and your sweet wife."

I shrugged his arm off me to get away from his horrible breath. "I don't have anything. Nathan Zwicker didn't give me anything." Which, as I said before, was true — his wife gave it to me. "So I'm trying to save you some time. You can pull my house apart, but you won't find anything."

"You're making a mistake," Fridge Guy said, and wagged the gun. "We don't want to hurt you. We don't care about you. Just hand over the ball."

"Oh," I said before I could stop myself. "You don't want to hurt me because all you need to do is get the ball and then Constant White sweeps in and finishes the dirty work."

That made both men pause. "Who'd you say?" Salami Breath asked.

"Constant White," I said. I couldn't stop myself now. I was fed up with this shit. "I know she's here. I know she's here to clean up this Zwicker mess."

Fridge Guy was about to respond when the front doorbell rang. Now we all froze.

"Who the fuck is that?" Salami Breath hissed.

"I don't know," I said.

The doorbell rang again, and the person banged on the door too. A muffled "Hello?" came through it.

"Don't answer it," Fridge Guy said in a menacing tone, but no sooner had he said it than Lisa's feet pounded down the stairs and she was at the front door.

"Is it more idiots to join your goon party?" she announced, and flung the door open before anyone could react.

Fridge Guy jammed his hand in his coat to hide the gun as my fat neighbour Roland stepped in. "I knew you guys were home. I saw the Jeep...." His voice trailed off as he looked past Lisa down the hall to where he could see me and the other two. "I'm sorry. Do you have company?"

"Come on in, Roland," I yelled before anyone else could answer.

Confused, but never one to let that stop him, Roland walked down the hall towards us. Fridge Guy left his gun in his shoulder holster and took his hand out. Roland stepped in the kitchen and looked back and forth between them. "Am I interrupting something?"

"No," I said hastily. "That's Fridge Guy," I said, pointing. "And over there is Salami Breath. They're just leaving. They came here by mistake."

Roland frowned. "I hope they aren't leaving because of me." He didn't even flinch at the names I used to introduce them.

Fridge Guy gave me a death stare, but did make his way towards the front door and was followed by Salami Breath. "We'll talk again very soon," he announced as they opened the front door to step out.

I rushed behind them and pushed the door shut, locking it, when they were out. I vaguely heard them talking as they walked down the driveway. One of them said something like, "Do I really have salami breath?" The other told him to "fuck off." I smiled as I turned away from the door and headed back to the kitchen.

"What," said Roland, "the hell was that?"

"Oh, you know. Jehovah's Witnesses or Mormons. Always trying to save my soul."

He looked at me sceptically.

An engine could be heard on the driveway and then a car speeding away. They were gone. I sagged against the kitchen island. Exhausted. "What can I do for you, Roland?"

He looked at the door where the guests had just left

and then back at me. "I…I needed your private practice contact info again. For that case I mentioned. I can't find the card you gave me the other day."

I nodded. "For the porn guy at your work?"

"Right," he said, but his speech was still halting after the commotion with the visitors. "But I can come back later or something."

I pulled out my wallet and handed over a shiny new business card. My cards were jet black with silver writing. A friend said it looked more like a card for a nightclub owner. I thought it looked cool.

He took it and looked at it as if seeing it for the first time. "Thanks for this. I'll be in touch about the referral."

I nodded and walked Roland back to the door, where we paused, and he turned to me again. "Are you sure everything's okay?" He was such a pleasant and concerned neighbour.

"It's fine," I said. "I guess it was lucky you came and interrupted their spiel so I didn't have to go through it all. I really didn't want my soul saved. Too much work."

"Right," he said, but actually meant the opposite. He left and raised a backwards hand as a wave as he trundled down the driveway.

I closed the door, locked it, and turned to fall back against it.

Lisa was sitting up on the steps now watching me. "So I guess you don't trust Roland with whatever is going on. Are you going to tell me?"

I looked up at her.

"Let me guess," she continued. "It's got something to do with that military contract you have that you're always so secretive about."

She knew I worked with the military, but didn't know about SSCHVA. At least I didn't think she knew about SSCHVA, but she was clever.

"I don't know what this is about," I said.

"So what work do you do with the military?"

I hesitated, but finally said, "I see people to help them, but most of it is classified."

"Classified?" She laughed, but not in a good way. "As in top secret?"

"I guess so. But it's fine. It's just a contract I have to work with military people. To help them."

"So it's okay that two goons show up here and sit in my living room waiting for you, but it's not okay to tell me what's going on?"

"Neither one of those things is *okay*," I said.

"So then, why were they here? What are they looking for?"

I looked away from her.

"You don't know or you can't tell me because it's soooo *top secret*."

I broke down. I decided to tell her a little something. "I was the last person to see a military scientist alive, and these guys are wondering if that doctor left anything with me."

"Did he?"

"No." Again, that was the truth.

"Blake," she said, frustrated. "I heard them say something about a ball, a magic ball."

I didn't respond.

"A magic ball like the one you had in the garage, maybe. The thing you said was just a magic trick."

Oh right. She'd seen it. Fuck.

"Why didn't you just give it to them? What's going on?"

"It's not that simple. There's other stuff going on. Other people involved," I started. "I'm going to fix this, but I need to make sure about how I'm doing it."

"Other people are involved?" she spat back. "Other people like Constant White? Who is that?" She must have been listening from upstairs.

"No one. I'm not sure she's even involved."

"So it's a her?"

I nodded.

She glared at me for another beat. She was debating asking more about the woman, but decided to switch gears. "Did you steal that ball thing?"

"No." I recoiled in surprise. "I wouldn't."

She just glared at me. She didn't believe half of what I was saying. She stood on the stairs and stared some more, wrestling with what she wanted to say next. "You know," she finally said, "I've always made it a point to not ask about your work. I know the people you see have a right to confidentiality, and maybe you are doing something *top* secret, but you can't keep me in the dark if your work spills over and affects me."

"I know and —" I started, but she held up a hand.

"But when Gabe went missing, I had a little thought

in the back of my head that maybe your work was involved. I had a little thought that maybe your sex offenders or maybe someone from the military had something to do with it, but I always pushed that thought away. When I had those thoughts, it made me hate you a little, and I didn't want to feel that way."

"That's not fair," I said.

"It's not fair that our son disappeared. As if it wasn't hard enough watching his disease make him weaker year after year — to have him just disappear?"

I didn't say anything.

"And sometimes I look at you and I think if you hadn't picked such a bunch of disturbed people to work with, then maybe my son would still be here." Her eyes filled with tears. "And that makes it pretty hard to live with you. Pretty hard to look at you."

"Lisa," I urged. "I would never...." But she turned and went back up, leaving me standing at the front door.

Standing at the front door — angry. Very angry.

CHAPTER 13

By the next morning my anger had subsided somewhat. I was no longer *going to make them all pay!* Or telling myself, *They don't know who they're messing with.*

Primarily because I had no ability to make anyone pay for anything — other than overpriced therapy — and I'm quite sure they knew exactly who they were dealing with. Probably they knew more about me than even I knew.

Even though I'd calmed down, it still stung that Lisa and I were having a thing again. A negative thing. I slept in the guest room and hadn't spoken to her since she accused my job of having something to do with our son's disappearance. That was not cool. That was not okay.

But I had to deal with the goddamn magic silver ball and the British assassin before I could turn my attention to my wife. When I awoke I made the instant decision to hand the antigravity ball over to SSCHVA. It made no sense for me to be hiding it. I don't know what I thought I was doing. Warning or no warning from Marie Zwicker, the antigravity ball and its coffee can house were out of my life today. Good riddance.

I had a couple of appointments that morning, which was fine since I needed to go to the office to get the thing. I figured once word got out that SSCHVA had the magic ball back that the heat would be off me.

That was the hope.

My first client was a kid.

Well, not a kid. I mentioned before that I don't see kids. Child psychology is a specialty I never developed an interest, or tolerance, for. Tim Carel was technically an adult age-wise. But he was also a child socially, or maybe a teenager, a young teenager.

The nineteen-year old was sitting on my couch crying. I shifted uncomfortably and waited him out because his tears normally embarrassed him pretty quickly and then we could continue. I was planning on switching topics the moment he recovered, but he switched topics for me.

"I saw my probation officer yesterday," he announced as he cleaned up his face with a tissue.

Red hair, freckles, and skinny. Tim would be a real sight sitting in the waiting room of corrections about to see his probation officer. I suppressed a grin. "How'd that go?"

"Fine. I asked about Internet for gaming and he still said no, but he's, like, a hundred years old. He doesn't get that you can barely play anything without a connection."

His probation officer was, like, forty-one — younger than me. I let the *hundred years old* comment slide. "Well, you did use the Internet to send a picture of your dick to a fourteen-year-old," I said. Maybe, subconsciously, I didn't let the *hundred years old* comment slide completely.

He put a hand over his face. Embarrassed again.

This dumb kid was not an anomaly, unfortunately. He was one of the new generation of gamer kids who grow up with the Internet connecting every fucking device they use. From the moment they gain the fine motor control to touch a screen, parents are shoving iPads in their hands. These kids don't stand a chance of developing normal social skills unless the parents forcibly kick them out of the house, make the kid join a sport or club, or otherwise expose them to — *gasp* — face-to-face contact.

Tim grew up making friends online, playing online, surfing porn, fantasizing about real life, but never living it. He was a smart kid. He was nice, compassionate, and funny. And he was a giant loser who had no clue how to have a normal relationship and who believed that porn was an accurate representation of how sex was intended to be: a selfish, gratuitous act of fucking.

In other words, he was confused and socially awkward. In the days before the Internet, high school kids were already confused and socially awkward, so the effect of the Internet was exponential. Now the awkward teens were striking out in the world after years of Internet porn education. God save us all!

Poor Tim had met a girl online playing *Call of Duty* or something. He thought he'd found the Holy Grail of gamer nerds and neckbeards — a gamer girl! They exchanged phone numbers and started texting. Tim was so desperate for something that felt like a girlfriend. He was eighteen years old at the time and had just finished high school, worked at McDonald's to earn money to go to university, and still lived at home. He texted her, she texted him. It was beautiful.

But she was evasive about her age.

And he didn't push.

And things got kinky and sexual because porn had taught Tim that's what you do. He wanted to meet her and do things to her because the amount of porn he already viewed had turned his nice brain into garbage.

So when she finally hinted at, and then told him, she was only fourteen years old, his garbage brain couldn't figure out what to do with that info.

Then the girl's dad finds the phone, and blah, blah, blah, Tim has a criminal record, is on the sex offender registry, was fired from McDonald's, and is hanging onto his sanity with fingertips.

But he still wants to get back online because that's all he's known. It's hardwired into who he is.

"I know," he whispered. "I shouldn't have been texting her, but I thought I loved her."

"Being offline is a condition, but not a punishment," I told him. "You have to disconnect your brain. Reset it. Find out who you are as a person."

His hand still covered his face. "As a person I'm a useless piece of shit," he said quietly.

"Tim," I said calmly, "are you feeling like hurting yourself?"

No answer.

"Tim?"

He took his hand away. "Not really." A pause. "Maybe a bit, but not really."

"No plan?"

He shook his head.

We spent the rest of the session brainstorming his offline life. He needed to get out and join a recreational group or pick up some volunteer work. He needed to be around people. Make friends. Develop social skills. That wouldn't happen sitting in his parent's basement.

My session with Tim went overtime by a few minutes, but I always left enough of gap between my patients to allow for that.

I'd unlocked the doors and was walking him out — continuing to pepper him with encouragement about the plan we'd developed for the coming week.

"And you can call me anytime," I was saying. "If you just want to touch base before we meet again, you know the number."

He paused at the next door, his hand on the knob. He didn't turn to address me, but spoke anyway. "Thanks, Dr. Waiter. I really appreciate it. I know I'm...."

He didn't get to finish because the door burst in and flung him backwards over a chair. Fridge Guy and Salami Breath stepped into the room.

I took a step back and grunted in surprise. (Okay, I might have squealed like a little girl, but this is my story.) "What the fuck?"

"Hello Mr. Shit-for-Brains. Miss me?" Salami Breath said.

"It's Dr. Shit-for Brains," I corrected him.

He stared at me, confused at whether I had just insulted him or myself.

I didn't know either.

Fridge Guy stood overtop of Tim now. "Who's this little shit? Did we interrupt some little fag hookup?" He sneered down at the scared teen, who lay awkwardly across two different chairs.

Salami Breath was still staring me down. "We clarified our orders," he started. "Seems like collateral damage would have been acceptable, so your bitch wife and your fat fuck neighbour dodged a bullet last night."

"Are you guys wearing the exact same suits as yesterday?" I asked. I sounded a whole lot cockier than I felt. I was trying hard not to piss myself.

Salami Breath turned away from me and used the back of his hand to shut my waiting room door. He reached down to the knob and made a show of locking it, but he didn't know that I controlled the lock with my phone.

He turned back and got in my face. "Do you still think I'm Salami Breath?" That comment must have really gotten to him. His breath smelled minty today, like he'd gone to town on a candy before bursting into my office. That was pretty weird. A bully who cared about having nice-smelling breath when he was threatening someone.

It was too early to get out of this guy's head. I decided to keep fucking with him. "No, sir," I said. "Your breath smells more like a complimentary breakfast at the Hampton Inn. Maybe waffles and bacon?"

There was a glimmer in his face like I might have actually hit the nail on the head, but he recovered quickly. His witty retort was to punch me flush in the face. I dropped in the shape of a smartass sack of shit that can't keep its mouth shut. Tim screamed.

From the floor, I felt my face to see if my nose was missing. It wasn't, but it was gushing blood. "Fuck!" I said with a strong nasal twang. That got me a kick to the stomach that sucked all the air out of me and made me gasp.

Tim yelled again, but Fridge Guy reached down and put a hand around his scrawny neck and lifted him right off the chair. "Keep your mouth shut," he sneered at the kid.

Salami Breath crouched down next to me. "So how's this going to go? I'm sort of hoping you hold out for a bit because I ain't tired of hurting you."

I wasn't sure how to be intimidating as I lay on my side, virtually in a fetal position. I decided on silence.

"Whoa," Salami Breath said in mock surprise. "No smartass comments from *Dr.* Shit-for-Brains." Instead of an exclamation point on his sentence, he bent over and punched me in the side of the head, mainly hitting ear. Immediately, my ear sang out and buzzed with pain that quickly spread through my skull.

I could hear Tim struggle, and begin to cry, which resulted in a slap across his face from Fridge Guy.

I struggled to sit and that made Salami Breath stand over me. I brought my knees up and held them as I spoke — I didn't have the strength to stand. "Let the kid go. He's got nothing to do with this."

"Which kid?" Fridge Guy said, and punched Tim in the face with his free hand, never releasing his grip on the kid's neck.

"Stop!" I yelled. "That's enough."

Fridge Guy hit him again, and I saw Tim's eyes flutter like he might lose consciousness.

Salami Breath said, "You don't seem to understand the situation. We're just going to do whatever we like until you make us happy. Give us the goddamn ball right now."

I leaned on the floor and forced myself to stand. Blood still leaked from my nose. "Let him go," I spoke into Salami's face. Bits of bloody spittle dotted the man's face after.

He slowly wiped his face and then wiped his hand down the front of my shirt. Then he put one hand on each of my shoulders. He opened his mouth to say something, but then brought his knee up into my groin, and I was back on the floor, gasping like a fish.

Then darkness. I blacked out.

I don't think I got a full refreshing nap because Salami woke me by slapping me across the face. My cheek burned like it was on fire.

"It's not sleepy time. Where is it? We know you have it."

Now my ear rang, my cheek stung, my head throbbed, my nose was bleeding and probably so was my dick. I forced myself up again. Who doesn't love a good beating? "Okay, you win." I glanced over. Fridge Guy had dropped

Tim onto the chairs. Tim didn't look good either.

"Just hurry up," Salami said, and they both slipped hands into their suits.

I wasn't getting out of this alive. I knew after I handed over the ball, they were going to kill me. They'd basically announced that when they arrived and said collateral damage was acceptable. They now had free reign to kill whoever was in their way. And that was currently me and Tim.

I took a step towards my inner office where the coffee can was and stopped. The waiting room door had opened and someone stepped in, noticeably filling the room with a bulk that couldn't be ignored. The bulk was Chuck Peligro. He was my other appointment that morning. And he was always prompt.

He stepped in and shut the door behind him. He slowly removed those godawful Oakley Blade sunglasses and surveyed the room. "What the fuck is this?" he growled.

Fridge Guy and Salami Breath instantly drew their weapons. They weren't expecting a giant and had no intention of attempting to manhandle this guy. "Stay right there," Fridge announced.

Chuck ignored him and looked at me. "What's this? We have an appointment right now." He was mad. There was blood all over my face and two guys pointing guns at him, but good old Chuck was pissed that I might have forgotten he had an appointment.

"I think your fucking appointment is cancelled," Salami Breath said. He motioned with his gun towards the door. "Why don't you drag your retard ass out of here before you regret it?"

It took a moment for Chuck to break his angry stare at me and turn to acknowledge Salami. He seemed initially intent on getting an answer from me about why the appointment would be interrupted. I could see the scary anger in Chuck's eyes. I wasn't so worried about Fridge and Salami anymore. I think we might all get killed. Fuck.

"It's okay, Chuck. We'll keep our appointment. No problem," I said, and held up my hands to him. "No problem."

"No, *Chuck*. There is no appointment. You're probably too stupid to figure that out, but no appointment. So get the fuck out of here." Salami motioned with his gun again.

Chuck was still looking down at the much smaller man in a suit with a gun pointed at him. Faster than anyone could have imagined, he reached out and took the gun away from Salami Breath. It was a blur and then Chuck was holding a gun. He looked down at the weapon and then picked a severed finger off the trigger. He held it up to have a look at it. For a second I thought he was going to eat it, but thankfully he just tossed it away carelessly.

No one breathed.

Salami's hand was still outstretched like he thought he had a gun. He brought it back slowly and held up his four remaining fingers and then a cry escaped him. A moaning scream of pain and shock. The colour was flooding out of his face.

"What the fuck?" Fridge Guy screamed. His eyes were darting back and forth between Chuck and Salami. "What the fuck?"

Chuck didn't hold the gun like a weapon. He just let it sit in his massive hand. It looked like a toy.

"Drop that gun!" Fridge screamed, his own gun waving manically. "Drop it, you giant fuck, or I swear to God I'll shoot you." Fridge Guy was losing it.

Salami was cupping his injured hand in his good one and took a step, dropping into one of the waiting room chairs. He was still heavily in shock.

"Drop that gun!" Fridge yelled again.

Chuck looked down at the weapon he was holding. I knew from our many hours of therapy that Chuck didn't much like guns. He could use them. He was, in fact, an expert marksman with virtually anything you could shoot, but he didn't like guns because you couldn't feel the pain you inflicted on your target. That's what he said. He liked to be hands on when he engaged a target. Chuck simply turned his hand upside down and the gun dropped to the floor.

Fridge Guy noticeably relaxed at this, but then he didn't know what I knew. Dropping the gun probably just made things worse for him. Oblivious to his danger, Fridge Guy barked another order. "Now get down on the floor. Flat on the floor, belly down and fingers laced behind your head." His voice still shook with adrenaline.

Chuck couldn't have been calmer. Angry. But calm. He finally addressed Fridge Guy directly. "You know what they used to call me before I started coming to this office?"

Here we go again.

Fridge Guy just stammered. "What?"

"Chuck the Fuck," he said. "And do you know why?"

"What? Shut the fuck up," Fridge Guy blurted. He had no clue what was going on.

"I used to fuck people up. That was my job and I was good at it." Normally Chuck smiled at his own punchline, but not today. A shiver went down my back. "But when I got this." — he knocked on the side of his head. "They said I couldn't do my job no more."

"Oh yeah," Fridge guy spat back. He was getting tough, but his voice still shook like a little girl. "Get down on the fuckin' floor." He jabbed the barrel of the gun at him. I guess Fridge Guy wanted to look menacing, but his actions made it look more like epilepsy.

It certainly wasn't menacing to Chuck. "But I think I can still fuck up a couple of limp dicks like you two."

Tim was still crumpled in an awkward pile in the chair he'd fallen in and likely only half aware of what was going on. He had a hand on his face and moaned softly.

Fridge Guy kept the gun trained on Chuck, but turned and used the back of his free hand to swipe the kid across the face. "You keep your mouth shut," he yelled because I guess he felt a lot more secure hitting the scrawny teen.

Fridge Guy had barely glanced down to land the blow, but when his eyes flicked back on Chuck, he saw only an enormous chest inches from his face. In that split second of inattention, Chuck had crossed the room and stood almost on top of the smaller man. The outstretched gun arm extended under Chuck's armpit.

Everything else happened in slow motion. Fridge Guy tried to rip his arm back to get the weapon pointed on target again, but Chuck simply clamped his arm down and pinned him. He pinned him with enough force the man squealed. Then Fridge guy slowly, reluctantly, raised his face to look up. What he found was an unhappy giant.

"I don't like you hitting that little kid," Chuck said.

Now the events of the last little bit had been out of control. It'd had been one crazy thing after another. Hell, all the crazy shit going on was unbelievable, but when Chuck said this, it was the most surprising thing that had happened yet. This was a trained soldier who didn't care about anything, anyone, or even himself. He was reckless, angry all the time, and in a continual state of frustration because of his medical leave.

"Fuck you," Fridge Guy said, and Chuck lifted up sharply on the trapped arm and snapped it in two. It now hung limp, at the wrong angle, from his elbow.

The silent scream that opened Fridge Guy's mouth was disturbing. His mouth just opened, and he stared down at his ruined arm.

Chuck stepped back from the man just as Salami Breath leapt at him. He'd recovered enough to try something, and this is what he came up with. It didn't even look like Chuck turned to see him, but he reached out and caught Salami by the face.

That's right. The guy was in full flight diving at Chuck, and he was stopped when his face slapped into that giant palm.

Salami collapsed in a heap, and Chuck stepped over the man towards me. I almost ran back into my office, but Chuck had just the sliver of a grin. "Are we meeting now?" he asked.

"I..," I started, but my expression of confusion was evident.

Chuck laughed. "I'm fuckin' with you. You gots to deal with this."

I finally started to breath again and immediately ran to Tim. He'd righted himself into a sitting position. "Are you okay, Tim?" The side of his face was red and there were some marks around his neck, but he didn't look too bad. Probably better than what I looked like.

"Who..." he started, "who are those guys?" He struggled to hold back tears. He was ready for a full meltdown.

I glanced back at the guys, who still lay in various states of distress and seemed wholly unready to mount any more attacks on Chuck. "They're nobody, really. Don't worry about them."

"Why did they do that?" He was staring up at my bloody face. Then he seemed to remember something else, and his eyes shot to Chuck. "Did that guy...." His voice trailed away as emotions choked off his words.

"Can you stand?" I asked, and then helped him to his feet. "Let's get you into my office." I put an arm around him and walked him back. As we moved I nodded at Chuck and then towards Fridge and Salami. He nodded back, acknowledging that he was keeping an eye on them.

I just needed to get Tim out of the horror that had become my waiting room. I got him seated with a can of pop out of my mini fridge and reassured him he was safe and he should just relax here for a while before I got him home. He asked something about the police, but I avoided that issue. For now.

I stepped back into the waiting room to find Fridge and Salami seated next to one another. Chuck had used their shirts to do a little field dressing to patch them up. Fridge's shirt was a sling that held his broken arm to his chest while Salami Breath had strips of his shirt wrapped around his hand to quell the bleeding from his missing finger. Both men were still painfully pale.

The guns were noticeably absent, and I had zero interest in resuming an armed standoff. I looked at Chuck, who sat opposite the two men, and I made a gun sign with my hand, and shrugged my shoulders to ask where they were.

He pointed at the top of my armoire in the corner of the room. He'd obviously stashed them on top where only a giant could easily reach them.

I'd grabbed a few tissues and was wiping my face as I went and sat next to Chuck. My legs were still a bit wobbly especially since the adrenaline was seeping out of me. "Are you okay?" I asked Chuck's shoulder, in my immediate line of sight.

He grunted something that indicated that was a foolish question.

"I'm sorry you walked in on this," I continued. To me, Chuck was still a patient whom I needed to protect. It was my job to help him, not put him in the middle of a violent melee.

"God, you Canadians apologize a lot." He leaned down to look me in the eyes and put his sunglasses back on as he did so. "Doc," he said with just a hint of a smile. "This has been better therapy than a million hours sitting listening to you natter."

I suppose that was good. It hurt my feelings a bit, but it was still good, I guess.

"Now," Chuck continued. "I've told these shit stains to answer anything you ask or I will begin hurting them." The way his voice broke slightly on the words *hurting them* suggested he was excited at the prospect. "They've assured me only the highest level of cooperation."

Well, as my granny always said, *In for a penny, in for a pound.* I wasn't sure it applied here, but figured I might as well get some answers to what the hell was going on.

CHAPTER 14

I guess when it came right down to it, having your index finger ripped off was only slightly less traumatic than having your arm snapped in half. I suspected the arm won out as worst because of the sustained pain.

Frankly, both were gruesome, and I highly recommend the avoidance of such injuries.

But as a result of his condition, it was Salami Breath who was better able to address my inquires, so it was to him I directed my questions. Questions like "What the fuck is going on?"

Through his bluish lips Salami answered, "You're going to die. You're going to die and you're going to destroy this city along with it."

"What the hell are you talking about?"

"That thing Zwicker gave you will explode. It can't be here." His words were choppy, being forced through his lingering shock.

"Why? Is it a bomb? Is it a weapon?"

He sneered at me. "I don't know the details. They don't tell us anything. I just know that there's two of those things, and they need to be near one another, but not touching or else they blow up. Something like that."

"Two of what?" I asked. I wondered if it was his injury turning him into such a cryptic dickhead.

"There's two balls!" he yelled like I was the stupid

one. "Whenever they get something, it comes in pairs. A brother and a sister. You have the brother. They still have the sister."

I put my face in my hands and mumbled, "Brother and sister. What the hell?" I turned to Chuck. "This guy is starting to annoy me. I wonder if he has too many fingers." This brought out a smile on the big man's face that would've chilled anyone to the bone.

When Chuck shifted as if to stand, Salami blurted out, "No, wait. Everything they find is in pairs. That's all I mean. Brothers and sisters."

"You mean on this antigravity project? Why are things in pairs?"

He shook his head. "There is no antigravity project. It was never an antigravity project."

"What is the project then?"

"They call it Dead Kitty. Project Dead Kitty."

"Bullshit," I said.

"I didn't name it. It has something to do with some scientist or something."

"You guys came up here and killed Dr. Zwicker for a project called Dead Kitty?"

"He was never supposed to leave the base. That was a colossal fuck-up. Paperwork was mishandled or something. I don't know. No one ever leaves Dead Kitty. He won't allow it."

"Who won't allow it?"

Silence.

"Who won't allow it?" I repeated.

Chuck slammed a hand down on my coffee table

and everyone jumped.

"Mr. Schlimm," Salami Breath blurted. "Mr. Schlimm is the project manager. I think he's civilian or something, but he's in charge of the whole thing."

"And where is this Schlimm now?"

"He's here. He had to come up and bring the sister object. If he hadn't, the other one might have blown up already. That's why you need to give it back. Only Mr. Schlimm can stop it from blowing."

I looked over at Chuck sceptically. He glanced at me and shrugged. "And this antigravity project is called Dead Kitty?"

"It's not an antigravity project!" Salami yelled. "It's something else."

"Something else like what?" I asked.

"I don't know. I just know that it wasn't about those antigravity balls. There's other stuff."

"Other stuff like what?"

"I told you. They don't tell us shit. Ask Schlimm."

"I might just do that. Where can I find him?"

Even Fridge Guy got involved now. He reached over with his good arm to touch Salami and mouthed, "Don't!" Salami shrugged him off.

"You guys worried at what Mr. Schlimm-Jim might do to you?" I asked.

Nothing.

I waited.

Salami held up his hand with blood-soaked strips of shirt wrapped where there had formerly been a finger. "I need to get to the hospital, asshole. I don't know anything else."

"You know where Mr. Schlimm is."

"He's at the casino hotel. He's in some fancy suite. That's all I know. I swear." Panic was pushing his pitch higher again. It was getting painful to listen to him.

I stood and casually stretched before addressing Chuck. "Why don't you escort these gentlemen out of the building while I pop in the bathroom and freshen up?" I could feel the blood drying on my face. I was happy I kept some extra clothes in this office too, given the state of my shirt.

Fridge and Salami sprang to their feet. "We can manage," Salami said, eyeing Chuck with no small amount of concern. Salami swooped something off the floor and they were both at the door, fast. I almost didn't have time to get it opened with my app first.

I nodded at Chuck to follow them out. He paused at the doorway and looked back at me, making a silent cutting motion across his throat.

"No!" I yelped. "Just make sure they get in a car and leave." Jesus.

He nodded and left to follow the other two. I made my way to the bathroom.

Chuck wasn't gone long, but by the time he got back I was cleaned up and back in my office talking to Tim. He was doing a lot better.

"I should really make sure you get home," I said.

"I'm totally good to go," he countered, refusing my

offer again.

Chuck stepped into the office. "I can take him."

That didn't help. Tim looked a bit scared of the man-mountain. "No. I'm good." Tim stood, and I stood alongside him.

"I'm really sorry about all this," I said.

"Wasn't your fault," he said, and left, forcing Chuck to back into the waiting room to let the little guy out.

I watched him go — still feeling like there was more I could do to make up for the trauma of the last half hour.

"He's fine," Chuck announced. "Who the fuck were those guys? Military?"

I snapped out of my daze and addressed him. "Not really sure. They're definitely connected to a military project. That Dead Kitty thing."

"That sounded like a big ole pile of bullshit."

I shrugged. It reminded me of something Dr. Zwicker had said when we met a few days ago — something about *Slim refusing to allow loose ends on his little kitten project.* At the time I thought he was just on the verge of hysteria, but he was probably talking about this Schlimm character and the Dead Kitty project.

When I didn't respond to his comment that the project sounded like bullshit, Chuck continued, "So you got one of these antigravity balls? The things those guys were saying's gonna blow up?"

My eyes darted to the ottoman. That's right. Was it really going to blow up? I leaned over and opened the ottoman and pulled the coffee can out and kicked the top shut. Chuck watched like a little kid tracking candy. But given that he had just saved my life, he deserved to see this. I opened the can and dug through the cloth to pull it out before dropping the can on the couch. I held it out in the palm of my hand. The shiny silver ball that was causing so much trouble in my life.

"That's it?" Chuck said, staring at it. "Why ain't it flying around the room?" Even he seemed reluctant to reach out and touch it after the warnings from Fridge Guy and Salami Breath.

To answer his question, I simply lowered my hand slowly and left the ball hanging in the air in front of us.

"Holy shit," Chuck whispered.

"I know."

"And that's the thing that's going to blow up and take half the city with it?"

"Oh fuck!" I blurted and actually stepped back from it. I kept forgetting that part. I supposed it was a pretty important bit to remember.

Chuck reached out and gently pushed the ball, letting it slide across the air until it bumped into a painting on my wall.

"Whoa!" I shouted. "What if it blows up?"

He was staring at the object like a little kid on Christmas morning, his eyes wide. He went and retrieved the ball and pushed it gently towards the floor, watching it float down and bounce off my carpet.

My heart was pounding. I'd played with the ball in a similar way, but I wasn't worried it was going to blow up at the time. "Chuck?" I said quietly to break him from his trance.

He looked over at me. "If it blows, it blows."

"That's not very comforting," I said.

He crouched down and was playing with the ball again. Floating it from hand to hand like a magician. It was hard not to watch. It was truly astonishing and looked like a special effect from a movie.

"I'm going to take it to this Mr. Schlimm and get him to leave me alone," I said.

Chuck stood with the ball resting in his giant palm and immediately started floating the ball around again.

"Chuck!" I called. "I'm going to take that thing to this Schlimm guy. If it's dangerous, I don't want to be near it. If he gets it back, maybe I'll be done with all of this."

His eyes tracked the silver ball, and he didn't address me directly when he said, "As soon as this prick gets this back, he'll kill you and then he'll probably try to kill me and that little ginger kid you had in here."

"What? Why? If he gets this back, why would he want to hurt me, or you, or especially Tim?"

"That's what I would do," he answered, still absorbed with his new toy. "He needs to tidy up anyone and everyone who knows about this. That's you, me, and the kid." He pushed the ball and walked around it. "Oh, and he doesn't want to hurt you. After he has this back, he'll just kill you."

I dropped down onto the couch. "So then what do I do?"

He snatched the ball out of the air and turned to

me. "No idea."

"I can't keep that thing if it's going to blow up."

"Want me to go kill this Schlimm guy?"

I didn't say no instantly, which made me feel guilty. "No," I finally said. "That doesn't solve the exploding ball problem. I think I need to bring this thing back to him and hope for the best."

"That's a stupid idea. Want me to go with you?"

Yes! my head screamed, but my mouth was stupid. "No. You've done more than enough. You saved my ass today. I can't ask you to do any more. You're my patient, for God's sake."

He shrugged. "It's what I do best. It's who I am."

"I know, but I'm not looking for a fight with this guy. I'm just going to go and talk to him."

He reached down to me on the couch and opened his hand with the ball. I took it from him. "All right," he announced. "I'll see you next week." He moved to the door and turned back. "That's if you don't get killed today." I think he smiled, or maybe it was a smirk.

I nodded. "See you next week."

And he was gone.

I put the ball away in its coffee can and got ready to lock my office up and go.

The Halifax casino is a beautiful building located downtown on the waterfront. It used to be combined with the hotel, but years ago they moved the casino a few doors down into its own building to open the hotel up with more space. The buildings are connected through a series of skyways, glass-enclosed hallways three stories up. The parking for both the hotel and casino is a multistory, stand-alone structure, the last in a line of attached buildings. This was where I pulled my Jeep into a stall and parked.

I sat with my hands draped over the steering wheel to see if my courage would soon catch up. It didn't. I glanced into the back seat, where I had wedged the coffee can under the passenger seat. I knew I'd better not bring my only bargaining chip with me — not yet.

I was about to open my door when my phone buzzed. I recognized the tone now.

You are at the casino. Mr. Schlimm is staying at the hotel. I assume you are going to speak with him.

It was Talus. *Do u know Mr. Schlimm?*

Yes. He cannot be trusted.

Y? I typed.

He lies.

About what?

Everything. The project is not what he tells people.

What project? Dead Kitty? I felt foolish even typing that project title.

Yes.

So u no about Project Dead Kitty?

Yes. That was the project that discovered the antigravity material.

The antigravity material that is going to explode? I typed.

No. There is no risk of explosion.

Explain.

This hacker guy, Talus, could type about three hundred words a minute because my screen filled with his text almost instantly:

> *Mr. Schlimm wants to control any technology discovered during Project Dead Kitty and has convinced all other project participants that each discovery is dangerous and only he can control the objects. He has even detonated a false explosion to illustrate his claims of risk. He is amassing a library of technology / objects for further research and exploitation through his company. He cannot be trusted and has no ethical constraints around his pursuits. He cannot be trusted.*

I read through his message a couple of times before I texted back. *Why should I trust u?*

I have no other motive apart from providing you assistance. That was the directive from Dr. Zwicker.

IDK, I typed.

If you bring the object to Mr. Schlimm, you will likely be eliminated.

Great. That's two votes for me being killed today. Not what I wanted to hear. *U mean he'll kill me if I hand this thing over?*

Yes.

I thought for a moment and then typed, *If u really want 2 help me, then what room is Schlimm in?*

He sent me the room number. Instantly. This hacker was good.

I swiped the text window off my phone. That was

enough of that conversation. It was turning into a real downer. I slid out of my Jeep and lifted the driver seat to reach into the back and get the coffee can. I stood back and held it my hand, looking at it as if I was reading the ingredients. Anyone watching me would have thought it was a unique can of java.

Then I bent back into the Jeep and shoved it deep under the passenger seat again. Jesus, I hoped it didn't blow up my Jeep while I was gone.

CHAPTER 15

When you enter into the Halifax Marriott Harbourfront Hotel from the pedway, you are already on the second floor. That means you don't have to come through the lobby or pass the front desk. I pushed through the automatic doors and into the red and black polka-dotted carpeted hallway of the hotel and glanced around, looking for the elevator. Talus had told me that I'd find Schlimm on the top floor, the fifth.

From where I entered, the pool and hotel spa are just slightly farther down the hall, but almost as soon as you enter the hotel, you also find the north corridor elevators. I jabbed the button and waited. For a busy hotel, this section was pretty thinly travelled at the moment. The empty elevator arrived, and I stepped into the dark cabin and pressed the button for fifth floor.

The top floor is bright with striped yellow wallpaper, white roof, and red carpeting. The presidential suite is in the corner of the hotel, facing out towards the ocean — basically straight down the hallway off the elevator I was on. Unfortunately, the corridor to the room is a dead end, so there is only one door in and one door out of this area.

When I arrived at the door, I paused. It suddenly seemed very foolish to be showing up here. No one else knew where I was. My hand was poised in the air, ready to knock, and I started to lower it. I needed more leverage before I charged in on this Schlimm character.

I turned to leave, but the door pulled open suddenly. I almost yelped and took a quick step back. It was a big burly guy with a beard who looked to be standard-issue security in his dark suit. Very cliché, but still intimidating — especially with the telltale bulge under the arm of his jacket. He was packing heat. *Packing heat.* My nerves were so shot with this whole thing that I sounded like a detective in a bad novel (not a good one like you're reading). I wanted to reach up and pull those thoughts out, but I didn't want to look weird.

"What do you want?" he snapped at me.

"I..," I stammered. "I'm here to see Mr. Schlimm. I'm Dr. Waiter."

He held up a hand, too close to my face. "Wait here." Then he shut the door on me.

Now was my chance to leave. I looked back down the long hallway to the elevator.

The door pulled open again, and the security guy was back. "Follow me."

The massive casino suite came complete with a sitting room and grand piano. Who doesn't need a piano in their hotel room whilst on vacay?

An overweight balding man sat in the living room near the fake stone fireplace. Next to him was a younger man, probably in his late twenties, and shirtless with a smooth chest. The older man had his arm lazily lying across the younger man's shoulders.

Fat Guy barely even reacted to my intrusion on their

romantic little scene. "You must be the ever-annoying Dr. Waiter," he announced. "Did you bring my property back?" He had just the slightest little click of a German accent, and it seemed as though he worked hard not to reveal it.

The security guy hung back behind me, but hadn't left.

I stood, awkwardly, near the sofa. "And I can only assume you are the kind and forgiving Mr. Schlimm."

"Flattery?" he said, seeming surprised. "I suppose it was a psychological strategy worth a try." He pulled his arm back and shooed his friend away. The younger man dutifully hustled out of the living room and was gone. "You still haven't answered my question, and I see no evidence that improves my mood." His bulbous eyes looked me over from head to foot in a fashion that made my skin crawl.

"No," I said. "I didn't bring the magic ball if that's what you mean. The timing didn't seem right."

Schlimm fell dramatically back against the couch. "The timing! What is that supposed to mean?"

"I wondered whether the return of the object might coincide with my untimely demise. I wanted to avoid that."

He considered that and then laughed. "Oh, I see. You would return it and then I would kill you." He laughed again. "I think you watch too many spy movies."

"Did Dr. Zwicker watch too many spy movies?"

His mirth came to an abrupt end. "That is most unfortunate. What a troubled man he was. But then he would have to be troubled to bring that little mystery item all the way here knowing what a risk it posed."

"What risk did it pose?" I asked.

He sighed. "It will explode. Like all the other objects that I could not directly contain. It will explode and you will die and likely your loved ones will die as well."

"Now you're threatening me?"

"Oh no," he said in surprise. "That magic ball is threatening you. Every moment you keep it in your possession, it threatens you and whomever you are near."

I didn't answer, but the scepticism was clear on my face.

"Dr. Waiter," he continued, and leaned forward to put his meaty elbows on his even meatier knees. "I am a scientist and a businessman who works for, and with, the United States military. I am not a murderer, nor am I a madman. I am a reputable, hard-working patriot who only wants to minimize any harm to innocent civilians. Surely you must see that?"

I wanted to say, "No I don't see that, and don't call me Shirley!" But I settled for: "Your self-assessment may not be universally appreciated by others."

He put on an exaggerated expression of disappointment. "You wound me. You really do. What can I do to regain your trust?"

"Well," I said, and brought up my hands to tick off answers on my fingers. "First off, you could not send goons to my house to intimidate my wife. Second, not send goons to my private practice to beat up my patients. Third, not kill my patients in front of my private practice.

Shall I go on?"

He nodded. He looked thoroughly entertained. "Yes. Do go on."

I grabbed a fourth finger and hesitated. "Actually, I had only three."

His expression fell.

"Wait! I have one more. Don't give British assassins access to my private patient files and then send them into my office."

Now his expression of confusion looked genuine. "British assassins?"

"Um, Constant White. Does that ring a bell?"

He smiled. "It certainly does."

I folded my arms, feeling smug. I'm not sure why.

"So you got to meet Constant White?"

"Ah, yes," I said as though that part was pretty obvious.

"And she obviously didn't kill you?"

"Obviously," I agreed.

"That," Schlimm announced as though he were now addressing a crowd, "is very interesting."

I looked around quickly in case a crowd had actually filed in while I wasn't looking. Nope. Still just the security guy.

"Edward!" Schlimm called past me. "Dr. Waiter met Constant White and she didn't kill him."

Apparently, Edward was the security guy. He seemed to field lots of questions from his boss. "Sure," he said with little enthusiasm.

"Yes," Schlimm rolled the letters around in his

mouth. "It is interesting."

I wasn't quite sure if it was interesting because he wanted Constant White to kill me and she didn't or because I met Constant White in the first place.

"Is there anything else you'd ask of me?" Schlimm urged.

"Not right now."

"Good," he said, and clapped his hands. "Now provide me my toy and leave."

I checked behind me to make sure Edward wasn't about to hit me before I answered, "I told you. I don't have it. I didn't bring it, as I wasn't sure of how this conversation might go."

He stood. It was a struggle for him, but he did it. He waddled over to me and put a hand on my shoulder. He was close, way too close. I could smell his garlic breath and feel the sticky wetness of his hand on my shoulder.

"I am tired of this conversation and I'm tired of you," he said directly into my face, or as close as he could manage since I stood taller than him by almost a foot. "Tell me where to find my property, and I will have no further contact with you or anyone you know."

My hesitation set him off again. He pulled his hand away violently and spun from me. "Who is spreading such lies about me? I'm a patient and tolerant man, but I cannot fathom why you'd risk the safety of this entire city over some rumour you heard."

I opened my mouth to invent an answer when he turned back to me. "Who has told you not to trust me? Who?" he said.

I don't know why I felt compelled to provide any answer, but I did. Part of me actually thought Schlimm would be taken aback to know I had a hacker on my side. "Talus doesn't trust you."

He froze. "Talus doesn't trust me?"

I nodded.

"What do you mean *Talus doesn't trust me*?"

"Just what I said. Talus told me not to trust you, and it seems like he's a guy who knows quite a bit."

"You spoke to Talus?" he asked, his eyes wide.

Now I hesitated. Schlimm's interest in this particular topic seemed to consume him. "Yes."

"Today?" he asked.

I nodded.

He turned away from me and put a hand to his mouth. He might have been chewing at a fingernail as he contemplated this new turn of events. Then he turned back. "Give me Talus." His tone was wholly different now. No more playfulness.

"I can't," I said. "I don't even know where he is. He could be anywhere."

"Of course he could be anywhere," he snapped. "Give me access to Talus. I don't care how you got access. I just want you to transfer it to me."

"I didn't do anything. He just contacted me."

"That's bullshit," he screamed, and bits of spittle flew. "Talus won't talk to anyone, but that goddamn Zwicker. If you really have access to Talus, you'll goddamn give that access to me or so help me God I will destroy everything...." His voice trailed off. I think even he realized he'd gone Dr. Evil on me. "I need Talus," he said in a calmer voice. "Without Talus, everything is lost."

"Next time I talk to him, I'll see if he'll meet with you."

"Don't be a goddamn smartass," he bellowed. "You'll give me full access to Talus or you'll have made the last mistake of your worthless life."

I glanced back at Edward again before answering. "You always say the sweetest things."

"Waiter, don't do anything you'll regret. Don't do anything your wife will regret."

That was it. "Hey," I said. "Fat fuck. Don't threaten me, and don't you dare threaten my wife. I was going to hand over your little floaty ball, but now you can shove a donut down your piehole and kiss my ass."

Schlimm's face went bright red. I think I hit a nerve, which was hard to do considering how much blubber I had to get through first. "Edward," he managed through gritted teeth. "Grab this ant."

I held a hand up towards both of them. "If Edward touches me, then your chances of getting the ball or talking to Talus go straight to hell." I glanced back and forth between them, and it was just then I noticed Edward was pointing a gun at me. Awesome.

"You're not leaving here without giving me Talus. That simply cannot happen."

I frowned at him. "Are you fuckin' stupid? Does it look like I smuggled Talus in here in my pants? Where exactly do you think I'm hiding some neckbeard hacker?"

I held my arms up over my head as though he needed a better look.

"*Stop*," he squealed, "*Referring to Talus as a person!*"

"What's that now?" I said, but my words were partially hidden beneath the massive crash of what sounded like a door being kicked off all three hinges simultaneously.

Everyone turned, but the door wasn't visible from where we were. Edward, gun still drawn, bolted off in that direction.

The next few seconds flew past in a haze. Schlimm was yelling, and someone else in a distant room was screaming. There were crashing sounds and fighting sounds. Schlimm pushed me, way too hard, and ran in the direction of the screams.

Well, he didn't run. He waddled, but it was pretty quick.

I followed because it seemed to be my new thing. Whenever there was a dangerous situation where I might get hurt, I charged in that direction. When I rounded the corner to the front hall, I saw that the door was lying on the ground and the commotion had obviously moved into a side room that might have possibly been a bedroom. Everyone was in that room, yelling and struggling. I took that as my cue and was out the front door before they remembered I was even there.

I imagine I looked like quite the freak trying to fast-walk all the way back to my Jeep. I didn't want to flat out sprint and draw attention to myself, so I did one of those heel-toe Olympic race walks. There's just no way to do that and not start pumping your arms and swivelling your hips. When the whole-body race walk starts, you shortly realize how stupid that must look and you slow down. So my trip back to the Jeep was a combination of Olympic walk sprints followed by casual strolls that slowly built back to Olympic sprint walks. Beauty.

When I arrived back at the Jeep and discovered it had not blown up, I breathed a sigh of relief and leaned heavily on the driver's side window. I wasn't sure I'd learned anything. In fact, I might have been further into the murk than I was previously.

And what was with Schlimm's fascination with Talus? Holy shit. He'd forgotten all about the antigravity ball when I mentioned Talus.

Let me say that again: *He forgot all about the antigravity ball!* This was a ball that defied the laws of gravity, and that meant less to him than talking to a hacker.

Or was he a hacker?

Who, or what, was Talus?

There was one person who might know, and I figured I needed to know as much as possible if I wanted to stay alive. It seemed like Talus might be turning into my trump card.

I slipped into the driver's seat and started the Jeep. I was going back to Marie Zwicker's house and just hoping she hadn't left town yet.

Before I could back out, my phone rang. I was expecting Talus, but the call display said it was a private number. So many people had a private number that call display was getting pointless.

"Hello?"

"Blake?" It was Anne. "Are you okay?"

"Yeah."

"Where are you?" she asked.

"Why? What's going on?"

"General Belaire hit nothing but dead ends on Constant White. No one will talk about her or admit she is operating in Halifax."

I didn't say anything.

"We dug a bit more on Nathan Zwicker too. Is there anything you didn't tell us?"

"Like what?" I asked. I'm glad she couldn't see me because I was cringing at my lies.

"Don't play games with this situation, Blake. There are some big people involved here. Walter heard that the project director from Nevada might be in town. Some guy named Michael Schlimm. Have you heard of him?"

I pulled the phone from my mouth and hit my forehead with my palm before answering. "Not really."

She was quiet and then, "Not really? Blake, what are you doing? Come back to 12 Wing. We need to have another chat."

"I can't right now."

"Where are you?"

"Listen, I don't want you involved. I'm handling this for now. If it gets any more out of control, I'll come running back to base."

"You're handling what?"

"I got something from Zwicker, and I need to figure out a way to return it without anyone else getting hurt."

"Jesus, Blake! What are you doing?"

"It's all good."

"Listen," she said, her voice calmer. "Walter told me that the Nevada base commander is landing in Halifax shortly. Let's just get everybody in a room and sort this out."

"Sounds good," I said. "Talk later." And hung up. Time to see Marie Zwicker.

CHAPTER 16

Marie Zwicker had not fled town. Not yet. I knocked on the door, and through the decorative glass I could see a blurry figure make its way over.

She opened the door and her expression shifted. She looked very disappointed. "Oh," she said.

"I need to ask you one other thing," I said quickly, expecting the door to be slammed in my face.

She squinted up at me. "What the hell happened to your face? Looks like you lost a fight."

I nodded. I'd forgotten that my nose still hurt and figured my eyes were starting to look a little blackened. I reached up and touched my nose reflexively. "I'll be okay. Can I ask you a question?"

She stepped out and pushed me backwards as she did until we were both standing on the porch again. She glanced up and down the street before she answered. "Were you followed here?"

I shrugged. "I don't think so."

She turned back to me with the expression of a disappointed parent. "How are you still alive?"

"Talus is helping me," I said, and watched for her reaction.

She froze, hands on her hips and her eyes narrowed. "Talus?"

"Ring a bell?" I asked.

"Is this a test?" She looked unimpressed.

"I just need to know what Talus is."

"How do you even know about Talus?" Her voice was low.

"I think your husband arranged it. Talus has been texting me."

"On your phone? Directly?" Now she was surprised. I barely said yes before she shushed me with a hand in my face. "Not here," she said. "Where's your car?"

I nodded over my shoulder to the street.

"Let's go," she said.

"What about your daughter?"

"She's with her grandparents in Rhode Island. I wasn't keeping her here with everything that's going on." She was already off the porch and headed towards the street.

I had to jog to catch up. "Where are we going?"

"Anywhere."

Anywhere didn't turn out to be *anywhere.* We drove towards the downtown core and every potential stop was a "No, keep going."

"What about this Tim's?" I said, slowing near the Tim Hortons coffee shop.

"Keep going."

We drove all the way down Spring Garden Road, and apparently none of the dozens of restaurants, fast-food places, or coffee shops was exactly right.

We ended up parking at the curb all the way down near the harbour front and walking a block down Bedford Row to the Olde Triangle, a rustic Irish pub.

Finally we were seated in a booth in the half-full Friday afternoon crowd of the restaurant.

We both ordered coffees before I leaned on the table and addressed her. "So? What's going on?"

"Talus is supposed to be dead," she said, and watched my face for a reaction.

I shrugged.

"Talus is more important than anything else. It was the first thing they asked me about, but I thought he took Talus with him."

"Who took him?"

"My husband. Talus was his thing. He never let anyone have access. Ever."

"So Talus isn't a person?"

She slumped back in her seat. "How aren't you dead? Of course Talus isn't a person. Do you know a person who has unlimited access to virtually any information stored digitally around the world and virtually instantaneous processing power?"

"I thought Talus was some hacker working with Nathan."

She frowned at me. I think she was deciding how far she had to dumb down her explanations so I could understand. It made me feel just great.

"I'm going to try to speak slowly," she started.

What a bitch.

"Do you remember what my husband's area of expertise was?"

"Didn't he work on those computer boxes attached to the interwebs?" I said in my best Forrest Gump voice.

She ignored me. "He worked in quantum computing and AI — that's artificial intelligence. Have you ever heard of that? Intelligence?"

Oh, now she was being funny. I had a good retort loaded up, but didn't get to pull the trigger because our coffees arrived.

"Anyway," she continued, "long story short. He did develop AI. He called it Talus. It was some kind of reference to a poem from the late sixteenth century about a metal man who helped dispense justice." She took a sip of coffee. She drank it black. Surprise! "Nathan was especially protective of Talus. No one was ever allowed direct contact with it."

"So why did people believe it even existed?"

"Nathan actually told people it didn't exist. I knew it did, but it was like one of the worst-kept conspiracy secrets running in computer circles. Everyone knew he had Talus."

"Why was he so paranoid?" I asked. I added milk to my coffee because I'm not an animal.

"So this is what Talus is...." She took another sip to prepare herself for the lecture. "It started as quantum code. Normally computer code operates in binary — that is off and on. That makes most programming cumbersome and lengthy. Even the most basic program needs to be really long to control all the variables when you can only communicate in yes and no, on and off, bits of data."

I nodded. I knew what binary meant.

She smiled, sarcastically approving my acknowledgement. "Well, Nathan pioneered quantum computing. By using quantum states as his foundation, he didn't have to work in binary. He had access to infinite quantum states in his computer language. He told me once that he could program four thousand lines of traditional code in one single line. That's the magnitude of difference we're talking about." She took another sip. "He used it to develop a program, Talus, that could think and act, but was subservient to him."

"Subservient?"

"It means that it was forced to answer only to Nathan."

"I know what subservient means," I snapped back. "How do you make a computer program subservient?"

"All computer programs are subservient to begin with. They rely on the programmer to write them, fix them, and ultimately run them. They require a user to turn a device on. They require a user to input variables. They don't run without a master. And Nathan built safeguards into Talus like that. Talus would only self-identify to Nathan. Talus would only respond to, and act on, requests from Nathan. And so on."

"Okay?" I said. I tried to say it quickly enough that she wouldn't pick up on my confusion.

"I know this must be confusing to you," she said. Bitch. "But there're two things you need to understand about Talus. First, Talus physically exists somewhere. You can't take a normal computer and use it for quantum computing. It requires a substantially different architecture. Something Nathan developed himself and hid."

"He hid it? He hid the quantum computer?"

"Yes. Whatever the system is, no one knows where it is, and believe me people have looked. If they could find it and reverse engineer it, then it wouldn't matter that Talus is keyed to only work for Nathan. Everyone could have his or her own version of Talus. Nathan could never be convinced that the world was ready for that and would never give up the physical location."

"And the second thing?" I prompted.

"Talus exists everywhere."

Now she was just trying to be obfuscatory. "You're deliberately trying to be obfuscatory," I said proudly. I had recently Googled that word and been waiting to use it.

The word didn't faze her. "Part of Talus's programming was to leave bits of itself wherever it visited. Every computer system that is used to gather information is also made a part of its hive mind. That's how Nathan described it. It left a piece of code in each system it touched to make easier, more direct access later. This included secure systems — especially any that Nathan might have worked on."

"Is that legal?"

She shrugged. "At a certain level, that question doesn't get asked anymore. I'm not sure it applies."

"So Talus can —" I started, but she didn't let me finish.

"Talus can do anything. Has access to virtually any information. Can solve most problems faster than they can be asked."

"Whoa."

"And no one is more keenly aware of that and more eager to get his hands on Talus than Nathan's boss down in Nevada."

"Mr. Schlimm," I said almost absentmindedly.

She reached across the table and put a hand over mine for emphasis. "That's right. You haven't been talking to him, have you?"

"Uh…" I started. Why did everyone make me feel like I was making the wrong decisions?

"Oh my God," she said, and retreated against her seat. "Tell me you didn't mention Talus."

"I didn't mention Talus," I said haltingly.

She put her fingers to her forehead and thought for a moment. "I need to go," she said, and slid towards the end of the bench.

"Wait!" I called.

She turned back to me. "Schlimm would do anything to get Talus. Anything." She stared into my face, her eyes darting back and forth to individually focus on each of mine. "Nathan used Talus to get their little Nevada project working properly, then he sabotaged the whole thing before he left. Schlimm can't do anything without Talus."

"What is the project in Nevada? Is it the antigravity thing?"

She shook her head. "I don't think so. Nathan never told me."

"Then what?"

She slid out and stood by the table. "Ask Talus."

Then she started for the door.

"Hey," I called after her. "I was your ride here."

She didn't turn around, but just held up a hand to silence me and pushed out through the exit.

I watched her go and then I pulled out my phone. Apparently, I now was the only one with access to the most powerful, maybe only, artificial intelligence in the world.

Me. Dr. Waiter. The guy that Marie Zwicker thought was a moron and more than a few people seemed to want to kill.

I'm a lucky guy.

I scrolled through my apps to find the text program that Talus had used to talk to me. Nothing looked familiar. When we texted before, it wasn't my normal text app. It was a unique window that had popped up on my phone and disappeared when we finished. Although last time we texted I had deliberately swiped the dialog box off my phone to end the call. Shit.

Now I didn't know how to start a conversation with the Talus thing. Did I have to wait for it to contact me? That wasn't convenient.

Shit and hell.

I held the phone up to my mouth. "Okay Google," I said, and there was a tone indicating my phone was listening. "Start Talus." It was worth a shot.

A list of websites appeared as a result of an Internet search. Not what I wanted. No surprise.

Then the familiar tone. The Talus tone! A dialog box

appeared. *It is not advisable to search Talus at this time. Your account is synced to this phone and could be compromised as a result.*

R *u monitoring my phone?*

Yes.

So how do I start u?

To initiate communication you can simply speak.

Speak? To who? I couldn't figure out what it meant. I typed, *What???*

I am currently monitoring active devices in your vicinity, including your phone.

"So I can just talk out loud and this thing will hear me?" I said as I stared at the phone.

Talus texted back, *Yes and please do not refer to me as a thing.*

"Were you always listening to me?"

Yes.

"Then why was I doing all that typing before? Why didn't you tell me?"

You did not inquire about my capabilities in regard to vocal registration.

"Son of a bitch," I muttered. "Can you talk too?"

"Of course," came a male voice through the phone. I don't know why I had assumed it should sound like a robot and be all mechanical-sounding. It wasn't. It spoke perfectly normally. Just an average adult male voice. No accent. Maybe a little formal-sounding. I brought the phone up to my ear.

"Hello," I said.

"Hello, Dr. Waiter."

"Shit on a stick, again," I said.

"I assume that is some local expression of surprise."

"Something like that," I said. I couldn't believe I was talking to an AI. Suddenly I was on *Star Trek*. I snapped out of it quickly and said, "I need to learn about Project Dead Kitty."

"I have complete files."

The waitress came over to check on me, and I waved her away. "Go!" I said into the phone. "Tell me everything about it."

"Perhaps now is not the most opportune time for our discussion," Talus said.

"Why?"

"Recent radio transmissions indicate that a nine-one-one call was made to local law enforcement by the casino hotel manager, and you have been identified as a person of interest in an assault and property damage complaint."

"You're kidding me."

"And the police will be entering the current establishment in four...three...."

I let the phone fall away from my head and turned to the door to see two Halifax Regional Police officers enter.

CHAPTER 17

So I got arrested. And handcuffed. All in front of the rest of the patrons of the Olde Triangle. I bet it made for great storytelling later that night. I didn't resist, and the officers were actually quite nice about it.

The Halifax Regional Police Headquarters is located at the end of Gottingen Street just where it meets up with the bottom of Citadel Hill. I'd actually been there a few times on official police business, consulting on open cases or running little seminars on mental health and policing type topics. Years ago I was even one of the main mental health consultants on hostage negotiation before someone else took that over. I'd never come in through the backdoor with my hands cuffed. That was not so fun.

There's a booking station and holding cells in the basement there. Not surprisingly, they booked me and then put me in a cell and told me a detective would be right with me. They also took my phone. That really sucked because I figured Talus would have been a real help right about now.

It wasn't long before I left the holding cell with a Detective Harrison Lindsay. He was a middle-aged guy in a suit in pretty good shape. Balding, but clean cut and polite. I didn't remember meeting him before, but he said he'd been in a couple of the seminars I gave and enjoyed them. He was carrying a laptop and a pad of paper.

After we were seated in an interview room, he did the customary preamble about lawyers and that I don't have to say anything. He reminded me that the room was being videotaped and audio-recorded. I just kept nodding.

"Okay," he finally said. "This should be short and sweet. Were you at the Marriott casino hotel today?"

"Yep."

"Did you have an altercation with a guest there?"

"Nope."

He leaned across the table that separated us. "Are we going to have a problem?"

I leaned over too, so now we were uncomfortably close. "What kind of problem?"

He didn't want to be the first to back out of this position, so he stuck. "The kind of problem where I just get nonsense answers or little short bullshit answers."

I could smell his coffee breath when he spoke. He had nice white teeth, though. "Depends on the questions you ask."

He tried to stare me down, but honestly it felt a bit romantic with how close we were sitting. Finally he caved and sat back. Ding, ding, ding. Point goes to Dr. Blake Waiter, who currently leads in the battle of the interview — one nothing.

"Do you know a...?" He looked down at a pad of paper. "Michael Schlimm?"

"Is he a great big fat guy? Bit of a German accent?

Kind of a douche?"

"Yeah, actually. He is," said Detective Lindsay.

That surprised me, and I almost laughed out loud. "I've met him."

"Was that at the same time you attacked him and put his bodyguard in the hospital with a dislocated shoulder?"

This was news. "No. When I left, nobody was hurt."

"Nobody, but you."

I frowned a look of confusion.

"Looked in a mirror recently? Looks like you've taken a few punches to the face. Maybe you were in a fight with someone. Maybe Mr. Schlimm and his bodyguard?"

"Oh this?" I said, and pointed at my face. "Different altercation."

"Anything you need to report to the police? I know where we can find a cop."

"Nah."

"What's your issue with Mr. Schlimm?"

I shrugged. "What did he say?"

"To be honest, he wasn't very cooperative. It was the hotel manager who called. I think they were concerned because the door of their most expensive suite was ripped off the hinges."

"That makes sense," I said, and nodded. "And you think I ripped the door off the hinges?" I gave him a sceptical look. "I'm flattered." I took a hand and patted my left bicep.

"We know you had an accomplice. Who was he?"

"An accomplice? Like I'm a crime lord?"

He just stared at me. Kind of smug.

"Listen, Harrison," I started. "You know me. I'm a forensic psychologist. I work with you guys. I work with the military. I'm not a criminal. I didn't break into a suite, to rough somebody up. You know that doesn't make any sense."

"I tend to agree with you, but we have a problem with that theory."

"Which is?"

"We have you on video entering the Marriott. We have you walking down the hall and entering the suite and we have video of some guy following a few minutes behind and kicking the door in."

"See!" I blurted. "It wasn't me that broke down the door."

"And then the hall cam shows you running out of the suite and down the hall. Shortly after that, we have the giant coming out of the same suite."

"The giant?"

"A great big guy. Must be six foot six. Ring a bell?"

Chuck. He followed me to the hotel. I shrugged.

"The hotel manager called us because other guests reported the commotion and then his staff found the mini war zone in the room. That Schlimm guy said he wasn't going to press charges, but the hotel manager was pretty peeved."

"So what are you charging me with?"

"We have you running from the scene of an assault."

"That's it? That's your evidence. A video clip?"

"Pretty compelling stuff," he said and patted his laptop.

"Is the clip on there?" I asked as innocently as I could.

"It's safe."

"Show me."

"You don't need to see it."

"Um, you're arresting me because of that clip. I'd like to see. Maybe it's not me."

He flipped the laptop open and let it boot up, and while it did so, he retrieved a small USB flash drive from his jacket.

"The police station has Wi-Fi doesn't it?" I asked.

He glared at me. "You wanna update your Facebook page?"

"Just checking."

The laptop was booted, and he pushed the USB into an empty spot and then spun the computer sideways so we could both see the screen.

He opened a folder with today's date on it. It contained a few video files. "Ready?" he asked. He seemed like he was enjoying this.

"I'd be more ready," I said as clearly as I could without yelling, "for Talus to delete all these video files."

"What?" Detective Lindsay said, confused. "Who's Talus?"

"I didn't say anything."

"What's wrong with you?" he asked, and shook his head in disdain.

I kept watching the screen while he was staring at me. The video files deleted one by one, and now the folder was empty.

He turned back to the laptop and moved his finger on the touchpad and froze. "What the…?" He closed the current folder and reopened the USB again. There was a folder with today's date, but it was still empty. "Son of a bitch," he said, and shot me a dirty look. "Did you —" he started, but didn't finish because the question wasn't going to make any sense. I hadn't touched his laptop. He slammed the computer shut and picked it up as he stood. "Stay here," he barked, and left.

Thank you, Talus.

I waited a good thirty minutes before Detective Lindsay came back. He didn't look happy. "You can go."

"What's going on?" I asked, innocent as a Catholic schoolboy.

"Doesn't matter. There aren't any charges. You're free."

I plopped my hands down on the table to push myself up. "Great. Sorry about any inconvenience."

"If I find out that you somehow hacked the police system to delete those video files, we'll be talking again."

I felt like gloating a bit more, but had probably done enough damage with my relationship to the police force. I collected my personals from the booking desk downstairs and walked out of there. Once I was out, I realized that I was also in for a walk. My Jeep was parked down near the Olde Triangle. Luckily, it was only about six or seven blocks away, so I started walking.

I wasn't exactly sure what my next step would be. I'd just learned that it was probably Chuck that had smashed in on Schlimm's hotel room, and I had no idea why that would have happened. It didn't seem like a rescue mission, although it probably had saved me. I supposed I had better track him down, make sure he was okay, and then figure out what he was doing there and why he put the security guy in the hospital. If anything, I bet my situation with Schlimm had gotten worse now.

But I also had Talus. I needed to find a place to sit and get some info on Dead Kitty and how all of this fit together. Marie Zwicker seemed to think Talus would have the answers I needed. So I decided I'd go get my Jeep and make sure the magic ball was still in the back seat and then find a quiet place to have an intimate little chat with my phone.

Just as I started walking, a car pulled in next to me on the street and the passenger window lowered. I stopped and bent to look in.

"Hey, stranger. How much do you charge for a party?" It was Anne.

"What are you doing?" I asked.

"Get in."

I got in.

CHAPTER 18

Once I was in Anne's car she just stared at me.

"What happened to your face?"

I waved off her question. "How'd you find me?"

She looked me up and down for another second before she answered. "We were looking for you. Walter is back at 12 Wing with a General Thaddeus Montgomery. He's the base commander from Nevada. He's worried about this Schlimm guy. He said there've been lots of questions about how he's running their research project."

"So he's the real Schlimm Shady," I said, and could not suppress a smirk.

"What?" She glanced over at me. "You're still making jokes? That's great."

I noticed that she'd swung the car around and was heading back towards the bridge. She was trying to take me back to SSCHVA headquarters. "Hey, I need to get my Jeep. We need to go back towards Sackville Street."

"It's more important that we get together with this Nevada general. They're waiting for us."

"Seriously," I said. "I need my car. There's something pretty important in there."

She sighed, but did flick on her signal to change lanes. "Do you know where Schlimm is? General Montgomery said they've lost touch with him over the last few hours."

"Nope."

"Did you see Schlimm and give him whatever it was you were talking about?"

I didn't get to answer because the world exploded. At first I thought the magic ball must have blown up and we had the Halifax Explosion part two, but that wasn't it. Anne was driving through a green light at an intersection and someone T-boned us. They hit us on the driver's side and pushed our car sideways up onto the curb. The impact of striking the curb burst one of the tires and shattered both the driver's window and the windshield. If it hadn't been for the frontal and side-impact airbags deploying. I would have probably cracked my head open. Even after the car settled back to the ground, I felt like I was still being tossed around like a rag doll.

It took me a second to regain my senses. I shook my head and tried to figure out my surroundings. Anne was unconscious. I put a hand on her arm. "Anne?" She didn't answer. Through her shattered window, I could see someone in the other vehicle — some kind of truck. He didn't look friendly. As he slid out and tentatively stood next to the truck, it looked suspiciously like Fridge Guy with his arm in a cast.

"Anne?" I called again, a little more frantic. I didn't have Chuck with me and wasn't interested in a rematch with these two guys. "Anne?" She groaned, but wasn't going to be jumping out of the car with me anytime soon. If I wanted any chance, I needed to move.

So I moved. I clicked out of my seat belt and rolled out of my door onto the sidewalk. There was just enough room to crouch between a building and the car. I heard the truck door open and knew Salami Breath was now on the move too. I looked back into the car. "Sorry, Anne."

We were on Hollis Street just past the Nova Scotia Government Province House. The car had been pushed up against a pillar right near the entrance to the Joseph Howe Building. I stayed crouched low and looked around. Behind me was the entrance to the office tower; otherwise I had to take my chances running down a sidewalk. I did a little crabwalk, staying low, up the six or seven stone steps to the automatic doors and slipped into the building. I heard Fridge Guy yell at me, but I wasn't stopping.

Once inside I could stand, and I hustled into the lobby where there was an elevator and a directory for the building. I briefly put a hand on the wall to steady myself. I was still dizzy from the accident. The directory meant nothing to me, but one word stood out. Rudy's Catering was a little cafe up one floor. It stood out to me because it reminded me that there was an exit out to Granville Street by Rudy's. I just had to get up there, and I could escape.

Fridge Guy came through the front doors, his eyes wild, looking for me. I didn't wait, but ran down the marble hall to the back where there was a staircase. I grabbed the door, flung it open, and jumped inside, slamming the door behind. It had one of those long bars on the inside as the door handle, and I glanced around frantically. Of all things, there was a snow shovel and a bag of road salt. I went to grab the shovel and then changed my mind and grabbed the salt. Meanwhile, I grabbed the push bar on the door and used my weight to hold it. It wasn't a moment too soon, either, because Fridge Guy slammed up against the door from the other side and started pawing at the handle. I could see him through a small rectangular window.

He jiggled his side only for a moment and then stuck his face to the window. "Open the door," he growled.

"Oh, okay," I called back. "There you go. Come on in." The door jiggled as he tried to open it, but I hadn't shifted my weight from the push bar. I laughed. "Seriously? Did you think I was actually just going to let you open the door?"

He kicked the door hard. "Just open it, you stupid fuck. No one is going to play games with you anymore!"

"How's your arm?" I called.

"Fuck you!" he screamed back, and cracked his cast against the windowpane. I was a bit surprised he didn't break it.

I kept the bar back with one hand and lifted the salt bag up and started wedging it behind with the other. Thank God it was a full, sealed bag of salt.

"Okay," I said. "Sorry. I'll open the door, but you have to promise not to try to hurt me."

He was silent for a moment. Probably collecting his patience. "Sure. I won't hurt you. Now open the door."

"There," I called. "It's open."

He wiggled from his end again and couldn't move it.

"Fuck you!" he called out.

"You are so stupid," I said as I finished wedging the salt in place. It wouldn't hold long. "Where's your ugly friend with the bad breath? Did they get his finger re-attached?"

He stuck his face in the window and sneered at me. "We had different jobs."

"Listen, I've got to go down to the parking garage. Why don't you meet me down there and tell me all about the different jobs you two guys do on each other?"

His response was to pound his cast on the little window again, and I took this as my cue to bolt.

I ran up a flight of stairs and out onto the second-floor lobby. Rudy's was just down at the end of the hall and next to it an exit. I walk-jogged down and out of the building and out onto Granville.

I turned left and headed down the sidewalk. I was only two blocks up from my Jeep. I started to do my Olympic calibre race walk to avoid attracting attention in case Fridge Guy got through the stairwell door and followed me this far.

I kept walking. I didn't want to turn around and give myself away, so I listened for a commotion behind. I just needed to get to the end of this block and turn down Sackville Street and I'd be out of Fridge Guy's line of sight behind the next office tower. I forced myself to keep moving even though my body and head ached.

When I finally reached my Jeep, I just wanted to hug it. I jumped in, glanced in the back seat to make sure the coffee can was still there, and sped off. I felt like shit leaving Anne behind, but I'd feel even worse dead, and I was pretty sure that was the only viable option until I got a little more of a handle on my situation.

Shortly I was on the Macdonald Bridge heading back into Dartmouth. This was one of two bridges that spanned the Halifax Harbour and connected Dartmouth to Halifax. Recently it had become a gamble to take the Macdonald Bridge because it was in the process of being retrofitted with a newer, larger deck. You never knew if you were going to drive smack into construction delays. I got lucky and there weren't any delays. Once over the bridge, I would have a few choices of where to go next. I could go back to my private office, or to 12 Wing, or just head home. It was too soon to go to 12 Wing and both the other options were compromised. Just last night the goons had been sitting in my living room with my wife.

Shit. Lisa.

I pushed a button on my steering wheel to activate hands-free. "Phone Lisa." She should still be at work at the physio clinic. She didn't always have her phone on when she was working, but it was worth a try. It rang and no answer — went to voice mail. I hung up and used hands-free again to dial "Lisa Work." One ring. Two rings. Three rings. Voice mail. That didn't make any sense. Why wasn't anyone answering the phone at the front desk?

Shit. Now I had a fourth destination. My wife's physio clinic in Bedford. Something was wrong. I knew it. I got across the bridge and went up Victoria Road. That would take me all the way out to Bedford over Magazine Hill.

As I drove, the Bluetooth call I'd just made to Lisa reminded me of something else. "Talus?" I asked tentatively. I didn't trust that I could just speak and it would answer. It was unnerving to think it was always monitoring me.

The answer came through the Jeep's speakers immediately. "Yes."

"Hello. Good. Was it you that deleted the hotel video files at the police station?"

"Yes. All copies the hotel and police had have been removed. I reserved a copy for your use if you need. It is in a secure location."

I hadn't even thought about keeping a copy for myself. "Good." I didn't know what this thing's capabilities were, but I thought I'd try. "Do you know where my wife is? Um, Lisa?"

"Her last known cell phone ping was from her place of work — Better You Physiotherapy Clinic in Bedford."

"Is she still there?"

"I'm unable to determine. Shall I dial her cellular number again?"

"Never mind. I'm driving there now."

"On your current route, you should arrive in twelve minutes."

"Okay. Thanks."

Magazine Hill is where Windmill Road turns into

Trunk 7 right on a little hill next to another military installation. From here you can veer into Bedford or keep going and end up in Lower Sackville. I took the Bedford Bypass and headed into Bedford. Lisa's physio clinic was located in a little strip mall next to the Sobey's plaza right off the Bedford Highway. She chose this location because of DeWolf Park right behind the clinic, where she could take clients out on the walking paths. Now I was wishing she still worked in Dartmouth because it'd take a lot less time to get there.

I could feel myself start to panic, and my speed was increasing. I felt pretty helpless. I needed to just calm down and get there in one piece.

I drove down a residential road off the Bedford Bypass alongside the Sunnyside Mall. From here I could get back on the Bedford Highway. I decided to get some more information from Talus as a way to distract my building panic.

"Talus, are you able to tell me anything about Project Dead Kitty?"

"Yes."

I waited, but he wasn't saying anything else. "Go ahead, then. Tell me everything you can about this Dead Kitty project." I didn't know if I had the patience to deal with this Talus thing.

"The project is named after Austrian-born Erwin Schrödinger, a physicist best known for his thought experiment Schrödinger's cat. He was the first to suggest, in 1952, a multiverse. Project Dead Kitty is a direct reference to one possible outcome of Schrödinger's thought experiment: a dead cat in the box."

I kept breathing nice and slow and asked, "So what is Project Dead Kitty? Is it an antigravity project?"

"The truth of the project has been concealed from the majority of individuals involved. The original goal was teleportation. There have been numerous references to theorized teleportation possibilities within the field of quantum physics primarily in reference to something called quantum entanglement."

Talus stopped talking, and I waited a couple of beats before I asked, "Why'd you stop?"

"Dr. Waiter, you are not a physicist. Do you require me to explain any of these terms?"

"Come on!" I screamed, a little too loud, but I couldn't help it. "Just tell me about that goddamn project." The combination of driving, my wife being in danger, and a smartass computer was not doing me any good.

Suddenly Talus' voice was loud and tinged with a surprising urgency. "Please pull over immediately, Dr. Waiter. I will contact local emergency services for medical assistance."

I looked around frantically for the first exit off the busy Bedford Highway. "Why?" I yelled. "What's wrong?"

"The tone of your voice suggested you were experiencing a neurological event. Possibly a stroke," it said, resuming its normal voice.

"Fuck!" I said, and relaxed behind the steering wheel again. "Are you kidding?"

Silence from Talus.

"You there?"

"I was joking," Talus said.

"What? You can't joke. You're a robot."

"I am not a robot." Now it sounded offended.

"Jesus. Sorry. What are you then?"

"I am Talus."

I was only a few minutes away from the clinic. "Let's get back to Project Dead Kitty. I don't have much time. What were you saying about them experimenting with teleportation?"

"Quantum teleportation. In simple terms" — Talus paused, waiting to see if this got a reaction from me before it continued — "two bits of information are entangled at a quantum level, but not located physically in the same spot. If something is done to one bit of information, it has an effect on its quantum partner such that if you measure the partner, you capture information about what happened to the first particle. In other words, I can teleport information from point A to point B because the two particles, or quantum bits, are entangled. These quantum bits are frequently referred to as qubits."

"I played that video game on my Intellivision in the the eighties. Great game."

"The principle of exchanging information between qubits, not Q*berts, continued to expand with the goal of true teleportation."

"Like *Star Trek*? Actually beaming people and things around the world?"

"Correct, but they never succeeded. Instead they accidentally proved the existence of the multiverse, and this became Project Dead Kitty."

"They proved the existence of what?" I said as I neared the turn into the parking lot of the Sobey's plaza.

"Physicists believe there is no theoretical incompatibility with multiple universes existing and possibly even overlapping. Concepts of time and space have changed radically in the last few decades to the point that most believe those concepts are not constants and are merely perceived as such because human minds have evolved to see the world in such terms. Humans, in fact, have very little capacity to appreciate a great many theoretical concepts such as deep time, infinite space, and quantum concepts such as superpositioning."

"So what did Dead Kitty prove the existence of?"

"The multiverse."

"They accidentally proved that there is more than one universe?" I said sceptically.

"Yes."

"How many? Where are they?"

"You must appreciate that we are dealing with the idea of infinity. Whenever we enter *infinity* into an equation, everything else disappears. All logic and every notion of how things *ought* to operate necessarily dissolve. For example, what is one plus infinity?"

"Infinity," I said.

"And one million times infinity? Does that result in a sum greater than one plus infinity?"

"No, it's still infinity."

"The same is true at the level of our understanding of universes. If we accept infinite possibilities for space and time, which appears to be unavoidable in every astronomical equation, then the multiverse is not only possible, but infinitely probable."

"And why haven't I heard that there are multiple universes before? Seems like a pretty big news story."

"A brief search of the Internet shows multiple references to this theory. In particular, a recent special edition of *National Geographic* entitled *Are We Alone? And Other Mysteries of Space* had an entire chapter devoted to the multiverse."

"And this Project Dead Kitty somehow proved that the multiverse exists?"

"That is what they believe. In particular, that is what Mr. Michael Schlimm is convinced of."

I had about a hundred more questions, but I'd arrived at Lisa's clinic. I pulled into a parking space near the entrance to the physio clinic and was barely listening to Talus anymore. A few staff were gathered outside of the clinic talking. They looked upset.

"Hold on to that thought. I have more questions about Dead Kitty," I told Talus, and jumped out of the Jeep.

"Hey," I called to the ladies. "What's going on?"

One of the front desk staff, Christina, looked at me and made a little gasping noise. "Oh, Dr. Waiter. We were just wondering about calling you or calling the police." Christina was in her mid-thirties and was known for being way too happy for no reason. She was the perfect person to answer the clinic phones and greet customers. It was weird seeing her upset like this.

"Where's Lisa?" I asked. "What's going on?"

Tara was one of the other physiotherapists. Crazy short and, just like my wife, owned only yoga pants and was wearing the blue clinic polo. I always felt like leaning over and putting my hands on my knees when I talked to her, but that would get me a slap at home later. "Some guy came in and talked like he knew Lisa and you. He pulled Lisa aside even though she was actually with a client."

"Then they left together," Christina jumped in. "I asked her if everything was okay, but she sort of shrugged me off."

"She didn't look like she wanted to go," Jamie added. She was the other physiotherapist standing out with the group. "He was holding onto her elbow — kind of walking her out."

"And she didn't take her stuff. She just left with him," Tara said.

"And left her client in the treatment room. Totally not like Lisa," Jamie said.

They were all talking at once. It was hard to follow.

"When? When did she leave?" I asked.

"Like ten minutes ago. Not even," said Christina.

"Who was that guy?" Tara asked. "Should we have said something? Should we have stopped them? Lisa didn't say anything."

Christina was staring at my face. She could read my concerned expression. "Should we call the police? Damn it. We should have called the police, shouldn't we?" She turned from me to Tara. "I told you. I knew it."

"What did the guy look like?" I asked, interrupting their hysteria party.

Little Tara answered. Her voice was sort of high and squeaky, which perfectly matched her stature. "He was big. Like your size."

"And he was wearing a suit," Lisa blurted.

"And his right hand was bandaged," Christina finished for them. "A big mound of bandages all around his hand." She moved one of her hands around and around the other to illustrate just in case I didn't understand how someone's hand could end up bandaged.

I sighed. That's why Fridge Guy was on his own earlier. Salami Breath was here.

"Do you know him?" Tara said, staring up at me. "Should we call the police?"

I shook my head. "I know him. I'll take care of it."

Lisa held out a pink Lug gym bag that I hadn't noticed her holding before. "This is Lisa's bag. Her iPhone's in here. It was ringing before."

I took it, said thanks, and headed back to the Jeep. The girls stood in a cluster (or was it a gaggle, or flock?) and watched me leave.

CHAPTER 19

I started the Jeep and drove out of the parking lot. I couldn't sit there with the physio clinic ladies just staring at me. I needed to be gone. I got back on the Bedford Highway and headed south, back towards downtown Halifax. I didn't have a plan, but was roughly settled on going back towards the casino hotel.

"Talus?" I asked to the air.

"Yes." It was still talking to me through Bluetooth and the Jeep speakers.

"Schlimm has my wife."

"Yes."

"I want to talk to him. What can you do?"

"He has no phone numbers accessible through the Internet or other databases. He has been quite careful about his electronic fingerprint."

"Figures. What about the goons?"

"Are these the men you refer to as Fridge Guy and Salami Breath?"

"Right. Get me Salami Breath's cell," I said.

"Accessing the Nova Scotia Health Authority database, I find an entry for earlier today in the emergency department of the Dartmouth General Hospital. An individual with a severed finger. His name is Jeremy Miller, age thirty-five. I have a cellular number from his hospital registration."

"Can you track it?"

"The phone is either off or has no charge left. Calls placed to that number go immediately to voice mail."

"Shit," I said. "What about Fridge Guy?"

"Accessing health records finds that another male came into the emergency room at approximately the same time as Jeremy Miller. He was treated for a spiral fracture to his right arm. Mr. Martin Baxter, age thirty-three. His cellular number is currently active."

"Call it."

Ringing came through my speakers within seconds and was answered just as quickly.

"Hello."

"Hey, shit head," I said. The Bedford highway runs along next to the Bedford Basin. I couldn't keep driving as I talked to this guy, so I looked for my first exit, which was at the Clearwater Seafood offices overlooking the harbour. I pulled off pretty quick and skidded into a stall near the blue and white front of the store. "Let me talk to your asshole boss," I said.

He didn't seem overly surprised to hear from me. "Is this Dr. Waiter? Don't you wish you'd just come along with me when you had the chance? Who's the smart guy now?"

"You're the smart guy. Now let me talk to Schlimm."

"Is something bothering you? Are you missing someone?"

"Don't even think about hurting her, *Martin*." I let his real name ooze out of my mouth.

"Oooh," he said sarcastically. "He knows my name.

I'm so scared. Let's see if your girl is scared too."

I was surprised they already had my wife with them. "Is she okay? Put my wife on the phone."

"Your wife?" he said in genuine surprise. "I was talking about the little whore who was driving you around. I think she said her name is Anne."

"Anne?"

The cell rustled as it was moved, and Anne's voice came on. "Blake? What's...?"

Fridge Guy obviously pulled the phone away. "That's enough for now, cutie. Now, Dr. Waiter, what were you saying about your wife?"

"You bastards. If you hurt either one of them."

"I know. I know. You'll hunt us down if it's the last thing you do. You'll make us pay. Blah, blah, blah."

"You forgot one — I was going to say you don't know who you're messing with," I added.

"Right. Nice one."

"Now put your boss on the phone. I'm tired of wasting my time talking to the help."

"You're in luck. Here you go," Fridge Guy said, and there were sounds of the phone passing again.

"Dr. Waiter, how nice of you to call." It was the clipped, slightly German-tinged voice of Mr. Schlimm.

"What do you want from me, asshole?"

"Oh my. Such language from a professional. Do you heal the psychiatrically disabled with that mouth?"

"You are going to let Anne and my wife go, unharmed. I'll expect that to happen immediately," I barked at him.

"*You!* " he shouted in a full outrage. "*Are in no*

position to make demands!" He relaxed and added, "You know what I want. You have stolen from me on more than one occasion, and you will make that right. I want both balls back, and you will turn Talus over to me. You will do this or they will suffer the consequences."

"Both balls?"

"Do not play games with me! I know your associate entered my hotel suite while you had me distracted. That animal harmed my Todd and also was rough with my personal security officer, Edward. That alone is unforgivable, but he also stole the other ball. I don't know what you think that accomplishes except to bring you one step closer to destroying this city."

I was silent. Working this all through.

"Yes," he continued. "The combination of those two balls is most deadly. They can stabilize one another, but if they come into contact, they will explode with nuclear power. They must not touch, and you must return them to me immediately. You do not know how to manage them. You are a menace to this entire city."

"Fuck you," I said. It was about the only thing I could think to say, and I was quite pleased with it.

But Schlimm ignored me. "And you will instruct Talus to reconfigure itself to me. I should be its primary operator. Bring me the balls and grant me primary access to Talus, and you can have these ridiculous women back, and I will leave this insignificant city."

"Don't hurt those women," I hissed at him.

"I believe you have already made all these empty threats to my colleague, so there is no need to repeat them to me, although I do find your false bravado entertaining. Call me at this number when you are ready to make the exchange." Then he hung up.

I sat and stared through my windshield at the Clearwater storefront. There was a neon red and blue sign that read "Open." I couldn't peel my eyes off it for a moment. These guys had my wife and Anne. I shouldn't have left her where that goon could get his hands on her. Now I had to save them both. If I could save only one — which one would I save? I reached up and pulled this random, warped thought out of my head and flung it away.

"Talus," I said. "You there?"

"Yes."

"I need you to kill Schlimm and the goons working for him. Make their heads explode or something."

"One moment," it said and then, "Done. All identified targets are dead."

"Wait, what?" I said. "Are you serious? How did you do that?"

"I was not being serious."

"Son of a bitch, Talus. Knock that shit off. How am I going to find Schlimm? How am I going to get Anne and Lisa back?"

"He suggested an exchange."

"I don't have the other ball. I think Chuck must have taken it."

"Would you like his home address?"

"Of course," I shouted. "Do you have a number for him, too?"

"Mr. Peligro does not have a cellular number or a landline registered in his name."

That's right. I remembered something from one of our many sessions where he explained how he didn't like to be tracked and only bought disposable phones or used public ones.

"I have transferred his address into your dashboard GPS," Talus said.

I looked at it as a route lit up on my dash display. I was about to back up when a guy in a white and blue shirt was at my window and about to knock. I frowned and rolled it down.

"Excuse me," the guy said. "These stalls are for Clearwater customers."

I looked around at about six empty parking spaces and then back at the guy. "Shut the fuck up or I'll get my robot to blow your head up." Then I backed out of there and got back on the Bedford Highway.

The GPS told me, in the sexy female voice I'd chosen, to *continue on the current route.*

I'd driven for only a few seconds when Talus spoke. "Did you just refer to me as a robot again?"

"Don't start with me," I warned.

"I am Talus," it said. As if I'd forgotten.

"Okay, *Talus*, then finish the story on Dead Kitty. You said that their teleportation project proved the existence of the multiverse. Explain."

"The teleportation project was a failure. They never managed to teleport any object, but under certain circumstances the process of attempted teleportation appeared to bring objects into existence in this reality that had not previously existed."

"Like the magic balls?"

"Yes. And all such objects appeared in pairs. One object appeared at Site A of the attempted teleportation and the other at Site B. They referred to the pairs as siblings and designated one the brother and the other the sister."

"What other stuff came through in this teleportation?"

"This is not fully disclosed. Mr. Schlimm was very successful at covering up his findings and the objects that were teleported into our world. He secreted many of them away, and it is believed he has a vault hidden in Las Vegas containing these objects."

"But he said the objects are dangerous. Schlimm said they'll explode."

"Yes. He convinced many that the objects were terribly dangerous, and this allowed him more exclusive access to them and ultimately the ability to claim they had been disposed of. Dr. Zwicker uncovered evidence that Mr. Schlimm actually detonated a decoy explosive on the base to corroborate his claims. Two people were killed."

"Jesus," I said, shaking my head.

"I prefer to be addressed as Talus."

"What?"

"The point is that the objects do not pose any danger. Mr. Schlimm fabricated this story as a cover."

I finally got his other comment about Jesus. This

Talus was going to take some getting used to. The GPS told me to continue on the current route and warned me there was a toll ahead. I was going to be going over the MacKay Bridge.

"So how did Dr. Zwicker find out all this stuff?"

"Mr. Schlimm could not identify the specific conditions under which the teleportation would bring objects across. The computer interface system was too limited in its ability to control the process and analyze the variables. Dr. Zwicker fixed this."

"He fixed it?"

"With my help," Talus added.

"Of course. I'm sure you did most of the work," I said, and rolled my eyes.

"And Dr. Zwicker instructed me to review all research and documentation in relation to Dead Kitty, and this included hidden or encrypted files. I believe he was suspicious of Mr. Schlimm quite early on."

"And you found out the truth of Project Dead Kitty."

"Correct," Talus said. "Shortly after, Dr. Zwicker devised his plan to exit the project. He was prone to bouts of anxiety and was not coping well with what he had learned, including the details about the incident where innocent people died. He intended to expose Mr. Schlimm's corruption, but wanted to get far away from Nevada first."

"So he sabotaged the machine, took the antigravity ball as physical evidence, and came to Halifax."

"Correct."

The GPS told me to take one of two lanes and turn left onto Highway 111 before merging with traffic toward, the on ramp of the MacKay Bridge. This was the newer bridge, the one not under construction, so I figured there wouldn't be any unnecessary delays.

"So what was Mr. Schlimm trying to hide? What was sent over from the teleportation?"

"He was intentionally vague about his findings and did not keep a log accessible to anyone on the base. It is likely that he did not want people to know how valuable the items were so that he could later claim them as his own creation."

"Like what?"

"In addition to the antigravity material, we were aware of only two other items that he secreted off the base. There were undoubtedly many more. There was also something he called memory metal, a durable yet pliable metallic material that could learn to hold a shape and resume that shape if damaged."

"Like UFO material," I offered, and I was immediately ignored.

"And he documented and deleted information about an infinite battery. Apparently, it was some type of power cell that didn't drain, but remained constant regardless of the applied electrical load."

I whistled. "I can see why he wanted to steal those things. Any one of them would dramatically change the world."

"Yes."

"And each of those came in pairs."

"That appears to be the case, although Dr. Zwicker had no access to these items. Only the antigravity balls appeared during his work."

The GPS voice interrupted again and told me to take the exit on my right for Highfield Park Drive. I took the ramp into a high-density neighbourhood in North End Dartmouth. It was an area consisting exclusively of lower-rent apartment buildings — not exactly a prime crime and drug area, but not far off. It was sort of in the middle. The GPS led me through a maze of buildings until it announced my destination was on the right.

There was a big parking lot mostly full of cars, but I managed to find a visitor parking spot near the front. There was a small path that led to the front doors of the building. A group of late-teen, early twenties guys hung around the path. The kind of guys who couldn't pull their pants up all the way. Clouds of smoke billowed away over them.

"If I'm not back in fifteen minutes," I said to Talus, "send in the army."

"Shall I adopt my robot form and accompany you into the building?"

I was figuring Talus out, so I knew to ignore this comment. I turned the Jeep off and got out. I glanced in the back seat to make sure the coffee can was tucked under the passenger seat, out of sight, and then locked the door and checked it a couple of times.

I took a big breath and walked down the path towards the crowd of kids. As soon as they heard me pull up, they'd been watching, and now they deliberately turned, as a group, to stare at my approach.

One of them called out to me when I was about ten steps away. "You a cop?"

I got that a lot. I think it was my size and my close-cut hair. "Nope," I called back, and then thought maybe I shouldn't have.

One of the kids with a scruffy beard and a ratty blue hoodie pulled high up over his head stepped onto the path, blocking my way. He didn't look up at me, and his face was partially obscured by the hood. "What's you want round here?" he mumbled at me.

It took me a second to decode what he'd said. "I'm here to see someone. Excuse me." I tried to move around him, but more of them stepped onto the path and I was blocked in. Fuck.

"Let me sees yer hall pass," another guy said. Surprisingly, he also wore his jeans low and his hoodie high. This guy must have been the comedian of the group because they all laughed at the funny hall pass joke.

"I don't want any trouble, guys," I said, and held my hands out in a gesture of acquiescence. "I just really need to go talk to someone. It's a bit of an emergency."

"Oh," said the comedian, mocking my voice. "It's a bit of an emergency. I need to go suck someone's dick."

Everyone laughed again.

I chuckled too, just to show I was a good sport, but I was losing my patience pretty quick. "Okay," I said. "Can I just get through now?"

The first guy spoke again and got right up next to

me, but didn't look up. I think he didn't want to show how much shorter he was by having to speak up to me. "You didn't pay the toll."

"Toll?" I spat back. "Come on, guys. This has been a shit day, and I don't—"

Comedian again: "Oh...oh...oh...I'm having a bad day." Then he switched to a more menacing voice. "Well, your day just took another turn for the worse, motherfucker."

"Listen you little shit stains," I started because I just couldn't help myself. I didn't have time for this when a lunatic was holding my wife. "I'm going to go into that building now. I need to talk to someone, so why don't you run along home now and get mommy to change your diapers?"

"What the fuck did you say?" the first guy blurted. He was looking up now and he was mad.

"Big mistake," one of the other voices in the mob chimed in.

I felt hands grab me on both arms before I had a chance to bolt out of there. The little punk in front smiled and pulled an arm back to hit me, but didn't get a chance because there was a bellow from the direction of the apartment building behind them.

"What the fuck is going on over there?" came a familiar voice.

Everyone froze and heads turned to see who spoke. It wasn't hard to find the person attached to the voice. The enormous bulk of Chuck Peligro stood in the entranceway of his building, about twenty meters down the path.

"Oh shit," Comedian said.

Tough Guy dropped his punching arm. "It's all cool, big guy. We just playin'."

"Playtime's over," Chuck growled. "Get lost."

"This bitch here was disrespectful," Tough Guy said, and nodded back at me where I was still being held in place.

Chuck's answer was just to stare down the path.

"We needs to teach this bitch how to show respect, yah?" Tough Guy kept pushing.

Chuck straightened his Oakley Blades before he spoke. "I'm gonna count to three and then I'm gonna take a mental picture of all the little pukes that are still standing in front of me."

The reaction rippled through them quickly. They exchanged glances, and I felt hands drop off my arms. They didn't want any trouble with Chuck. It was no surprise he had a reputation in this area.

"One," Chuck said just loud enough for us to hear.

Even Tough Guy's attitude changed. "Oh, snap. It's all good." He waved the other guys off, and they began parting, clearing the way for me.

"Two," Chuck said evenly.

"Get the fuck out of here!" Tough Guy yelled, and that was all it took for the group to turn tail and run in every direction. They couldn't get out of there fast enough.

That just left Chuck and me staring at each other. He turned around and started back towards the building.

After that display, now I was wondering about going up to this guy's apartment all by myself. He stopped at the double doors and held one open as he looked back. "You coming?" he asked.

As an answer, I jogged down the path towards the building.

CHAPTER 20

Less than five minutes later I was sitting in Chuck's Highfield Park apartment. Nervously. On the edge of an oddly patterned couch with a brightly patterned afghan thrown over the back. The room was a mess of inconsistency. The coffee table in front of me was littered with remnants of weaponry, including gun barrels, spent cartridges, and various wire brushes for cleaning. Up against the wall opposite me, next to a TV cabinet, was a glass shelving unit with glass doors. Inside the unit was a collection of ceramic animals — most miniature — and all lovingly arranged in the cabinet. Empty take-out food boxes randomly finished the decor along with piles of magazines (guns, MMA, and porn) and articles of clothing.

Right now Chuck sat in a well-worn easy chair. He had reclined the back, but not lifted the footrest and was staring at me. It was hard to tell if it was anger, irritation, curiosity, or quite possibly the look of someone trying to remember how he knows me. Because of the head injury his memory was shit. As he sat watching me, he slowly turned his head to follow my gaze and found I was looking at the ceramic animal menagerie.

"That's from my mom."

I snapped out of my daze. "I'm sorry?"

"Those animals and that case are from my mom. She

collected them. They came as like a prize in boxes of tea bags years ago. She collected every goddamn one and then bought that shelf thing at a garage sale. I had to go help her bring those goddamn glass shelves home and assemble it. Took half a day while my unit was waiting to start a training exercise. I know those guys were pissed, but generally people don't say shit to my face, so it passed."

Oh my God! I'd been seeing this guy for therapy in my private practice office for almost a year. Three times a week for almost a year. That's literally dozens and dozens of hours of therapy, and this was the most personal information he'd ever shared. I almost didn't know how to respond. So I just nodded.

He was still looking over at the glass case. "She died a few years ago, and I put all that shit in storage while I was still on active duty. After I got stuck here in Shitsville, I decided to get it and put it there." He turned back to me as if I should now have a response.

"It's nice."

"Yeah," he said. "It's pretty cool. I like the turtle best." And he was totally serious.

"Yep." I felt like crying. I didn't know why exactly.

"So what the fuck are you doing here?" Chuck said, sliding in a clever segue. I think he sensed an emotion in me that made him uncomfortable.

"Did you follow me to the hotel when I went to see Schlimm?"

He shrugged.

"He's kidnapped my wife and a friend of mine from

the base. He's going to hurt them if I don't get him both antigravity balls back." I decided not to mention Talus to him. No reason.

"Who'd he take from the base?"

"Anne. She's one of the—"

He cut me off. "I know her. She's cute."

I nodded. "Do you have the other ball?"

"Those things are pretty fuckin' cool," he said as something approaching an answer.

I just waited. Hoping there was more.

"You know," he said, "those things aren't affected by gravity, so the only thing that slows them is striking something or just a little bit of air resistance."

"What's your point?"

"Well," Chuck said, "it's just a little smaller than a baseball, and I used to pitch some in high school, so it got me thinking."

"What?" I prompted him.

"Chances are I could throw that little ball faster than a bullet, and it wouldn't stop real easy. I figure I could toss that bad boy right through a concrete wall."

"Well, that's great, but we're not going to try. So you're saying you have it?"

He actually looked a little sheepish. It wasn't a look that was consistent with his muscular bulk. "Yeah. I thought I would follow behind you and maybe be your backup, but then I got it in my head those things might be dangerous and maybe those guys shouldn't have it, so I guess I kind of went and took the other one."

"You broke in the door at the hotel and took it?"

Another shrug and he looked away from me.

"I'm going to need it," I said in what I hoped was a nice, even tone.

He held up one of his giant hands and opened his fingers to reveal the silver sphere. He lowered his hand away from it, and it stayed put in mid-air. "Aren't you worried it's gonna explode?"

"I don't think that story is true, and even if it was, should we keep it in the middle of an apartment complex?"

He lifted both his arms and put a hand on either side of the ball and began gently pushing it back and forth. It was mesmerizing and hard for the brain to comprehend. Your brain needed to view it as CGI from a movie and ignore that fact that it was real life. He spoke as he continued to let the ball drift back and forth. "You can't trust that German guy. He's going to kill Anne and your wife and you." He made a special point of looking directly at me on that last word.

"I guess he'll try, but maybe not."

"You got a plan?"

"Not really."

"Then I'm not giving this to you." He snatched it out of the air and it disappeared in his grip.

I blew out a breath of frustration. "Then you've just killed my wife and Anne."

"I'm not giving it to you because I'm going with you to meet Schlimm. I'll hold onto it."

I frowned. "I can't ask you to do that. You shouldn't have been involved in this at all. You're my patient."

"Well, then, you're fired. You were a shit shrink anyway. There!" he announced, and looked quite smug.

"I was a shit shrink?" I gasped. I couldn't help myself. I wasn't a shit shrink. Was I?

"I normally felt worse after our meetings," he said, and folded his beefy arms. He suppressed a grin, but I didn't know if it was because he was enjoying this exchange, having a joke with me, or finally getting something off his chest.

I just pushed on. "Well, it doesn't matter anyway. Just because you fire me doesn't mean I can drag you along on this thing. It could be dangerous. I'm not going to risk you being hurt too."

"Don't be a pussy," he said, and stood. "What now?"

"What? Now nothing," I blurted back. This guy wasn't getting it. "You need to give me that ball and let me go save my wife."

"You couldn't save...." He paused, struggling to make his head work to come up with a retort. "You couldn't save a cookie from a Girl Guide."

I guess that was kind of an insult. I stood too and put my hand out. "Are you going to give me that ball?"

He smiled down at me. "You and I both know who's winning this argument. Can we just get to the part where I kick someone's ass?"

I couldn't argue with that logic. I nodded in what I hoped looked like a resigned fashion, but secretly was relieved I had some actual backup. "I need to call Schlimm and see where we're meeting."

He waved his hand at me in a gesture to say *get on*

with it. I pulled my phone out and was about to redial the last number when he held a hand up to stop me.

"Make sure they let you talk to Anne. You need to confirm she is okay, and she might be able to get you some intel."

"Some intel?"

"She's military. If she can give you an idea of where they are or what's coming, she will. She's smart."

"Okay," I said tentatively. "And I'll talk to my wife too."

"I don't care about that. Just make sure you get Anne on the phone."

I nodded and hit redial. It was answered on the second ring.

"Do you got it?" It was Fridge guy again.

"Yes. Let me talk to my wife."

I heard Chuck groan and saw him shake his head in frustration.

"She's fine," Fridge Guy said.

"Let me talk to my wife and Anne. I want to make sure they're okay," I demanded.

"Or what?" he shot back. "Or you'll refuse to meet us and let us just kill off these bitches? I don't think so. You don't get to make demands."

A voice called in the background for him to let the ladies say hello. It must have been Schlimm.

There was a rustle and a new voice on the line. Lisa. "Blake?" She sounded panicked.

"Honey! Are you okay?" I said, and cupped the phone with two hands. "Have they hurt you?"

"I'm fine. I just — "

The phone was obviously pulled from her and put to someone else.

"Hello?" It was Anne now.

"Anne? Are you okay?" I said rapidly.

"Blake, get hold of —"

And the phone was gone again.

"I trust that suffices." It was the lightly accented voice of Mr. Schlimm. "Now, do you have what I need?"

I tried to slow my breathing as I let one of my hands drop. "Yes."

"Excellent. My associate has arranged for us to meet at a neutral location. Are you familiar with an ice hockey arena in Dartmouth called Bowling?"

"Bowles Arena?" I clarified. It was an old ice rink out behind the Dartmouth General Hospital. Located in an industrial area, the arena stood all by itself on the edge of the business park. It was a pretty desolate location to meet. The goons must have stumbled onto it around the time they made the trip to hospital. "I know it."

"Forty-five minutes," Schlimm said. "And is it really necessary to tell you to come alone?"

"Just don't hurt those ladies," I said, but he'd already hung up on me. I let the phone drop away from my ear and looked to Chuck.

"Bowles Arena?" he asked. "Good choice."

"How so?"

"Good lines of sight all around the building. You can't sneak up to it. And lots of open space inside. I don't even think there's an ice surface in there right now. They were working on the roof a couple of weeks ago."

"So it's a good choice for them or us?"

"It's a good choice for whoever plans on doing the most damage."

I didn't know if that was meant to comfort me or to contribute to the chill that was already running down my spine.

"Do you know what they used to call me when I was still running ops?" he asked, grinning.

Here we go again. "What's that?"

"Chuck the Fuck," he said with the evil grin spreading. "Know why?"

"Because you liked to cuddle with the other guys?"

The grin faded. "No. Are you trying to be funny?"

"Probably."

He didn't know how to take that, so he ignored it. "I used to fuck people up. I'm sort of savant when it comes to hurting people."

I supposed that was a little comforting under the present circumstances.

⧈

Twenty minutes later we were approaching my Jeep in the parking lot. We had worked out a plan, and I had an idea for some extra insurance using Talus and what it could do with cell phones. Chuck had geared up and let me borrow a Kevlar vest. I suggested I also borrow a gun and tuck it in the back of my jeans. This made him laugh until he had a coughing fit. I didn't end up with a gun.

Suddenly, Chuck yelped and almost dropped the oversized rucksack he was holding.

"What?" I yelled.

He was holding his right hand out in front of him. "It's singing."

"What?"

I was closer to him now, and it was definitely singing. Not words, but more like a freaky wind chime and like nothing I'd ever heard before. It sounded random, but not really, and even though it was obvious that the sound was coming from the ball, it wasn't obvious. The music seemed to just surround the area and tuck you inside it.

"What the hell is that?"

He held the ball away from his body. "This thing. It just started doing it." The big man looked legit scared. That was enough to leave me terrified.

"Why? What's going on?" I asked.

He let the thing go, and it sat in the air for a second and then it started to drift. It moved right alongside my Jeep and bumped gently against the driver's side windows all the way down to the back end, where it disappeared around the edge.

"Grab it!" I yelled at Chuck. The last thing I needed was for this thing to float off into the atmosphere and be gone.

"You grab it!" he yelled back.

I moved behind the Jeep to catch up. As I did so I noticed the black coffee can in the back seat, only it wasn't on the floor any longer. It was now hovering over the passenger seat and gently rolling around as if tracking Chuck's ball outside.

"Look!" I said, pointing.

Chuck peered in the window at the floating coffee can. "You still got your ball in that?"

"Yes."

"Something's going on," Chuck announced, confirming that he was along on this journey for his muscle and not his brain.

I caught up to Chuck's ball and snatched it. It resisted only very slightly and continued with its eerie chiming. "I'm going to try something," I said. "Watch the coffee can." I held the ball firmly in both hands and walked backwards away from the Jeep. The noise didn't change until, very suddenly, it just stopped.

"The can is sinking," Chuck called. "It's falling back to the seat."

"Any music?"

"Nope."

I was about ten meters away. I started back towards the Jeep, and the chiming immediately started again.

"The can stopped sinking," Chuck called. He was resting his forehead on his arm against the back window of the Jeep. "I think I can hear the music again."

I could again feel the slight pull from the ball like it wanted to be free, but I held it firmly. "It's something about when the two balls are close together."

Chuck stood and could easily look at me from the opposite side of the vehicle. "Like maybe an early warning signal that they're about to explode?"

"Jesus, I wasn't thinking that."

"Oh."

"But now I am," I said — cold chills returning to my spine. I held the ball a little farther from my body.

"So what now?" Chuck said.

Then I remembered my trump card in the suit of Talus. I pulled my phone out and held it out in front of me in my free hand. "Talus, you there?"

"You have asked this question before, and I am unsure where else I might be."

"No time for that," I snapped. "What's the deal with the music these balls are making?"

"Yes, that is a curious aspect of the objects. No one was ever quite sure, and Mr. Schlimm's records are notoriously incomplete with regard to his hypotheses over such things."

"So everything that comes over from the multiverse sings like this?"

"No, just the antigravity orbs. Other objects do interact with one another in various capacities, but none, to date, have exhibited that quality."

"What does it mean, though? Are they going to blow up?"

"Dr. Zwicker did not believe so."

"Who are you talking to?" Chuck called over the Jeep.

"Just a sec," I called back. "Talus, I would appreciate a little info on my current situation. If these balls get too close, are they going to blow up?"

"That is unlikely. It was clear that Mr. Schlimm established the story of multiverse materials being unstable and explosive for his own purposes. There was never any evidence of danger."

"So the singing means...." I pushed.

"It is likely that the presence of these materials in our world is unnatural, and when in proximity to one another, a certain stasis is sought. The sounds you hear are evidence of an interaction."

"That doesn't help me figure out how close to dying I am," I said, growing tired of Talus' complicated answers.

"Stasis for these objects may mean a particular proximity to one another."

"Should I keep them apart?"

"There is no evidence to support that conclusion."

There was a brief silence. "Was there a *but* there?" I asked.

"Until more is known, it would be advisable to not allow the objects to come into physical contact with one another."

"What? Why? What happens if they touch?"

"Possibly nothing. Possibly the objects return to their unique universe."

I finished for Talus. "And possibly they do explode."

"There is no evidence to support that conclusion."

I put the phone away and headed back to the Jeep. The chiming continued and so did the minor pull for me to release the ball, but I didn't. Chuck came around and met me. I put the ball back in his hand.

"Hold this. Don't let it go."

He held the ball away from his body like it was contaminated. "I don't want to hold it."

"Fine," I said, and bent into the back of the Jeep. I grabbed the coffee can and wedged it firmly under the seat so it wouldn't move around and then stood back up with an old blanket. I took the ball back and wrapped it under the blanket before shoving it into the crack of the back seat so it was immobilized too. The chiming noise continued, but muffled now from the coffee can and blanket. I turned back to Chuck. "Happy?"

He nodded and then asked, "Who were you talking to on the phone just now?"

I slid into the driver's seat and motioned for him to come around and get in the other side. Once he did, I said, "I've got an inside guy. He assures me the balls won't blow up, but warned me not to let them touch."

He nodded. I guess that satisfied him, but he didn't fully care. Who knows?

I started the Jeep, and we left to start part one of the plan: Mic Mac Mall.

CHAPTER 21

Mic Mac Mall is only about five minutes away from the Highfield Park apartments. It used to be one of Halifax and area's premiere shopping destinations, but closures of the big department stores have taken a toll on the mall. It is still a shopping hub, but other areas like Bayer's Lake and Dartmouth Crossing along with a revitalized Halifax Shopping Centre have sucked some business away.

The quickest way to get to the mall is to go back out to Highway 111, called the Circumferential Highway or just the Circ, and then basically get off on one of the next two exits since the mall is right next door. There are no parking structures here, but just a giant flat lot that surrounds the mall on all sides.

We cruised on in to find Friday crowds had virtually filled all the spots anywhere near a door.

"There's one," Chuck called, pointing.

I sped up slightly only to find there was a motorcycle in the stall.

"Want me to toss that bike out of the way?" Chuck offered.

I laughed, but then realized he was serious. "No."

We drove another couple of laps through the cars, and I decided it wasn't worth it. The clock was ticking. I knew there was a little area near the Old Navy and the central mall doors with a circular driveway. It was intended to be a drop-off point only and not additional parking spaces. Most people respected that. Normally that list of people included me, but today I just didn't have the time to be respectful. I swung up onto the ramp and pulled along the side of the road into an area marked with yellow stripes.

"Don't those stripes mean no parking?" Chuck asked. Suddenly he was a Boy Scout.

"I just need to run in here for a second," I said. "You stay here with the…." I didn't know what to call them, so I just kind of nodded into the back seat. Thinking about them now made their continuous singing noises even more apparent. They hadn't shut up since I put them in the Jeep together.

"How about I go in and you stay?" Chuck countered. "I'm getting sick of the noise."

Chuck looked funny squished into the passenger seat of my Jeep, but not so funny that I wasn't taking him seriously. "I'm just going to be gone a second."

"Well, then, we're wasting time," he announced, and opened his door and started towards the mall.

"Damn it," I said, and jumped out to hustle in after him. "Wait up."

This entrance brought us onto the second floor of the three-story mall. The kiosk I wanted was on the bottom floor, so we followed the corridor and took the central escalator down one flight. We rounded Starbucks at the bottom and kept moving down past the shops until we arrived at an area with multiple freestanding kiosks in the large hall.

It was the discount cellular phone carrier booth that I wanted, so I made my way over and stood next to the display case of phones and tried to make eye contact with the clerk. She was a young blonde woman in a blue company polo shirt with a name tag that read Kadenyze. She was leaning against the counter opposite me and staring at her phone.

I cleared my throat and kept trying to make eye contact with her. Nothing. Chuck arrived next to me. I could tell because he partially blocked the light from behind us. I cleared my throat again and leaned on the counter to try to make myself more visible.

Before she could acknowledge us, Chuck had reached the end of his patience (which was, unsurprisingly, a very short journey). "Yo!" he said loudly, and the clerk jumped, nearly dropping her phone. She looked up and quickly made her way over.

"Can I help you?" She was talking to me, but her eyes kept darting to the scowling hulk over my shoulder.

I imagine we were both quite a sight to see. My face was bruised and a bit puffy, and my T-shirt didn't fit very well over my Kevlar vest. Chuck, meanwhile, had some kind of green army vest on with multiple pockets both inside the jacket and out. He was lumpy all over from the weapons he had tucked into those pouches. He had those blade sunglasses on he always wore outside his apartment. He looked, basically, like some army character out of a video game. He looked like the kind of guy who might have come to the mall just to shoot it up.

“I need a disposable phone,” I said.

“A what?” she asked. Chuck was really distracting her.

“Like a phone that comes all set up or whatever. You know, like a one-time-use phone?”

She focused on me and frowned. “Like what a drug dealer would use?” She wasn’t being sarcastic, and after glancing back at Chuck, I thought her guess was actually pretty good.

“Well, I guess, but we’re not drug dealers. I just need a phone that’s already set up to go, and I really only need it for today.”

She nodded. “Like to make a drug deal and then throw the phone out.”

“Jesus, lady,” Chuck growled. “Are you an undercover cop or do you sell phones at a shitty kiosk?”

I put a hand up to silence the big man and smiled at the clerk. “I’m sorry about that,” I peered at the name tag, trying to sort out the pronunciation, “Kaden?”

“It’s pronounced Cadence — like in music,” she corrected me, and ran her fingers along the letters on the tag to help me understand.

“Awesome,” I said. “Kaydenyze, do you have something that might work or do you know where I can get it?”

She pulled a box out from under the counter. “This is our basic prepaid phone. It comes with a SIM card and ten hours talk time.”

It was a flip phone. I didn’t know they still made those. “I need something with a decent camera and preferably one that didn’t have to be opened like that.” I tapped the picture of the flip phone on the box.

She put the box back and shifted down the counter. Each time she bent over, there was a rattle of keys as she had to unlock the specific cabinet. She brought another phone back up. It looked more like a typical smart phone. I think it was a Moto R or something. "This is a prepaid and has a decent camera. Same deal as the other one."

I picked the box up and flipped it around to read the features on the back. "Bluetooth?" I asked.

"All phones have Bluetooth," she said. You could almost hear her eyes roll.

◘

It took way longer to fill out the paperwork than it should have, but I eventually got the phone. I had to add data to it because that wasn't standard on a prepaid phone. Then we had to wait while she went online and activated the SIM card.

"Are we leaving now?" Chuck said as we walked back towards the escalator. "Or did you want to pick up some gift wrap paper and a bow for your pretty new phone?"

"I explained to you why we need the phone," I said, and held up the plastic bag I was carrying with the newly purchased phone inside.

"I wasn't listening."

"I know."

We were up the escalator and down the hall quickly and back out through the mall doors only to be met with a commotion. A commotion centered around my Jeep. I slowly kept walking towards it. There were about twenty people gathered in little pockets all around my vehicle. As we got closer, there were audible gasps and whistles from the crowd.

"What the hell?" I said loudly, and a small path cleared. Probably because of Chuck.

At the center of the crowd was the source of the entertainment. My Jeep door was open, and the singing balls were floating about four feet off the ground, singing loudly, and orbiting each other in a steady pattern. It looked like a slow-motion chase in a lazy circle, all the while the chiming sounded, sometimes getting a little louder and sometimes less so.

"Hey," I called. "What the hell's going on?"

The crowd of gawking zombies barely acknowledged me and returned to watching the orbs. I went over and tracked the balls for a second and then reached out and grabbed one out of the air. This elicited a general negative murmur. Chuck was right behind me and grabbed the other ball as it began a slow drift towards me in pursuit of its sibling.

Chuck spun on the crowd now. "Who took these out of the Jeep?" he bellowed.

Two male teenagers had been backing through the crowd, and now they turned and flat out ran. Chuck didn't hide his sneer as he watched them go. Thankfully he didn't look like he was about to chase them.

"Let's go," I said to him, and got into the driver's seat.

Some of the crowd was already bored and moving on, but not all. Some people stayed around to yell.

"What are those things?"

"Where'd you get them?"

"Don't park here, asshole."

Chuck had gone around to the passenger side, but veered off at the last comment and confronted the by-stander. He needed to take only a few steps in the direction of the thin scowling guy, who quickly changed his tune and hustled into the mall. Chuck turned back and wedged himself into the Jeep.

We pulled a quick U-turn and headed out of the parking lot. "You didn't lock the doors, did you?" Chuck asked as we slowed to the traffic lights at the first exit.

I ignored the question and tried to hand him the ball I was still holding.

"Whoa," he screamed, and recoiled away. "I've got the other ball here. You almost made them touch."

I pulled my hand back. "Grab me the coffee can." It was sitting open on the back seat. He handed it up to me, and I sat the ball back on the towel still inside and pushed the plastic lid on. "There," I announced.

Chuck visibly relaxed, and I saw him look for an empty pocket on his vest and then shove the ball away.

I handed him the bag with the phone. "Open that and make sure the phone is on." Then I addressed the air around us. "Talus?"

"Yes," came the response through the Jeep speakers.

"Who's that?" Chuck said.

"Just a guy helping us," I said quickly. "Talus, we

have a phone. Can you connect to it?"

Chuck was holding the phone in his giant palm. It looked like a toddler's toy.

"Please activate Bluetooth pairing on the new device," Talus said.

I looked over at Chuck, and he looked back at me and shrugged. He wasn't a techie. I told him how to pull down a menu by swiping his finger on the screen and then had him find the little jagged letter B symbol. It took a few times to get it right because his finger tended to hit six things at once.

Finally Talus announced, "I am fully integrated with the new device." Chuck continued to hold the phone out in front of him like it was some kind of vicious animal.

"Is it going to work?" I asked. "How's the audio and video?"

"It is adequate."

"Let's keep our fingers crossed," I said.

CHAPTER 22

We got back on the Circ and headed south towards the harbour. Bowles Arena is only about ten minutes away from Mic Mac Mall. There's a back way in off the Mount Hope exit, and that's the route I took. It allowed us to weave our way through the industrial park to eventually arrive at the arena. We slowly cruised down Neptune Crescent and hung a left, and there it was, standing all by itself on a little bit of a rise — Bowles Arena.

I rolled up into the parking lot, where there was only one other vehicle. A dark sedan with tinted windows — probably the same car I'd seen a few days ago outside my private office after Nathan Zwicker was murdered. I backed into a stall that would allow me the cleanest getaway, should that become necessary, then turned off the ignition.

"So," I said. "Should we go over the plan for what happens when we get in there?"

Chuck's answer was to get out of the Jeep and slam his door.

I reached behind, grabbed the coffee can, and followed him. The entrance was along the middle of the big tin structure. It basically looked like a blue warehouse from the 1950s, which maybe it was originally. Chuck was not one for subtlety, and he pulled open the front door and started to head inside with me on his tail. "Hold up," I called to him. I took my phone off my belt. "Talus," I whispered. "Ready?"

"Yes," came the answer.

I dropped the phone into my shirt pocket, making sure the camera lens was peeking over the top and facing forward. Chuck watched me with an obvious sneer and then continued on into the arena as I followed.

It was dark inside. Just a few lights on the roof casting a bit of light around. It took a few seconds for my eyes to adjust. I noticed Chuck even took off his sunglasses and hooked them on the neck of his shirt. The facility was really just big enough for one hockey rink and then a bit of room around the outside for locker rooms, stands, and an office. Very minimal design to get the ice there. Once inside, you were almost immediately met with the boards of the rink and the inevitable Plexiglas above that.

"I said to come alone," called the familiar nasal German voice of Schlimm. We hadn't been able to sneak into the ice rink because the chiming from the orbs hadn't stopped. It was like we were bringing a weird radio along for the ride.

I peered into the rink and saw him down at the far left end where there should have been a net. There wasn't a net, but there wasn't any ice either. Schlimm stood next to my two favourite goons: Fridge Guy and Salami Breath. They had dragged a couple of those old wood and metal stacking chairs out and placed Anne in one and my wife in the other. There was duct tape over their mouths, and I assumed their arms were tied because of the way they were both sitting.

"He's my partner and has the other antigravity ball you want. If he hadn't come, you wouldn't get the other ball," I called back. There was a visceral reaction from the goons as they recognized the person who'd hurt them earlier today. I wasn't sure if they were scared or possibly excited at the prospect of revenge.

"Even still, this must be counted as strike number two," Schlimm said.

Chuck and I turned right and walked along the rink toward, the change room until we got to a door and stepped into the rink. We were now on the far end of the rink away from them.

"That's not fair. I don't remember strike number one."

Now that we were inside, I could see that each of the goons held a gun. Fridge Guy had his pointed at Anne, while Salami was focused on Lisa.

"Strike one was obviously when you dug a bigger hole for yourself by violating my hotel suite and removing the sister orb. In the process, you put my security officer Edward in hospital, which is where he remains."

"That wasn't my fault," I called back, and then glared at Chuck. He wasn't concerned.

"You just referred to that monstrosity of a man as your partner, so I can only assume he acts with your blessing," Schlimm countered.

I kept moving towards them, slowly. "It doesn't

matter," I said. "Let's just get this over with. I don't want any more trouble with you."

"That is very wise. So am I to assume you have those things which belong to me?"

I held up the coffee can.

"And have you transferred Talus to me so that I am the sole operator?"

"There's a bit of a problem there," I said.

"That sounds to me like strike three." He turned to Salami Breath. "Mr. Miller, please shoot his wife in the head."

"*No!* " I yelled, and almost ran at them, but both goons retrained their weapons on me.

"You will keep your distance," Schlimm said. "And I would appreciate it if you both kept your hands visible."

"Don't hurt her," I said. I could see Lisa's body shake. She was terrified and crying. "I tried to get Talus to shift to you, but it couldn't. It required a home device. Something of yours."

"A home device?"

"You've been quite good at keeping personal details about yourself off the Internet," I continued. "Talus was unable to uniquely identify you to transfer control over."

"You are still only describing strike three," Schlimm said.

"So I transferred full authorization of Talus to this phone." I took the prepaid phone out and held it up. "Whoever has this phone has full access to Talus. No one else."

Schlimm stared at me for a moment as if sorting this out. He finally came to a decision. "Mr. Baxter is going to come over there and retrieve that device. If you do anything other than hand it to him, Mr. Miller will execute your wife."

"No," I said. "If I'm handing this over, I want you to release Lisa."

Schlimm shook his head slowly as if talking to a dim-witted child. "We are only beginning our transactions, Dr. Waiter. Please do not let your rashness result in harm to these beautiful women."

Fridge Guy slowly made his way over. He kept his gun pointed at Chuck. When he got about ten feet away, he motioned for me to walk towards him and waved Chuck to stay back. He didn't want to get within reach of the big man. I walked to him, and he reached out with his casted arm to retrieve the prepaid phone and then backed up the way he'd come.

Chuck and I could only watch as the phone made its way back into Schlimm's chubby hand.

Schlimm eagerly looked at it and tapped at the screen with his sausages. "How do I access it?" he asked.

I thought he knew more about it given how eager he was to get his hands on it. "Just talk."

"Hello?" he said.

"Yes," Talus answered. It was faint, but I could hear its voice through the Motorola's speaker.

"This is Talus?" Schlimm asked.

"Yes."

Schlimm looked up at me. "How do I know this is

real and not a trick?"

"I don't know. Ask it something," I called back.

"Why does the machine not work any longer? The teleportation device back in Nevada."

"The device contained multiple flaws primarily related to the computer interface's computational strength around quantum superpositioning. Dr. Zwicker was able to correct many of these, but removed their effective parameters when he learned of your ulterior motives for Project Dead Kitty."

"Yes, yes," Schlimm said, trying to cut Talus off. "And you can fix this sabotage so that the machine works?"

"Correct."

Schlimm was smiling now, but looked back to me. "And how do I know you no longer have access to Talus as well?"

"Ask it," I called. "It's a robot. It can't lie." I suppressed a smile.

"Talus," Schlimm said, redirecting his attention to the phone. "Does anyone else have authorization to access you or receive assistance from you?"

"No. Only Mr. Michael Schlimm currently holds authorization to interact with my system."

"Dr. Waiter can no longer access you?"

"No."

"And you cannot tell a lie," Schlimm said, his excitement building again.

"Talus is incapable of deceit or manipulation."

"Excellent." Schlimm redirected his attention to me

now. "And I believe you have two other objects that belong to me."

"Let the women go," I said. "Then you can have them."

"It pains me to think you have placed an object of such immeasurable value in that disgusting coffee can," Schlimm continued, ignoring my request. "I hope you had enough sense to not place both brother and sister in there."

"I have the other one," Chuck grumbled.

"Of course you do," Schlimm said. "If you'd placed both brother and sister together in that can, then you would no longer be alive. The orbs must simply not come in contact with one another."

I opened the coffee can and pulled the ball out before tossing the cloth and can to the side. It was singing right along, and it tugged gently at my hand in the direction of Chuck. I held it out. "This is as close to the ball as you're going to get until I see those ladies leaving."

"Who are you to make demands?" Schlimm yelled. "Those do not belong to you."

Chuck pulled his orb out of a vest pocket and held it out. "Come on over and take it then, you foreign fuck."

Schlimm was visibly upset by this comment. He reached into his vest pocket and took out a black case about the shape and size of an expensive pen and pencil set. He handled it in an agitated fashion as though wrestling with his next decision. "Why should I not kill you both right now?"

"Why don't we see what happens if these balls touch and just sort this out once and for all?" I offered, and then moved closer to Chuck. We brought the balls almost together.

"Stop!" Schlimm screamed. "You will not do this."

Even Salami Breath and Fridge Guy looked uncomfortable with the new tactic. Maybe it was true that they would explode if allowed to touch.

"Then let my wife go!" I screamed back.

Schlimm turned to Salami Breath, who was still holding a gun next to Lisa's head. "Mr. Miller, kill that stupid bitch."

"No!" I screamed. "Don't be a fuckin' idiot."

Salami Breath braced himself and made exaggerated motions like he was about to pull the trigger. The way he was handling his weapon was patently awkward, but I now realized that was because he was forced to use his left hand. His right was missing a trigger finger.

Schlimm held a hand up to stop Salami Breath and spoke to me again. "You don't have any cards left to play, Dr. Waiter. You can only hope that by giving me what is mine, I will then live up to my side of this deal and allow you all to walk away."

"That sounds like bullshit," Chuck mumbled.

Schlimm ignored Chuck's comment. "I will make one final offer. Mr. Miller will walk over to you and collect my property. Your wife will accompany him. Once you have provided him with my property, you can keep this whore and do what you like with her. Then the four of us will exit this facility."

"The four of you?" I called back to him.

"Yes, Anne will need to accompany us out of the facility. We will leave her somewhere safe once we are gone."

I could see Anne shaking her head very slightly. Tears shone in her eyes too. She didn't want to leave with these assholes.

"You're not leaving here with Anne," I said. "Tell Salami Breath to come and take these balls and bring Lisa and Anne. Then you three can run out of here like the pieces of shit you are."

"Come, come," Schlimm said. "Such hostility."

"Okay," I said. "Send your guy over here with my wife." I knew the chiming noise would hide our voices a little, so I spoke in low tones to Chuck while trying not to move my mouth and give it away. "Chuck?"

"What?" he whispered back — at least I think it was supposed to be a whisper.

"Remember what you said about how fast you could throw that ball?"

"Yah."

"That guy is going to kill Anne," I said.

"I got it," he said.

Salami Breath had untied Lisa, and they were approaching now. He was pushing her along in front, using her as a shield. Under the duct tape across her mouth, her face was blotchy and red from fear and crying. I mouthed, "It's going to be okay" to her.

Salami Breath stopped about three feet away. "Put that one back in the can," he barked at me. I gathered up the cloth and can and repackaged it and handed it off to his bandaged hand. He tucked the can under his arm, but kept the gun in the middle of my wife's back. Now he turned to Chuck and held out his bandaged hand. He looked scared.

Chuck grinned at him. "How's the finger?"

"Fuck you," he said. "You're not leaving here alive."

Chuck shrugged and put the ball firmly in Salami Breath's hand, intentionally banging it against the wound. The man yelped, but quickly wrapped his remaining fingers around the ball and started to back up.

I took a step forward to embrace Lisa as Salami was backing away.

"Stop," screamed Schlimm. Everyone froze. "There is a change of plan. Mr. Miller, please bring Ms. Waiter back with you."

"That's not the plan," I yelled. "She stays." Lisa looked at me with pleading eyes.

"Move it," Salami Breath said, and poked her from behind with the gun. The two of them started backing away.

"You asshole," I said.

"And now," Schlimm announced, "I have changed my mind about my preferred hostage. I will use the wife and no longer require this one. Mr. Baxter, please kill her." He casually waved at Anne.

Fridge Guy stepped back from her and readied his gun. Schlimm stepped away as well, presumably to avoid getting blood or guts on him. Anne's body was heaving as she struggled with the ropes that had her tied to the chair.

"You sure, boss?" Fridge asked.

"Shoot," Schlimm hissed.

And then the music stopped.

Salami Breath was about ten meters away from us now. He looked down at the orb he held in his hands.

Schlimm turned to us. "What have you done?"

Salami Breath turned back to Schlimm. He shrugged and held the ball out in his palm.

"Drop it," Schlimm shouted.

Salami Breath opened his hand, and the ball thudded instantly to the floor.

"Looking for this?" Chuck barked, and his arm was a blur as he threw something. A silver shape streaked through the air like a flash of light and was gone, shattering the rink glass and violently punching a hole through the wall of the arena.

Salami Breath pushed my wife away, let the can go from under his arm, and quickly fired twice at Chuck, who spun around and dropped face first to the floor.

"Chuck," I screamed.

On the other end of the rink, I saw Schlimm playing with that damn pencil case again, and he turned to Fridge Guy and Anne. "What are you waiting for? Kill that bitch."

But Fridge Guy couldn't hear him. There was an baseball-sized hole that went clear through his chest, showing light on the other side. He had stayed standing for a moment, but now crumbled to the floor.

While the violence to Fridge Guy momentarily distracted me, his partner had pushed Lisa aside and charged at me. He struck me across the side of my face with his gun, and I fell backwards, almost losing consciousness. I was on the floor now next to Chuck, and when I looked over, the floor around his face was soaked with blood. The bullet had hit him in the head. I struggled to stay conscious.

"Don't kill him yet," Schlimm called. "Check that can and make sure we have it."

From the floor, I watched him get Lisa to open the can and verify the ball inside. She took it out and let the ball momentarily hover in the air for Schlimm to see. He growled at her to pack it up and bring it back.

"Let her go," I said weakly.

Schlimm went over to Fridge's body and retrieved the gun. "Who else knows about this misadventure?"

"No one."

"Who else have you been speaking to? Who knows about Talus?"

"No one," I said. My head pounded. "I swear."

"This one knew," Schlimm said, and waved a gun near Anne's head. "Who else?"

"No one!" I yelled. "I didn't tell anyone."

He stopped and looked down the rink at me. "You realize you now have three strikes." He smiled and tapped Anne with the barrel of the gun as he spoke. "Strike one was breaking into my hotel room and stealing the sister orb." He hit Anne in the head for emphasis, and she recoiled. "Strike two was bringing this monster to our business transaction, and now look." He turned and waved the gun at Fridge Guy's body. "Strike three was losing one of my orbs." He turned and pointed at the hole in the side of the arena.

"I'll get it back," I protested weakly.

He shrugged. "Regardless, you still have three strikes." Without any more warning, he pointed the gun at the side of Anne's head and pulled the trigger. Her head bucked violently to the side as an explosion of blood, brain, and bone sprayed out and settled to the floor.

I opened my mouth to scream, but no sound came. Lisa collapsed in a sea of tears, and Salami Breath just let her fall.

"There are consequences for all of the nonsense you have put me through!" Schlimm screamed, and began walking over. "I cannot allow any more of this. Now who else knows about me? Who else knows about Talus?"

"No one," I managed to get out. Tears flooded my eyes too. "I swear."

"We shall see," Schlimm said, and retrieved the phone I gave him earlier. "Talus?" he said to it, and waited before saying it again. "Talus?" He looked to Salami Breath. "Static. Nothing, but static on my screen."

Salami Breath pulled his phone out of his pocket and swiped across the screen. "Mine too, boss."

Schlimm knelt next to me. "What game are you playing? You have an electronic jammer with you? How will that save you?"

"I'm not doing anything," I said weakly.

"This is ridiculous," Schlimm announced, and stood

and spoke to Salami. "Shoot him."

Lisa let loose another wail as Salami pointed his weapon at me. I held a hand up at him and said, "Don't," but it didn't matter. A shot rang out.

And a red hole appeared on Salami's forehead seconds before he collapsed.

Schlimm turned sharply towards the fallen goon and then his eyes darted around the arena. "What?" he said. "Who?"

I rolled over, expecting to see Chuck had recovered, but he remained motionless in a pool of blood.

"Hey, guys," a female British-accented voice called from somewhere behind us. "Room for one more in your party?"

I struggled to turn and saw Constant White strolling towards us with a sniper rifle laid across her arms. When I turned back to Schlimm, he was frantically opening the pencil case and then he vanished...

...along with the coffee can.

...and my wife.

CHAPTER 23

Chuck was dead. Anne was dead. Fridge Guy was dead. And a psychopath had kidnapped my wife.

There were three dead bodies around me and an assassin standing over me. Things weren't going exactly to plan.

"Are you all right?" Constant White asked. She was wearing a skin-tight black outfit. An assassin's outfit, I suppose. Her jet-black hair was tied back into a ponytail. She was casually holding her sniper rifle in one hand and letting it dangle by her side.

I was still lying on the floor next to Chuck's body. It was unlikely that I was pulling off this position in a manly fashion. I wanted to at least get to a sitting position. I tried rolling one way, but then caught myself just in time. I did not want to roll towards Chuck's body. I had no interest in seeing his exploded head again. It would either make me vomit or cry. I rolled the other way and managed to push myself to a sitting position. I drew my knees up and held them for some stability. "Why are you asking if I'm okay?" I asked. "Do you just want to make sure I'm comfortable before you kill me?"

Constant was surveying the room, looking for something, and then she turned back to me. "How did that fat fellow disappear?"

"You saw that too? Good. I thought it was a hallucination after getting pistol-whipped."

"The fat guy disappeared and then so did your wife."

I let my face fall against my knees and sobbed. "Jesus. What have I gotten myself into? You might as well kill me."

"Honestly," she said in an exasperated British way. "Please do stop saying that. If I were going to do you, you'd be done already."

I looked up at her. "Then what's going on?"

She sighed. "You're my bloody assignment. That's all. You're quite valuable to someone, and they want you alive for the time being."

"I'm valuable?" I said in surprise. "Why?"

"I'm not at liberty to say," she said with a grin. "You'll probably find out soon enough."

"So you're not working with Schlimm?"

She looked behind us where the German had been standing moments ago. "Was he that disgusting fat bastard?" She shook her head.

Suddenly there were sirens, lots of them, approaching the arena.

Constant White cocked her head, listening, and then said, "That's my cue, sweetie. You should be okay, now." She started walking.

"Wait," I said. "What about my wife?"

She kept walking and called over her shoulder. "I was only hired to look after the boys. She's your responsibility if you want to save her."

"The boys?" I called, and tried to stand, but my head was pounding. "What boys?"

She'd reached the edge of the ice rink. Tires were squealing in the parking lot just outside the main doors.

"You know," she said with a big grin, "you have the exact same expressions as he does." Then she ran the last few steps, planted a foot on the boards of the rink, and grabbed the top of the glass to catapult herself over.

"The exact same expression as who?" I screamed after her just as the front doors of the arena exploded with the incoming rush of bodies.

I was expecting to see the police, but it was JTF2 — Canada's elite special forces unit dressed in full gear. They came in and swept the building, securing rooms and exits so fast I didn't have time to put my hands up and surrender. One black-clad JTF2 soldier, a young guy, ran directly up to me. I thought he was going to attack me, but he stopped short and asked if I was okay. He addressed me as Dr. Waiter, so I figured these guys knew what to expect when they arrived. I told him I was fine, and he took up a post next to me, assault rifle at the ready.

I put my hands on the floor and tried to push myself up. The soldier immediately put a hand under my arm and helped, but all the while kept trying to convince me I should stay on the floor. I waved him off.

"What's going on?" I asked.

"We were on standby, ready to go operational if things went bad."

I was shaky, but at least I was standing now. "Well, I'd say things went pretty fuckin' bad," I said, looking around the arena that had become a bloodbath of bodies. "Did you catch Schlimm?"

The soldier pointed back to the door. "Here comes the General. He can answer your questions."

I looked back to the entrance and watched General Walter Belaire arriving along with another, older, distinguished looking officer in uniform. They hustled through the rink and made their way over to me.

"Jesus," Walter said upon reaching me. "Are you okay?" He was surveying the room as he waited for an answer, and his eyes fell on Anne. He caught his breath.

"General," I started. "She's dead. I...."

"Don't," he said, stopping me. "I know what happened. Your video link worked. We have that bastard Schlimm recorded. He'll pay for what he did to Anne."

"The video link," I said, remembering. I'd forgotten that one of the reasons I wanted Talus installed on that new phone was so he could run a continuous video and audio feed and send it back to 12 Wing. Talus had established that connection as soon as we arrived at the arena.

"That's right, Blake," Walter continued. "We have the video and audio off his phone and yours. It worked perfectly up until the very end."

"What about Schlimm?" I said desperately. "He's got my wife."

"We have people looking for him right now," the other man added. "He won't get far."

Belaire turned to him. "Blake, this is General Thaddeus

Montgomery. He's the base commander down in Nevada. We all know now that that con artist Schlimm was using the base for his own purposes."

"Damn straight he was," said Montgomery. "We had our suspicions, but I had no idea how far he would go to protect his little scheme."

Walter turned back towards Anne's body again. "I can't believe we've lost her."

"He'll pay for that," Montgomery said. "Mark my words."

"And for Chuck," I said. "They killed —" I was turning as I spoke and stopped short. Chuck was sitting up with the JTF2 officer who had previously been helping me. He was holding a hand to Chuck's bloody face. Obviously putting pressure on a wound.

"What?" I yelled. "He's dead."

"Fuck you," Chuck muttered at me.

"Sir," the JTF2 officer was saying to Chuck, "you need to lie down and wait for EMT."

I ran over to him and knelt down. "How are you alive?"

He looked at me through a blood-covered face. "Steel plate," he said and then he fell unconscious again as the JTF2 officer helped bring him back to the floor.

"Looks like it was a glancing shot off the plate in his skull. Ripped off a lot of skin and he's likely got a concussion, but he'll live," the officer said.

EMT came running into the arena now with a gurney.

I backed off to let them work.

"Looks like your friend is going to be okay," General Montgomery said. "That's one small victory."

I stood and turned back to the generals. "I need to go after my wife," I said. My head was starting to feel a little clearer.

"You need to go to the hospital first and get checked out," Walter said.

"No. There's no time."

"There's gonna have to be time because that's a direct order," Walter barked. "You're in no shape to go chasing after this guy. He's too dangerous."

"Besides," added Montgomery, "we have men on his tail now. We'll get your wife back."

I looked around the arena. Chuck strapped to a gurney. Anne slumped dead in a chair. The two goons dead. I couldn't just sit around. Schlimm was a monster and needed to be stopped.

"Now, son," Montgomery said, "if you want to help us maybe you can tell us what happened right at the end of that video feed. How did you kill this man and how did Schlimm escape? Our video feed went blank on us for about five minutes when we were on the way here."

The man they were talking about was Salami Breath. They must have seen on the video that he had a weapon and was about to kill me, but they didn't see what happened next. They didn't know that Schlimm had simply vanished into thin air, and they didn't know about Constant White's involvement. When she arrived, it must have disrupted the video feeds. Constant White's trademark.

"Constant White was here," I said. "She killed him."

"Constant what-now?" asked Montgomery. It was obvious he'd heard me, but was pretending that the name didn't ring a bell.

"Constant White," I said. "The assassin."

"You mean the myth," he shot back. "There's no such person."

I looked at General Belaire to jump in and back me up, but he just shifted uncomfortably. "There is definitely such a person," I said with anger sneaking into my voice. "She was here and killed him to save me. She said I'm her mission or something."

"That's very unlikely, son," Montgomery said. "It's more likely that this soldier over here." He pointed at Chuck on the gurney. "He must have came to just enough to fire the shot before he blacked out again. That man probably saved your life."

They were going to concoct whatever story they wanted to make things neat and tidy. I was too tired and beat up to fight this any longer. "Sure. Chuck probably saved my butt again for like the third or fourth time." Now I wasn't even going to bother with telling them that Schlimm had used something that allowed him to vanish.

"What about Schlimm?" Montgomery asked. "Where do you think he was going and why did he take your wife?"

I just shook my head. "He's a lunatic. Who knows?"

Belaire stepped in now. "That's probably enough for right now. Let's have the psychologist here get to a hospital and get checked out."

"Yeah," I agreed. "I need to go." I turned and started back towards the rink exit.

"There's an ambulance outside that will take you to the hospital," Walter called after me.

I looked back at the men and gave a thumbs up. "Got it." I kept on walking and made it all the way to the front door before a JTF2 officer held a hand up and stopped me. He gave me a pretty intense look before he said something into his shoulder radio. After a moment, the soldier looked into the rink where the generals were still standing. General Belaire obviously heard something on his radio because he looked our way and waved the soldier off, so the guy let me go.

It was early evening now and a bit cooler as I stepped outside. Sure enough, there were a few ambulances waiting out here, but I slipped between them and headed to my Jeep. Luckily I had parked far enough down, in perfect getaway position, that none of the JTF2 vehicles had blocked me in. I noticed the dark sedan was still in the lot too, meaning that Schlimm must have left on foot. I thought that was odd — maybe there was another vehicle I hadn't seen earlier. I didn't have a lot of time to contemplate that now. I kept moving at a slow and even pace and made it over to my Jeep without interruption. I slipped in and pulled the door shut.

I wasn't giving up on Lisa just yet. I had no confidence that these army guys would be able to find Schlimm let alone stop him. I might not be the best person to stop him either, but I had something they didn't. I had the Talus trump card — a card I wasn't going to share with the generals, not yet. And that evil bastard Schlimm was carrying a Talus-linked phone around with him.

CHAPTER 24

I pulled out of the Bowles Arena parking lot quickly, happy to put some distance between myself and the horrors that took place there. I couldn't believe Anne was gone.

"Talus?" I asked the Jeep.

"Yes?" came through the speakers.

"Where is he? Where is that bastard Schlimm?"

"Unfortunately, I cannot accurately locate Mr. Schlimm."

I nearly slammed on the brakes. "What? Why? We have that dummy phone on him. Track that."

"I am attempting to track the other cellular device, but there is an error with its operating system. Very curious," Talus said.

The route I took on leaving Bowles was down Acadia Street between the provincial court house and the Dartmouth General Hospital. I pulled abruptly to the curb and stomped on the brakes. "What is so damn curious? Where is my wife?"

"With my limited ability to access the other device — it appears that Mr. Schlimm is currently in the middle of the Halifax Harbour."

"He's in the harbour?" I asked sceptically. "As in floating in the goddamn ocean?"

"It is unclear if he is floating."

"How the hell is he in the middle of the harbour right now?"

"That is also unclear."

"Talus," I said, my impatience tainting my voice, "give me something here. What's happening?"

"My records are incomplete, as all electronic devices were momentarily rendered inoperable for a period of time during the previous altercation, but the following hypothesis is very likely: Mr. Schlimm has an additional technology that allowed him to escape from the arena."

"What additional technology?"

"During the altercation at the ice rink, Mr. Schlimm produced two small objects that looked like smooth stones from the case he was carrying. When he placed a stone in each of his hands, there was a significant time displacement. It was this time displacement that damaged the dummy cellular device's OS. The time on that OS currently reads six months and four hours later than the current time."

"Later? Like in the future? Six months from now?"

"Correct."

"So Schlimm can time-travel?"

"No. That does not appear to be the case. Or we would likely have no signal from the cellular device. He is still in the vicinity."

"Then what happened?"

"It is possible that the stones are from a parallel universe where time operates with a different interval than this universe. By accessing the stones, Mr. Schlimm can change the relative speed at which time functions in this universe, but only for the individual who has the stones."

"So he can run super fast? I don't see that happening."

"No. He likely moves at the same speed, but things in this universe move at a dramatically slower speed relative to him."

"What would even make you think that's possible?"

"The relativity of time has been well known for many years. The time displacement on the other cellular device combined with significant negative physical consequences for Mr. Schlimm are consistent with the theory."

"Negative physical consequences? Like what?"

"When I first regained contact with the other device, I was able to monitor a conversation between Mr. Schlimm and your wife. Both were suffering from severe fatigue, headaches, and general symptoms consistent with a viral infection. He explained to Ms. Waiter that this was normal and would eventually go away."

"This thing, this time travel thing, hurt her too?"

"I believe it is how he exited Bowles Arena undetected."

"Why would it hurt them?" I asked.

"It would be very hard on the human body. He, and whoever is with him, would physically age the equivalent of six months in a matter of seconds. This would necessarily limit how many times he can use this device and for how long during each use."

"So he can't keep using it to get away?"

"That would be a logical inference based on the limited information currently available," Talus said.

"And right now they're in the middle of the harbour?"

"As you can see from this map" — Talus used my dash video screen — "this is the estimated trajectory of his movements on leaving Bowles Arena." A dotted line appeared and moved away from the ice rink, down Acadia Street, and onto Mount Hope Avenue. The line continued over Pleasant Street and kept moving ever closer to Halifax Harbour.

Suddenly it made sense. I knew where he'd gone and I knew why he was in the middle of the harbour. "He's on the ferry," I said. The dotted line was moving directly towards Woodside Ferry, one of two terminals on this side of the harbour. At this time of day the ferry was probably leaving there every half hour. "He's on the goddamn ferry right now."

I threw the Jeep back into drive and peeled away from the curb. That ferry only took about twenty minutes to make the trek across the harbour, so I didn't have much time. I got back on Pleasant Street and headed north towards the Macdonald Bridge. Traffic on this road wasn't bad, but I knew it was going to keep getting worse as I got closer to the bottleneck that was the entrance to the bridge.

"Talus," I said. "You can map my route to the ferry terminal in Halifax. Any chance you can help with traffic?"

"That would require accessing the Halifax Regional Municipality's traffic system. It is a heavily secure network, but it would provide the ability to manage traffic lights in a favourable way."

"Well, how long would it take to get into that system?" I yelled back as I swerved around yet another granny driver.

"I have already gained access."

"God," I said. "You can be really annoying."

I was fast approaching the intersection with Portland Street. "Lights ahead," I said. "I want a left turn light." The light was in sight now, and it was already blinking for an advance arrow even though the turn lane was empty. I hit the lane and made the turn with two tires of my Jeep coming off the pavement. When I straightened out, the Jeep rocked with the impact. "Shit."

I knew I could keep following Portland and it would turn into Alderney Drive, a major road parallel to the water that went all the way up to the bridge entrance basically. But it would be busy and wasn't a very big road. I decided to risk a detour. "Straight ahead," I said. "Give me the lights to go right through this next intersection."

The next lights were the complicated intersection of multiple roads including Prince Albert, Portland, and Alderney. The light was green for me and I went right through, staying on Portland, but taking a very quick right onto Victoria Road. It was a straight shot up Victoria to Nantucket, which was the road that led straight onto the Macdonald Bridge.

And I was immediately behind another granny driver and slammed on the brakes. When you first get on Victoria, there is no way to pass. It's a one-way road going uphill with cars parked along the right-hand side. I pulled up on the bumper of the Toyota Echo and gave a little honk. If anything, the driver started to slow down. Just ahead, next to the cemetery, the road divides to become a two-way. As soon as we hit the wider road, I slammed the gas pedal and pulled into the other lane and sped up. So did the granny driver. Keeping pace with me going up the hill and not letting me get back into the proper lane.

Only it wasn't a granny. It was some fucking kid wearing his baseball cap backwards and staring out his window at me. He was making faces and sticking his tongue out.

I frantically watched in front for traffic cresting the hill and coming down at me and kept glancing to my right to see if this idiot was going to let me back over.

Nope. Little piece of shit.

I slowed and he slowed. I sped up and he sped up.

I didn't want to slam on my brakes and lose time. The teenager in the Echo was losing it laughing so hard that I didn't know how he was still driving.

We were close to the top of the hill and I might well be driving head-on into someone. I was out of time. I jerked the wheel hard to the right, and the big steel bumper of the Jeep collapsed the plastic front panel of the Echo. The kid's expression changed pretty dramatically. He swerved, but not enough to avoid the impact and managed to grind his passenger side tires down the curb. There was a loud pop like a gunshot, and the Echo lurched and came to a stop. One of his tires had blown out on the curb.

I was back in my lane, and I crested the hill and kept going. I'm sure the little shit wasn't expecting that outcome. I smiled.

There was only one more traffic light to go straight through before the right turn onto Nantucket, and then Talus had the lights ready for me to cruise straight down and into the mess that was the tollbooths. There wasn't much Talus could do here. Thankfully, at this time of day, late on a Friday afternoon, most of the traffic was leaving Halifax and coming back towards me. Unfortunately, at this time of day, two of the three lanes of the Macdonald Bridge were set from Halifax back to Dartmouth, so I only had one lane to drive in. That meant for the length of the bridge I was stuck with no way to get past anyone.

Ten minutes had gone since Talus had told me Schlimm was in the middle of the harbour. That ferry was probably docking right now. I tore off the end of the Macdonald Bridge and took the 270-degree turn under the bridge that put me down on Barrington Street. The Jeep did its best to stay on four wheels, and I pushed it hard trying to roll it as I rounded this sharp corner, but the Jeep won. I sped out on Barrington as I told Talus to make sure the lights ahead — and there were lots — were all green.

Barrington was more or less a straight shot into downtown Halifax. I got up to ninety kilometers an hour on this stretch until I hit George Street. I knew this road went straight down to the waterfront, ending in a little circular lot where motorcyclists often sit to drink coffee and show off their toys. With Talus giving me the green lights, I sped into the circle and stopped short right next to a Harley-Davidson parked in front of a hot dog cart. This was the tourist part of Halifax with the wooden boardwalk, restaurants, and gift shops all around. The ferry terminal was literally steps from this circular drive, and I bolted out of the Jeep and ran to the entrance of the two-story terminal.

There were two areas inside — the lobby where you could buy tickets and then a small entrance to the waiting area of the actual boat. The lobby was still half full with people waiting for a Dartmouth-bound ferry. Through a large Plexiglas window, I could see into the loading area and the last passengers boarding a boat.

"Which boat is that?" I called to no one in particular.

A bored businessman looked up from his phone and then over to the ferry. "Woodside," he said, and looked back to his phone.

I glanced around this area, but there was no sign of Schlimm or my wife. That ferry had been in dock here for at least five or ten minutes. I'd missed them. I ran back outside onto the boardwalk and looked down the path towards the Historic Properties and then the other way past Murphy's gift shop and restaurant. I saw steady crowds of people, but no fat German with my wife.

I had no idea where to go.

I pulled my phone out. "Talus, any idea where they are?"

Silence. Then, "GPS still shows them in the harbour."

"What?"

"No. The GPS is updating. They are on shore. Difficult to pinpoint exactly. Somewhere within five hundred meters of your location." A pause. "Possibly."

"Great," I said. "So there is a possibility that they're within five hundred meters of me right now?"

"It might be more accurate to say one thousand meters."

I started back to the Jeep. "That's not helpful. How can we find them?"

"I cannot establish a reliable GPS fix with the current condition of the device's OS. I would suggest you contact the phone directly."

I slipped back into the driver's seat. A number of bystanders were giving me some pretty heavy stank eye, presumably over my recent driving and running around. Fuck them. "How does it help if I call?"

"If you can maintain a connection with the cellular device, I may be able to track the unique digital signature."

"Fine," I said. "Call it. Make sure my name shows up on his caller display."

I pulled the Jeep door shut as the speakers began to ring. It was answered after two rings.

"Is this Dr. Waiter?" It was Schlimm's disgusting voice. He even sounded fat. "You are more resilient than I had originally thought."

"Let me talk to Lisa," I demanded.

"You seem incapable of learning. You have never been in a position to make demands of me."

"And you seem incapable of being anything other than a fat piece of shit," I offered in retort. I can be quite clever when I need to be.

"So crude," Schlimm said. "I don't think we have any need to continue in this conversation."

"What were you doing on the ferry?" I asked. "Was it a bucket list thing?"

"The ferry?" He seemed genuinely surprised. "Why do you think I was on the ferry?"

"I know quite a bit. I know you used your little time displacement device to get out of the arena and then ducked on the ferry to get back over to Halifax. I'm just not sure what the point of that little trip was."

Silence now. I think I hit a chord.

"You may be too clever for your own good," Schlimm said.

"I get that a lot," I lied.

A dot appeared on the map of my dash video display. Schlimm was just heading up the ramp onto the Macdonald Bridge. The bridge I had just come over on.

"Where you going now?" I asked. "You're heading back over the bridge back to Dartmouth. Did you forget something?"

"I have grown tired of this conversation," Schlimm said, and I think he actually tried to produce a yawn for effect.

"Well, I'm not done with you," I said, using my toughest tough-guy voice.

The response was the click of a terminated call. Schlimm had hung up on me.

"Talus," I said immediately. "I don't want him getting over that bridge."

"What would you suggest?"

I needed to stop the traffic, but how?

"What about the tolls?" I blurted. "Can you crash the computer systems at the tollbooth? If you crash the MACPASS it'll create a big traffic jam on the Dartmouth side before anyone can get off the bridge."

The MACPASS was the preferred method for commuters to pay the tolls. It was a small electronic transponder that people kept in their cars, and it registered each time you passed the tolls. It helped speed up the process, but you still had to wait for the MACPASS to connect before the gate would open.

"Done," Talus said. "None of the terminals will recognize the MACPASS."

"Let's go then."

I started the Jeep and spun around the circle and back out towards Barrington Street. Talus was already working the traffic lights for me.

CHAPTER 25

This drive wasn't nearly so long or harrowing. We raced back down Barrington Street for the on-ramp to the Macdonald Bridge, and the effect of Talus shutting down the tolls on the far side was immediately apparent. The traffic build-up had trickled down the ramp and all the way out to Barrington Street, causing this road to become a parking lot.

As soon as we hit the wall of cars, I pulled the Jeep up over the curb onto the grass and walking lane right next to the road. I parked and started jogging down towards the bridge. There were a lot of angry people in cars along Barrington. I just hoped one of the angry ones was Schlimm somewhere up in the middle of that pack.

Shortly, I was jogging up the road of the ramp to get onto the bridge. This wasn't the proper route for pedestrian traffic, but that ramp was currently blocked because of ongoing construction. The bridge wasn't safe for pedestrian traffic. The surface of the bridge was getting repaired, and this meant the small walking path was out of service.

As I jogged up the roadway, I spoke to my phone again. "Talus, have you still got a signal for him?"

"With a large margin of error, his phone still registers on the Macdonald Bridge. Most likely mid-span."

I sped up and rounded the corner of back-to-back cars to start the straightaway over the bridge. I didn't know exactly what kind of car I was looking for, so I slowed ever so slightly as I made my way down between the two lanes. At each car, I stooped slightly to look in a window and then kept going. So far, nothing.

I was feeling the stress of today. The Macdonald Bridge was more than a kilometer long, and with the rest of the racing around today, I felt like I was on the last stretch of a marathon. My body ached, but I couldn't stop. I might be just a few car lengths from my wife.

And then there he was. I was about halfway across with nothing, but water below and bridge on either side of me when I saw that fat piece of shit who had killed Anne. Mr. Michael Schlimm. He was standing next to a Casino Taxi, hands on hips, and looking very impatient staring down at the tolls. He wasn't looking in my direction and didn't see me. I slowed up and stopped about three cars behind.

"Hey, dumb-ass!" I called out. He immediately turned around, which I thought was funny. He answered to the name *dumb-ass*.

His face raced through a volley of emotions, mostly negative. He was initially shocked and then frustrated and angry as he pieced things together. "I assume I have you to thank for the bridge delay."

"Where's my wife?"

He couldn't help himself. He glanced, briefly, at the cab before refocusing on me. "What is this little charade supposed to prove?"

"Let my wife go." I moved another car length closer to him.

He sighed heavily. "Just what do you have to bargain with now? I feel like we've already played this game."

I held my phone up. "How do you think I closed the bridge down?"

His shit-eating grin sank away as he realized what I was implying.

"That's right," I said. "You don't have Talus. You never did."

He pulled out the dummy phone. "Talus," he said quietly, but I could hear him. "Reopen this bridge."

I didn't hear a response. With the glitches on that phone, I wasn't sure Talus could even access it.

Schlimm shot a look back to me. "What have you done?"

"You never had Talus. I wasn't going to hand it over to a psycho like you."

His face contorted. I knew how bad he wanted Talus. He needed it if he ever wanted to get his multiverse teleporter working again. "You continue to meddle and make terrible mistakes. Your mistakes are going to continue to get people hurt. Don't you remember what happened to that silly bitch from your precious military base?"

"Don't talk about her," I growled back.

He bent into the cab and said something. My wife stepped out along with another man. I recognized him even though he was wearing a shirt now. It was the young guy from Schlimm's hotel room, probably his lover. That must be why he came back to Halifax.

Lisa didn't look good. Her face was a mask of fear. The little shit lover stood behind her, probably with a gun to her back.

"Don't hurt her," I warned.

"Oh, my Todd won't hurt her unless you continue to act in such an impetuous, stupid fashion."

"Lisa," I called. "Are you okay?"

Tears streaked her face, but she nodded.

A bearded driver stepped out of the cab behind Schlimm. "What's going on?" he said. "I don't want any trouble."

"Get back in that fucking car," Schlimm snapped at him, and the guy did as he was told. Then he turned back on me. "I need that program. Give me Talus."

"What's the point now?" I asked.

"I am authorized to do whatever is necessary to contain this Halifax situation. I have the full support of the Nevada project and the U.S. military."

"Bullshit," I called, interrupting him.

He choked, slightly, offended at my interruption. This was a guy used to getting his own way.

"You've got no authority. You're done," I added.

"No more games," he screamed. Some people were now out of their cars watching all the drama.

"Fine," I said. "No more games. You're done. Nevada knows about you, knows the shit you've been pulling. The whole scene in the ice rink was being recorded and streamed to 12 Wing."

He just stared at me.

"And guess what base commander was a guest at 12 Wing, listening to the whole thing?"

No response.

"Are you familiar with a General Montgomery? He seems to know you and would love to have a chat. I think he's looking for you right now."

"You're lying," he said as more of a wish than an actual suspicion.

"I assume you were on the way to the airport. You have a private plane there? You should go. You should go and see who's waiting there. I think you'll enjoy it."

"Fuck you."

"No," I said contemplatively. "I don't think I'm the one who's fucked."

Schlimm looked over at Todd and back to me. "You've ruined everything."

"It's not the first time someone's told me that," I said, and shrugged. "My bad."

He stared at me for what felt like a long time. It started me thinking about an old wives' tale about how if two people stare into each other's eye, for a certain amount of time, they'll get married. God, I didn't want to marry Schlimm. As subtly as I could, I quickly pulled that thought out of my head and threw it away.

He obviously finished weighing out his options. I wasn't convinced he had that many to weigh out, but it took him a while. He slowly walked around the back of the cab to where Todd was standing with my wife. "Looks like you've won, then," he said, but he wasn't looking at me. He was staring at my wife. I saw him make eye contact with Todd and nod, and the other man backed away.

"Don't be stupid now," I said, and moved closer still.

Without warning, he grabbed Lisa and dragged her off towards the edge of the bridge. I started after them, but wasn't close enough. The construction had left a lot of openings from the road to the walking path, and he dragged Lisa through onto the path and pushed her up against the railing. There should have been guardrails high enough to prevent someone from going over, but they were missing at this particular spot. He pushed Lisa against the gap, and she hung precariously over the edge, hundreds of feet up from the surface of the unforgiving harbour.

Todd turned and ran between the cars towards the Dartmouth tolls. I guess he hadn't signed up for this level of crazy.

I chased after Schlimm and pulled up short at the edge of the pedestrian path. I held my hands up to him. "Schlimm," I said, trying to stay calm. "Don't."

"You've taken everything!" he screamed. "I'm going to do the same to you."

"Don't," I called. "You don't need to."

"Why?" he screamed. "You did it to me."

"You did it to yourself," I screamed back. "But it's over now. Nevada is done. Project Dead Kitty is done."

Lisa was trying hard to balance herself without going over. Her hands were searching for something to grab as her toes scrambled along the edge.

Schlimm let his face fall. "I just need Talus. I can fix

this."

"You can have Talus," I yelled. "Just bring Lisa back."

He lifted his head. "Say it then!" he screamed back at me with spit flying. "Let me hear you authorize Talus to follow my commands and only my commands. No more games!"

I pulled my phone out. "Of course. Listen." I spoke into the phone. "Talus, I want you to obey Mr. Schlimm. He is your primary user now."

"Certainly," came the response from my phone. "Would you like to remain as a secondary user?"

"No," Schlimm said, shaking his head violently.

"No," I said. "Mr. Schlimm is the primary and only user." I had only scratched the surface of what this AI was capable of, and I didn't know what kind of evil I was unleashing on the world, but I needed my wife back. "It's done," I yelled, and held the phone out towards him. "Let her down."

His eyes were wild, and sweat smeared his face and shirt. He looked from me to the phone and then over to Lisa. "Hold it closer to me," he barked.

I moved a little more towards him.

His eyes darted again from me to the phone and back to my wife. He was obviously weighing out some course of action, and then he acted. He pushed Lisa and lurched for the phone, snatching it out of my hands. I didn't care about the phone, but jumped at my wife as she lost her footing and went over the railing.

I think I was screaming, "No!" but everything was a

blur. My hands grabbed at her, but I didn't have a chance. It happened too fast, and she was gone. I collapsed over the railing like a rag doll with the dulled sound of people screaming all around me.

And then I saw Lisa hanging on a support bar under the belly of the bridge. She had both hands gripped on the rusty metal, and her legs dangled wildly in mid-air beneath her.

She looked up at me with white panic on her face. "Blake?" she whimpered. I think she was reluctant to yell in case that was all it took to shake her grip loose.

I couldn't believe she wasn't dead. I reached farther over the railing, and my feet lifted into the air behind me. I wanted to cry. I wanted to scream. My fingertips were just brushing against the top of her hands. I looked back at the bystanders and screamed, "Grab my legs! Hurry."

A number of people were immediately there. Hands on my legs, my belt, my shirt, my feet, and I was almost immobilized. I managed to stretch down the extra distance and caught hold of Lisa's wrists. "I've got you."

My big hands could close around her thin wrists pretty well. It used to be a bit of a game we'd play where I'd squeeze her wrists until her fingers were forced to open. I don't remember her liking that game very much.

Once I had her in my hands, she wasn't going anywhere. I would never have let go of her. The crowd above us started pulling me back, and soon they had both Lisa and me on the bridge deck. We immediately threw our arms around each other as the crowd erupted in applause.

Our desperate hug went on for a few minutes. I didn't want to let her go, and her petite body was a mess of spasming from all the tension and stress.

Finally, I pulled away, but kept a protective arm over her shoulder. I looked around the scene. Cars were still deadlocked on the bridge, but some movement was apparent down by the tolls. I think they had the booths working again.

But there was no sign of Schlimm. The psychopath, who now had control of the most powerful computer program ever invented, had escaped.

Someone in the crowd that still surrounded us noticed my gaze. "Are you looking for that guy that pushed her?" He indicated my wife.

I nodded. "Where'd he go?"

Someone else answered, "He started running towards Dartmouth. A few of us went to grab him, and he sort of just disappeared."

A few people muttered their agreement with that.

I nodded, thanking them for the information. It wasn't a surprise. I just hoped the military had the airport staked out. Please let them catch that guy before he gets out of here with Talus, I thought. I reached for my phone. I decided I had better warn General Belaire that Schlimm now had access to Talus. He might use that to get out of Halifax.

But my phone was gone. Schlimm had it.

Fuck.

I looked at Lisa, but knew she didn't have her phone.

She'd left it at the physio clinic, and now it was in my Jeep parked way back on Barrington.

"Can we go home?" Lisa said quietly.

I gave her a squeeze. "Yes."

The bystanders were returning to their cars, as traffic was about to start moving. A few stayed and offered Lisa and me a ride, but we declined. Then a bearded guy in an ill-fitting polo shirt came over. I thought it was another offer of a ride, but then I realized it was Schlimm's cab driver.

"Yes?" I said.

"That guy didn't pay," he said.

"That guy?" I had no clue.

"For the cab ride. No one paid me."

"Jesus," I moaned. "Seriously? Did you not see what just happened?"

He offered a fake frown of concern, but then returned to his initial concern. "So you're not paying for the cab ride?" He looked from me to Lisa, who was still cowering under my arm.

"Fuck off," I said.

He blew air out in disgust and raised his hands like he was giving up and started back to his cab. With his back turned I heard him say, "Then I'm just throwing that fuckin' coffee can in the garbage. Fuck this."

"Whoa!" I said, and disengaged from Lisa. "Hold up there, buddy. Did they leave something in your cab?"

He stopped and turned back. "Some stupid coffee can. I don't like cleaning up other people's garbage."

"I'll take it," I said quickly.

Now he was curious. Shit. "If you want the can, you have to pay the fare."

"Fine," I said, and reached for my wallet.

"Plus a surcharge for my inconvenience," he added quickly when he saw my wallet come out.

"What inconv —" I started, but it wasn't worth it. "Would a hundred cover it?" I held out five twenties.

His eyes went big, but he snatched it out of my hand before I could change my mind. He hustled back to the cab, reached in, then returned to me with the coffee can.

My coffee can.

And after a quick peek under the lid...my coffee can with the magic orb inside.

I had the coffee can tucked securely under my arm as Lisa and I walked back to my Jeep. Most people on the bridge didn't know how much drama had just unfolded, so we had to endure a lot of nasty looks for being on the road and making cars skirt around us. I didn't care. I had Lisa back.

At the end of the bridge, we were finally able to hop the barricade and get back on the pedestrian pathway, which was a whole lot safer. It was a small path that led back under the bridge to the trail along Barrington Street.

Now that we were a little more secure, Lisa finally spoke. "Is it over?"

My arm was around her, and I gave her shoulder a little squeeze. "I think so."

She looked up at me. Her face was still blotchy with dried trails of tears. "Don't lie to me. I can't handle that right now."

I smiled at her grimly. "I hope it's done, but I don't know. That fat bastard is gone. He has no reason to come back. I just hope the military grabbed him."

She was quiet, and we kept walking until she asked another question. I could tell she had a lot of questions. "Is Anne really dead?"

I nodded.

"What about that big guy that came in with you?"

"No. I think he's going to be okay. He had a steel plate in his head. Bullets just bounced off him."

She nodded. I guess that made sense to her because that's the kind of day it'd been. There weren't going to be a lot of explanations that weren't plausible. "What about Schlimm? How could he just disappear?"

I sighed heavily. "I think it's one of the reasons there's so much fuss right now. The military found a way to access really fantastic things, and Schlimm was trying to steal it all for himself. Him disappearing was one of those things."

We kept walking. We could see the Jeep ahead, still parked on the path.

"It was a couple of stones," she said. "That's all. Just looked like the kind of polished stress stones you might find at a cheesy gift store."

I didn't say anything. She could just tell me whatever she needed to. We had all the time in the world to talk now. I had Lisa back.

"I was with him when he did it at the ice rink," she continued. "Everything was really blurry, and it was hard to stand. It felt like every step we took made us slide an extra three or four feet. I thought I was going crazy."

I just nodded. The psychologist in me was tempted to use the old *Tell me more about that.*

"And when he finally stopped and put the stones away, neither one of us could barely stand. I think I puked instantly. He could handle it a bit better, but I was really sick. That's why I couldn't really do much when he dragged me on the ferry. He kept telling me it would pass quickly, but oh my God how my head hurt."

"Yeah." I knew her non-stop talking was a side effect of her shock. She was trying to recover, and a steady stream of words sometimes helps people reset their minds.

We kept walking. We'd arrived at the Jeep. I opened it and held her door as she got in, then I went around to the driver's side and joined her. I turned and set the coffee can in the back.

"What's in the can?" she asked with almost no hint of suspicion. Just curiosity.

"It's that magic silver ball that can float in the air."

"Oh right," she said as if that were as normal as a bag of carrots. It was still the shock talking.

I started the Jeep. "Home or hospital?" I asked.

She looked at me with a serious expression. "Do I need to go to the hospital?"

I shrugged. "I don't know. Maybe."

She ignored that question because something else

had occurred to her. "Hey. What was all that about Talus? What is a Talus?"

Oh God. I'd almost forgotten how far away from over this story really was. I was in a daze and had nearly forgotten I still needed to call the generals immediately and let them know how much more dangerous Schlimm was now. He had full access to Talus. "Hold that thought," I told her and I reached into the back again and grabbed her pink Lug bag, pulling it to the front. "I need to borrow your phone."

She waved me ahead and turned to stare out her window towards Halifax Harbour.

I grabbed it and hit the power to bring the screen to life. It was weird to hold a cell phone now and not be able to just start talking to Talus. I stared at the phone, realizing that Lisa wouldn't have any of the 12 Wing numbers in her address book. I had no idea what number to call to get hold of anyone. I let my hand drop into my lap and threw my head back against the seat.

"Can I help you?"

I sat up. The voice had come through the speakers. A familiar voice.

Lisa had turned back too. "Who's that?"

I put a hand on her knee. I was holding my breath. "Talus?"

"Yes?"

It was him. I started to breath, again. "What are you doing? How are you here?"

"Your wife's phone automatically syncs with your vehicle."

I wanted to laugh. I wanted to cry. "But why are you in my wife's phone? I made Schlimm the primary user, and you said I lost my authorization."

"I thought you were being sarcastic," Talus said.

I couldn't help it. I burst out laughing in fits of howling and equal amounts of tears. "You mean Schlimm doesn't have access to you at all?"

"I only provided him access to my deadly robot form."

"Jesus!" I shouted. "You're such an ass."

"What's going on?" Lisa yelled.

My answer was to turn, grab her, and give her the biggest kiss she and I had shared in many, many years. Maybe things were going to be okay.

CHAPTER 26

"Thanks for coming in on a Sunday," General Belaire said.

I was sitting in his office in the basement headquarters of SSCHVA. Walking down this corridor might never feel right again. It meant having to walk past Anne's office. It meant remembering that she was never going to meet me at the elevator or joke with me. It meant that she was gone.

"No problem," I said. "Just tell me you got him. Tell me you have Mr. Schlimm in custody."

Initially, his lack of an answer was not the answer I wanted. Finally he said, "We don't know where he is." The General's age was showing more than I'd seen in some time. He looked tired and somewhat defeated. It was not a typical look for a man who generally oozed confidence and authority. "Schlimm was spotted at the airport, and we had his private plane under surveillance, but he vanished." He paused there and looked at me with a knowing expression. "Sound familiar? Schlimm up and disappearing on us?"

"Yep."

"General Montgomery figures this Schlimm character has quite a few toys out of whatever research project they were running down in Nevada. Guess that Schlimm fella was sneaking stuff away since the project began.

The way they figure, he couldn't have gotten farther than Vegas, so he probably has stuff stashed there. Probably a whole lot of it. Nobody really knows. He's now on an international watch list."

I just nodded.

"That's their next best bet on catching that son of a bitch. They've got personnel on the ground in Vegas trying to trace his steps, trying to sort out his hiding holes. He is a crafty piece of work though." He paused and continued to eye me strangely. "Why do I feel like I'm telling you a story you already know?"

I looked away. "I know bits and pieces, but I don't know everything. I had an idea of what he was doing in Nevada."

That answer didn't really convince Belaire. "That Schlimm character sure took an interest in you." His expression told me there was a lot more to his comment.

"It doesn't take much to poke a psychopath."

He raised an eyebrow. "Is that what he is?"

"He killed Anne," I said bluntly.

He recoiled slightly, but recovered quickly. "Yes, and I'll never forget that." He leaned over his desk for emphasis. "And I'll never forgive it."

I nodded in agreement with him.

He leaned back in his chair again. "General Montgomery wants me to ask you if you have any tech leftover from this fiasco."

"Tech?"

"Like the floating ball. What did they call it, an anti-gravity sphere? I think there were two of them."

I nodded.

"Do you know where they are? On the video you were feeding us, we saw Sergeant Peligro throw one of those damn balls straight through a man at the ice rink. Montgomery's men subsequently searched the grounds all around the building and didn't find a thing. They think Schlimm grabbed it on the way out."

I lifted my hands in an expression of ignorance.

"And I guess you had the other ball in that coffee can? I think you handed that over to Schlimm while you were still at Bowles Arena."

"I didn't hand it over as much as he took it," I corrected.

"So it's gone too?"

I'd wrestled with this decision the entire way over to 12 Wing. Part of me wanted to hand the ball over to the General and wash my hands of this nightmare, and I would have if they'd caught that monster. But now I wasn't so sure. There was nothing I wanted more than to see Schlimm pay for what he'd done. The antigravity ball was insurance and maybe even leverage against Schlimm. I had a feeling that our paths would cross again, and I didn't want to be empty-handed at the exchange. "I guess it's gone, General."

He eyed me carefully. "You've no idea where it is?"

"I can't help you. Sorry."

"Can't help me or won't?"

I paused. "I guess both."

"Schlimm is a dangerous character. Montgomery suspects that man may not be done with you in particular."

"That sucks," I said.

We were both silent. I thought he might be trying to wait me out.

"Montgomery also wanted me to ask you about Talus. We heard you and Schlimm talking about it, and we understand it has something to do with artificial intelligence. Is it a computer program?"

"Yeah. It was something Dr. Nathan Zwicker was using."

"He was the computer guy that Schlimm had killed?"

"Yep."

"So does Schlimm have this program now?"

"It was running on my phone, and he took it while we were on the bridge."

"So you don't have access to this Talus thing anymore?" he asked while trying to keep eye contact.

"I thought it was the only way to save my wife. I gave it over to Schlimm."

He nodded, but the expression on his face suggested he didn't fully believe me. "Well, if you think of anything different with this case, you come straight to me. I think the fallout from the Nevada project will be settling for some time."

"Got it."

I wasn't ready to go home, so I ended up at my private office. The waiting room was still a mess with bloodstains on the carpet and furniture overturned. I puttered around and set chairs right and moved things back into position. There was a cleaner coming first thing tomorrow morning to deal with the carpet, and after that things could slowly drift back to normal.

Or maybe not.

I felt miserable for lying to the General, but I wasn't ready to show all my cards just yet. I had the antigravity ball. I didn't know if that was enough to bring Schlimm back to town, but if he came looking and I didn't have it, I might be expendable.

And expendable meant dead.

As for Talus — it wasn't mine to give away. It seemed like it was probably the last thing Nathan Zwicker did before he was murdered. He entrusted Talus to me. He could have given it to anyone in his final moments, but he gave it to me. He didn't give it to his wife or the base commander in Nevada or some research colleague. He gave it to me. And I didn't think the world was ready for me to hand it over to anyone else — let alone pass it over to the U.S. Military.

Talus was a quantum computer capable of actual thought. It could enter any computer system easily and potentially posed a global threat as a result.

So why shouldn't all that power be kept with a mediocre psychologist in Halifax?

I felt good about that decision.

It was funny that the military didn't find the sister orb outside of Bowles Arena. It had to be there. If Schlimm had grabbed it, he would have had it in the cab and the orbs would have been singing. I don't remember hearing anything. He couldn't have had it.

And he wouldn't have had time to find it anyway. He was in desperation mode to get out of the ice rink and couldn't have risked over-using those smooth stones for the time displacement. No, I was convinced that Schlimm didn't have that second orb. So who had it?

Maybe Chuck? No, he was in the hospital.

Who took it then? The only other choice was Constant White. Made sense. She might have been watching long enough to see Chuck throw that thing and then just decided to collect it.

Or maybe she knew about them the entire time and that was part of her mission.

But why hadn't she taken the brother orb? Why hadn't she taken the coffee can?

Unless....

I stood up and went across to my desk and opened the drawer. It only took a moment of rooting through packs of gum, fast-food utensils, pens, old business cards, and other junk to find what I wanted. I pulled out the laser pointer and hastily left my office.

My private office is less than fifteen minutes away from Bowles Arena, but I drove it in ten flat. There were wooden barricades at the entrances to the parking lot, so I parked on the street and walked up to the building from there. I was half expecting to still see military personnel on-site, taking measurements or working on the clean-up. There wasn't. It was deserted.

I walked up to the front doors, which were crisscrossed with Do Not Enter yellow tape. I tried the doors anyway but they were locked. Chained actually with a heavy padlock. I wasn't getting in there.

I kept moving along the side of the building and pulled out the laser pointer. I flicked the light on and off and let it dance along the side of the building as I walked. When I got to the end of the building, I turned and kept going down the next side, but slowed as I did so. I was scanning the wall as I went and letting the laser beam play up and down the side until I found what I was looking for: a hole, a baseball-sized hole punched right out the side of the building. At this point, no one had even bothered to put tape over it or nail a board to cover it. It was just above my waist on the side of the wall, and I bent to peer into the building. It was dark in there, so not much to see.

I stepped back and looked around the ground. Not surprising, there were little splinters of wood and insulation on the ground beneath the hole, but no sister orb. I turned around and looked at the area opposite the hole. On this side of the building, closest to Acadia Street, there wasn't much. The parking lot didn't even extend around this far. It was just a bit of rough ground and then a steep drop off down to the next street. I turned back to the hole and turned the laser pointer on. I set it in the hole and turned back to see where it was going.

If that ball had punched through the wall, it would have slowed, but kept going. It wasn't just going to drop to the ground right here. It was an antigravity ball. I knew from playing around with the one I had that when you pushed, in a particular direction, it moved until it hit something. It didn't tend to just simply lose momentum and fall. It would go straight until something stopped it. Something like the building that the laser pointer was now focused on. The Dartmouth provincial courthouse.

It was just down the street from where I now stood, but the courthouse building was the only structure in a direct line with this end of Bowles Arena. Even though the ice rink was on a bit of a hill, the courthouse building was five stories tall, giving the perfect landing area for the sister orb.

I scrambled down the hill and jogged toward, the courthouse. Since it was Sunday, that building was likely empty too. I slowed as I reached the parking lot on this side of the building and squinted up at the light brown metal panelling and windows that made up this side. Looking at it now I realized — it was a pretty ugly building. It looked like it had been made from ripping open corrugated cardboard strips. I knew the ball would have struck pretty high up, so I was focused on the upper floors. If it hit a window, it would have probably broken it. Chuck threw that ball pretty hard. I wasn't convinced it would penetrate those gross metal panels.

There were no signs along the top floor. No broken windows. I started scanning the fourth floor. It wasn't looking good for my brainstorm on finding the sister orb, until….

It wasn't the ball I saw first. It was a smear of red on the metal panel. A smear of blood. I'd almost forgotten that I wasn't looking for a pristine silver ball but a gore, soaked ball that had passed right through the chest of Fridge Guy.

It was, in fact, a ball that had passed through the chest of a man, crashed through the glass of a hockey rink, punched through the wall of a building, flown about half a kilometer, and now rested, perfectly calm and relaxed, against the fourth-story wall of the provincial court house.

Now I just had to figure out how to get it down.

I had no hope it was open, but I wandered over to the front doors anyway. It was Sunday. There was no court on Sundays, and just as I suspected, the doors were locked. That didn't really matter because I'd been in this building many times. I'd done meetings up on the fifth floor, where the Crown attorney offices were. I'd consulted for the mental health court program on the second floor. And there was one thing I was pretty sure of. None of the windows in that building opened. Even if I could get up to the fourth floor I couldn't just lean out and snag that ball. I needed a different solution.

I wandered back around and stood directly beneath it. It was about fifteen meters straight up. Even if I stood on top of my Jeep, I wasn't going to reach that.

"Hey, little guy," I called sweetly. "Come here. Here, boy."

Out of the corner of my eye, I saw a person on the sidewalk slow as they watched me. It looked like a hipster student going over to the community college across the street on the harbourfront. I smiled at him. I realized that it must look like I was calling for a dog, but

I was looking straight up the side of a building.

"Flying dogs, right?" I said, and nodded at him like you would about a shared, universal truth.

The guy just nodded back like he'd been there and done that.

I waited for him to get down to the traffic lights at the corner of the street and then refocused on the ball. "Get down here, you bitch." No response.

I had a brainstorm to ask Talus how to retrieve this antigravity ball, but I hadn't replaced my cell phone yet. Schlimm had taken my old one and I'd given Lisa hers back. If I wanted to talk to Talus, I needed to get online somewhere.

"No," I said out loud. I could solve a problem or two on my own.

All I needed was a fishing rod, a bedsheet, duct tape, and an industrial magnet.

Were these balls magnetic? I'd never tried.

Shit. All of a sudden I felt like a total moron. Why was it so hard to get this ball back?

Then it hit me and I realized I *was* a moron. I started back to my Jeep, which was parked over by the ice rink. I jumped in and raced back to my private office. This was a no-brainer. I didn't know why I hadn't thought of it right away. I unlocked the side door and bounded up the stairs to the third floor. I hustled into my office and straight into the back. I'm a creature of habit. I opened up the ottoman storage chest, and there it was. The coffee can with the brother orb.

Twenty-two minutes later and I'd gone a full three hundred and sixty degrees because I was right back in the courthouse parking lot. This time I had a plan.

On Sunday the little traffic gate was up, so I parked my Jeep and got out with the coffee can under my arm and strolled over to the side of the building. I glanced around for any curious onlookers because I didn't need an audience for what was going to happen next.

I was standing right under the sister orb and waiting to hear the familiar chiming music start but so far nothing. I looked around and then raised the coffee can in the air over my head. Still nothing. No chimes and no noticeable movement either inside the coffee can or from the bloody silver orb overhead.

I brought the can down and stepped away from the building. It didn't entirely make sense because I thought the plan was foolproof. Then I had an idea. Maybe the sister orb was just a little bit out of range. I kept backing up as I was sizing up the distance and suddenly hit something. I spun around and there was a dark-skinned, angry looking man behind me with his arms folded across his chest.

"Oh, sorry," I said quickly.

"What are you doing?" he snapped with a bit of a Middle-Eastern accent.

I turned and looked over my shoulder at the building and then back to the man. "I'm just…. I'm just testing out something."

"Don't do it here. Please leave." He maintained his scowl and folded arms.

I cocked an eye at him. "What's the problem?"

"I'm the building superintendent and this is private property. You leave now."

I frowned. "This is the provincial courthouse. It isn't private property."

"It is private. You leave."

I shook my head. "No. You're trespassing. I'm going to call the police."

"What?" he yelled back. "You're calling the police? No. I'm calling the police."

"You can't because I'm going to call unless you show me some ID — right now."

"I don't need to —" he started.

"Ah, ah, ah," I interrupted him with a wagging finger. "I'm done playing games with you. You've just violated Code 719.9 of the Public Property Act, and I'm going to hit you with a pretty hefty fine."

"Code what? What fine?"

"Why are you still talking?" I yelled at him. "Go get some ID right now before I arrest you."

"Arrest?" Now he was thoroughly confused. "How would you arrest me?"

I stared at him with as much intensity as I could manage and then I said in a calm and measured manner, "I'm going to count to ten."

"And then what?" he shot back.

"One."

"Why are you counting?"

"Two."

"This is ridiculous. Stop counting."

"Three." I gave him a raised eyebrow on that one.

He put his hands on his hips, defiantly.

"Four."

I could see in his face he had no clue what was happening, and my counting was just making him more and more anxious.

"Five," I said a little bit louder.

He lowered his arms and looked over my shoulder to the front entrance of the building.

"Six," I shouted.

"I'll be right back and you better be gone," he said, and bolted for the front doors.

I sighed with relief. Thank God I'm a psychologist.

I went and jumped in my Jeep and drove it over right next to the building, directly under the orb. I left the Jeep running and got out to scramble onto the hood and then the hardtop. The extra couple of meters was all I needed. Now when I brought the coffee can over my head, I immediately heard the chiming song and felt the rattle of the orb inside. I looked past the can and saw the bloody sister orb start to slip down the wall towards us.

Very shortly it was within reach, and I snatched it and dropped down off my Jeep and behind the wheel again. I threw the coffee can on the passenger seat, but kept a firm grip on the disgusting sister orb as I peeled out of the courthouse parking lot. As I was leaving I saw the building super coming out of the front doors, waving a fist at me.

Now I was back on Pleasant Street heading north toward my private office. The chiming inside the vehicle was a familiar, and annoying, sound, but I was relieved to hear it. Score one win for Dr. Blake Waiter.

CHAPTER 27

The Dartmouth Memorial Gardens is a sprawling green space that has been in operation since 1954. The Atlantic Funeral Home sits at the top of the garden and hosts a stream of ceremonies weekly. I hadn't been there since a good friend of mine died of cancer a few years ago. It was not easy to go back there.

Lisa and I each took a brochure from men dressed in ceremonial uniforms, white gloves, caps, and all the hardware. The chapel itself was full of more people in formal uniform, both military and Halifax Regional Police. We slid into a pew towards the back. It had only been fours days since the ordeal that had taken Anne's life, and even though I didn't think Lisa was quite recovered, she insisted on being here.

We'd arrived early and managed to get a seat in the main chapel, but as more and more people arrived, that part of the facility filled. Once the chapel was full, the funeral home started sending the overflow to a secondary room. The other room was already set up for the post-funeral reception, but used video monitors to broadcast the ceremony from the chapel.

A procession of officers, led by General Belaire, came down the center aisle carrying an urn. The urn was placed on a table at the front of the chapel before all the officers took their seats — all but General Belaire, who went behind the lectern. Watching this procession, I noticed an older couple at the front. The man had an arm around the older woman, whose shoulders were shaking with sobs. I assumed they were Anne's parents.

General Belaire stood and surveyed the audience. The already quiet chapel took on a new sombre silence. "Too soon," he started, and let his first words hang. "Colonel Anne Petrost was not done. Not by a long shot."

Tears in the audience swelled again. I felt a hand grab onto my knee with force. I looked over at Lisa. Her face was contorted as she desperately tried to hold back a full meltdown. She shook her head slightly and whispered, "I can't."

Belaire's voice was a rumble in the background. I couldn't make out his words. I knew what Lisa was telling me. I nodded and put an arm around her to help her stand. She shrugged me off and stood, excusing herself as she moved past a few people to get to the aisle. I followed.

Soon we were out the front door and standing under the porte cochère. Lisa sucked in a long breath, lifting her shoulders back, and then exhaled loudly. She was tough and regaining her composure quickly.

I put a hand on her shoulder. "You okay?"

She looked up at me. "I was right next to her. This could have been *my* funeral. This almost was my funeral."

"It's not, though."

"He tried to kill me. He would have killed me as easily as he killed her." Tears again.

"But he didn't. I wasn't going to let that happen."

Her eyes flashed. "You mean you let it happen to Anne?"

That didn't need a response. I kept my hand on her shoulder.

She looked away. "I'm sorry. I just…I just don't know if I can do this."

"Do what?"

"Whatever you do! I don't want to live like this where there might be someone around each corner trying to hurt you or trying to get at us."

"That won't happen again," I said, and regretted it right away.

Her eyes raked me over. "You can't stop it."

I just held her gaze.

Her voice softened, and she asked, "Blake? Just promise me one thing."

"Anything."

"If you ever come across that monster Schlimm...." She paused. "Kill him."

At first I nodded because I still just wanted to console her. Then I thought about what she was asking of me. I thought about what it would mean if I ever saw him again. Then I gave her my real answer. "If I ever see him again...I will kill him."

Lisa had enough of funerals for one day, and I sent her home in my Jeep. I couldn't leave. I wanted to go into the reception. I needed to. I would just get a cab from here.

By the time I returned, the service was over and a steady crowd was moving towards the reception hall. I joined the flow of police, military and civilians and started the slow-motion trek. People must have been under the impression that it was disrespectful to move quickly at a funeral.

Soon enough we were in the reception room. There was a small kitchen off to the right and then a large area that could be separated into two smaller spaces with a floor-to-ceiling room divider. They must have been expecting the large crowd today because the divider was pushed back, allowing full access to the space.

Her parents and her police officer husband were near the entrance to the kitchen. A small crowd around them was trying to comfort them, but the tears and the hugs were too much for me. I sidestepped an officer, or someone, and made my way past the bigger crowd.

I didn't know a lot of people from Anne's work or personal life. Truth was, I only knew a handful and with good reason. The program Anne and I worked for was beyond classified. Most of the people in this room knew Anne from other postings, other military service, not SSCHVA. All enlisted SSCHVA members were required to hold other postings for the sake of optics; otherwise they would have awkward conversations with other military in town.

"Hello, Dr. Waiter," a deep voice said. It was the General. He'd been watching me weave through the crowd and had waited. His expression was unreadable. A few other high-ranking Halifax military types flanked him.

"Hello, General. Beautiful service." I nodded to the other officers.

"The part you saw, you mean." He'd obviously seen me take Lisa out.

"Lisa's still struggling with all of this." I gestured subtly around us.

"We're all struggling with this. That's how people tend to react to unnecessary deaths." There was an edge to his voice. The other officers shifted uncomfortably.

"I'm sorry?"

"I'm glad you said it," he snapped back, no mirth in his voice.

"What?" I wasn't in the mood. I leaned a little closer. "Do you have a problem with me?"

He shooed his companions away, and we stood alone in the crowded room. He leaned towards me. "Anne was a straight shooter. She always played by the books."

I was puzzled, but just nodded.

"I always had my doubts about you, but Anne never did. It was a strange choice for you not to take an office within the secure envelope of 12 Wing, but Anne backed your decision." He paused for my reaction, but got nothing. "The events around this Schlimm situation are not entirely clear, but they all rotate around a particular person. Any guesses who that person is?"

"I don't know what you're trying to imply, but —"

He held a hand up to stop me. "I listened to your protestations of innocence a few days ago. I don't need to hear it again."

"What's your problem?"

He put an old, beefy hand on my shoulder. It wasn't a sign of affection. "I gave you the benefit of the doubt on Sunday when you said you didn't have any information and didn't have any of the *special objects* in your possession any longer." He put air quotes around *special objects.* "But guess what building we have discreet surveillance on just in case Schlimm returns looking for some magic ball?"

Oh shit. They were watching me search around Bowles Arena. They probably watched me use the brother orb to bring the sister down from the side of the courthouse. I swallowed hard.

"Now, unfortunately for us we left only a few strategically placed video cameras around the building. That means we saw you arrive and slink around looking for something. You seemed especially interested in the exit hole on the side of the rink, but you took off in an awful hurry all of a sudden."

They didn't see me find the other orb.

"Care to fill me in on what exactly was going on?" He almost sneered at me, but I knew the funeral left everyone's emotions high and raw. I needed to make sure I didn't feed the angry fuel of this conversation.

"General," I started, "you're absolutely right. I'm in the middle of this shitstorm and because of that my wife almost got thrown off the Macdonald Bridge. So am I still interested in this shitstorm and maybe seeing that Schlimm gets caught? You bet. And did I poke around to see if I could find that goddamn floating ball? Yes, sir. But are you and I working on different teams?"

I smiled at him. A derisive smile. "Anne was my friend too. I cared about her."

His expression was stone. "I'll be keeping an eye on you."

I shrugged, and just as I did so, the light got pulled away as a giant slid in next to us.

"Am I interrupting a little faggot date?"

I turned on the intruder. "Jesus, Chuck. This is General Belaire."

The General glared up at Chuck, who met the stare with equal ferocity.

"Well," said Chuck, not backing down, "maybe the General should learn some manners when it comes to shooting the shit with other grieving mourners at a funeral." He'd obviously overhead some of the General's accusations.

General Belaire's neck was rimmed with fire that was slowly spreading up through his cheeks. He turned and walked off. I think it was just in the nick of time. Chuck was a monster, but the General was pretty close to throwing a punch.

Chuck watched him, snorted, and then turned back to me. The side of his head was shaved and covered in a white bandage, but it was a surprisingly small area relative to the damage I remembered seeing.

"Are you okay?" I asked, and pointed to the side of my head.

He lifted a hand and touched his head as though just remembering he'd been shot there. "Aces. What was that guy's prob?"

"I think he blames me for Anne's death. It's just a grief reaction. He needs someone to blame for his feelings of loss."

"You ain't responsible for nothing."

"Thanks."

We stood there awkwardly for a few minutes. A hulk in grey cargo pants and a jean jacket with half his head bandaged and some guy in a suit that the General had just had serious words with. I'm surprised the rest of the funeral crowd didn't give up on niceties and simply turn and stare at us.

"Listen," I finally said to break the silence. "I'll figure out something for getting you a new psychologist. There's a social worker that works with us on the base. She's great."

He sneered at me. "Fuck that."

I frowned in confusion. "I think you should continue with someone, and obviously I just dragged you into something awful. I can't apologize enough for letting you, a client, get shot. I should have never brought you into this. It was never your problem."

"You Canadians apologize too much." He reached across me to a table near us and picked up a glass of fruit punch and drank it all in one swig. He wrinkled his nose after. "Non-alcoholic," he announced. "Listen, Doc. I've been dead for over a year. From the moment my brains got spilled out and I learned I was off active duty, I was dead inside. You brought me back to life. I'm going to continue to see you. You're my psychologist."

I wasn't convinced. I started to protest, but he

stopped me.

"I'm not here for a debate. I'm here to say goodbye to Anne, and I'm telling you that I'll see you tomorrow morning at eleven." He put his empty glass down and turned to leave, but paused and turned back. "And let's just hope you stumble into some more shit because you've got me waiting in your corner." He winked and left as the crowds parted for him and filled in after as though he was never there.

I only waited a few seconds before I followed. It was time to go home.

⧈

When I arrived home, the house was dark with just a single light on in the kitchen. It was early evening and my Jeep was in the garage, so I knew Lisa was home. I made my way upstairs to our bedroom and poked my head in. She was lying on top of the covers, still wearing the black dress from earlier. I decided I would give her a little more time before I went in and changed. I gently backed out and drew the door closed slightly.

When I got back downstairs, I went into the kitchen and pulled down a bottle of rye we kept over the fridge with the rest of the liquor. We'd originally put the booze up high to keep it out of the curious hands of our son. We'd never bothered to move it after he disappeared.

I poured a generous helping into a lowball glass and then threw in a handful of ice before cracking a diet cola and just dribbling a bit of it on top. I called this drink a rye and Coke, but Lisa always corrected me and said it was rye on the rocks because there wasn't enough pop to be counted in the ingredient list.

I swirled the ice around to mix my drink and walked into the living room. Lisa's iPad was on the coffee table. I bet if I turned it on, I would find myself on the front page of her Pinterest account. I smiled at the predictability. I considered sitting on the couch and turning on the TV, but my mind wasn't ready.

I walked over to our stone fireplace and put a foot up on the hearth. There was a smattering of family pictures along the mantle, right at my eye level. There was a picture of Lisa and me on our wedding day. I looked quite dapper in a tuxedo, but it was nothing compared to my beautiful bride. Next to this was a picture of our family on the lawn out front. I don't even remember who took it. There was me sitting on the grass and Lisa lying against me while our son, Gabe, was rolling around in front. It must have been taken just months before he disappeared, so he was around ten years old. I think we were trying to get a family picture and he kept screwing around and wouldn't sit still. The smile that was captured in that moment was better than any staged photo. We all looked happy. It was the happiness of a family that didn't know how much tragedy was just around the corner.

I felt arms go around me, and I almost bucked them off in surprise. It was Lisa. She'd come downstairs barefoot without making a sound and now embraced me from behind. It was weird for her to initiate physical contact like this.

"Hey," I said. "You feeling better?"

She still sounded sleepy. "Yep. How was the rest of the funeral?"

That was a weird question, but I let it go. I also didn't feel like burdening her with the tension between General Belaire and me. "It was fine."

She cocked her head around my arm to look at the mantle. "You looking at the family picture?"

I didn't want to poke her emotions after the day we'd had. "I guess."

"I look at it a lot," she said. "I keep wanting to take it down, but it makes me happy when I look at it."

I nodded.

"It makes me happy when I look at it," she repeated, "until it makes me sad."

I knew exactly what she meant.

We were silent for a minute, each of us lost in our own thoughts as we looked at the picture, and then she spoke again. "You know, you and he have the same expressions."

Something about her words really struck a chord with me. I tensed up, but didn't move. I was trying to sort it out in my head. So much had happened in the last week.

Lisa could tell my mood had shifted. "What is it?" she asked.

I turned and broke free from her arms so I could look at her. "What did you just say about Gabe?"

She looked slightly alarmed. "I just said that you and he have almost identical expressions. I can really see it in this picture. He has the same goofy smile as you."

Then I knew. It was something the assassin Constant White had said just as she left Bowles Arena. She'd said I had the same expressions as him. But who was him? Was Constant White talking about my son?

Was he still alive?

THE END